PANGLOSSIAN

QUASI-DAISY

PANGLOSSIAN
QUASI-DAISY

M. K. Bingman

First paperback edition March
2021
Cover Design by Leatrice
Rosenplatz-Boe
Edited by Sara Kelly

www.mkbingman.com

DEDICATION

For my grandfather, Roger Keelean, who will always be remembered for his curiosity in every topic, rest in peace. For my grandmother, Silvia Bingman who will be remembered for her will and perseverance, rest in peace. And for my high school journalism teacher, Patrick Shannon, who taught me how to write at a professional level, thank you.

M. K. Bingman

VOIDTRISS

"Hope always shines the brightest when the world is engrossed in darkness and that hope is the greatest gift."

CHAPTER 1

STATIC RONDURE

In the distance of the tar-black night, the whine of a passenger train could be heard. The air was frozen, as if made of static electricity.

For any normal human, the night was the same as every other fall night, and not a single being could tell that something of great importance happened that could greatly impact their lives. For them, it was just a normal evening they shrugged off as another non-historically significant day, like every day; but who could blame them?

~~~

Meanwhile, a man of no importance stepped off the public transit, holding a black briefcase; the same any business representative would be carrying. His shirt previously tucked, now untucked, wrinkled below the last ivory button. The tie, underneath the collar of the shirt, was moved down in an attempt to wipe the day's history from the man's memory.

His stride was quick, to keep with the pace of the other pedestrians out that night, as if he were trying to go unnoticed. He kept his head down, to prevent him from looking into the eyes of the other paranoid people, who were doing the same.

As he walked, he could feel his stomach tighten, like an external force was grasping it and squeezing it to juice the remains of his late lunch out of his system. The arm without the briefcase swung underneath to support the gut and to ease the pain a bit as he grimaced. He slowed his pace for him to recover from the pain that disturbed his insides.

What's going on? he wondered as his vision started to blur, and he felt as if he were on a spinning carnival ride.

His briefcase hit the sidewalk with a dense thud that was soon followed by the rest of his body.

~~~

In a field near the city limits, an altercation took place a few hours prior. This altercation seemed strange, one like no one had ever experienced. A man of average height and average weight stood there in fear while a woman a few inches taller than him screamed at him. The Man was without a shirt and shoes while the woman was dressed in a dark blue, strapless sundress that seemed to bounce light off every one of her curves. The man's expression was a mixture of apologetic and confused, as if he didn't know where he was and how he got there. His knees collapsed from underneath him, he fell backward, and broke his fall with his hands.

"Get away from me!" the woman demanded as she forcefully placed her foot into the soft topsoil and proceeded to take a step towards the man, in hopes that he would be scared off.

The moonlight reflected in her eyes. Her left hand clenched, forming a fist while her right hand was flat and open, almost like she was creating a platform for something to happen. She stood still in this position for a few seconds and then took another step towards The Man.

"I do not know why you are mad, miss, I have done nothing to anger you; in fact, we have just met, so I know I have not done anything to upset you," The Man said as he gripped the topsoil in his hands to brace himself as he stood up. He placed one hand on one of his knees and balanced himself.

3

The woman looked at him with disgust and said calmly, "You are correct in thinking that this is the first time we have met, and you are correct in thinking that you have done nothing to anger me; however, I just get a feeling that I absolutely do not like you for some reason." She closed her eyes and maintained her pose.

The palm of her hand started to glow, like if she had embedded an LED into the center of one of the creases. As the light became brighter, it sounded like a bag of popcorn was being popped to perfection in a microwave.

The Man could feel the electricity build up in the air, and he knew something awful was about to happen; however, the fear he felt prevented him from taking action.

"Look," he said while he took a step closer to her. "I promise I will not do anything to hurt you, so you can knock that off right this instant, Miss Faith."

The brightness intensified in her hand as he stumbled those last few words out of his trembling lips. "How do you know my name?" she asked with her eyes wide open now, filled with terror. "Are you some sort of stalker perv that has been peeping on me through my window at night?"

"Not at all, Miss Faith. While you have your tricks, I have mine."

"Even more reason to not like you, sir!" she shouted. A small breeze swung her long, straight, rust-colored hair in front of her sapphire eyes. Even in her fit of rage she could be considered attractive.

One final popping sound came from her palm. The air seemed thinner while she stood there in the breeze. Total silence rang in the two people's ears while they waited for what was going to happen next.

~~~

A combination of screeching brakes and flashing lights halted the traffic where the man was now lying on the sidewalk. Two paramedics jumped out of the ambulance in a panic. The one that jumped out of the driver's seat looked to be the more serious and seasoned one of the two—he wore a gray lumberjack beard that was cut short, probably to make it look more presentable. The crow's feet at the edges of his eyes showed that he had seen a lot of activity while being a paramedic. His partner, probably no more than twenty-five, seemed excited. His head was bald, but from an outsider's perspective he seemed like a nice enough guy. They both were determined to save the guy's life.

"What happened here?" the older paramedic asked the woman who had dialed 911, after she had witnessed the guy kiss the eggshell-colored cement after his tumble.

"I don't know," she said in a southern drawl. "He was walking, he slowed down, and he toppled over like a cougar in a beer barrel. I dialed 9-1-1 afterwards. I didn't wan' to hurt the guy by movin' him."

"Ron, I need your help over here," the younger paramedic yelled over the traffic, which had picked up again. "We need to get him to the hospital immediately."

Ron swiveled his stance and ran towards the younger paramedic, turning to look behind him. "Thanks, we will take it from here," he told the lady who had dialed emergency care, who was now more interested in the reporter van just pulling up to the scene.

The young paramedic pulled a stretcher out of the back of the emergency response vehicle. The two men loaded the unconscious, injured man onto it and then proceeded to buckle him into it for his ride to the hospital. Lights and the deafening siren on top of the truck started whirling around to alert oncoming traffic to pull to a stop.

~~~

As the two people stood in the field, time seemed to have stopped. They both provided each other with their undivided attention, remaining alert to the next move their opponent was going to make.

"What is your name?" the woman demanded as she continued to collect static in the palm of her hand.

"I have no idea," The Man responded as the look of confusion returned to his face. "I do not even know where I am at the moment or how I got here."

"Cut the crap, jackass, what is your name?" Faith shouted. She had a murderous look in her eyes, ready to slaughter the man if he made another move. "I would like to know who it is I am about to kill."

"Miss Faith, if I knew, I would have told you already." The Man was completely on his feet again, grimacing from his pain with the unknown origin. His pants were torn, mostly in the knee region; beneath, his knees looked as if a cheese grater had been used to make a freshly grated pile of knee cheese. The scrapes looked somewhat fresh; however, the blood had dried and clotted to a degree, so that the slightest irritation would cause the wound to restart the healing process.

"Fine you don't have to tell m—" She was cut off as The Man lunged at her. He pushed her to the ground, cutting off her concentration; the static ceased while the air thickened. "What are you doing?" she shouted as she pushed her hair out of her eyes and attempted to sit up but was thwarted due to the man, now on his hands and knees above her.

"I am sorry, Miss Faith, but right now you need to be quiet; we are in grave danger. You need to do everything I say."

"What are you talking about? The only danger I see is you." The Man placed his hand over Faith's mouth to muffle her shouts and complaints.

"Look, Miss Faith, I will try to explain everything after we are safe, but right now I am going to need you to be quiet, and I am going to need you to listen to me." His face no longer resembled the deer in the headlights look, but instead it had taken a more serious look, one of concern.

Faith attempted to push his dirt-covered hand off of her mouth. Her eyes looked as if someone had started a fire in them.

"Now I am going to remove my hand and help you up. I am going to need you to start your static trick again, but it has to be big and it has to be powerful; we are only going to get one chance at this," he whispered into her ear, constantly looking up and forward, like someone who was paranoid. "Two more things: do not freak out when you turn around—I need you to remain calm, cool, and collected; and secondly, remain quiet—this thing we are facing is drawn to loud noises." Faith's eyes changed. The fire that was there was replaced by two oxidized slivers of sapphire filled with terror, her face was flushed, and she had a feeling something awful might happen any second.

The Man did exactly as he said he would: removed his hand, helped Faith up, dusted her off, and reminded her to start collecting static in her palm. She was going to need more electricity in her one palm than the almighty Thor could muster with a single flatulence after chili night Thursdays.

"Slowly turn around now," The Man whispered to her. "Do not make eye contact and aim directly for its chest. Throw it when you are ready."

Faith's face changed to a bright red color out of embarrassment. "Hey, um, jackass, I can't do it," she said it a quiet tone, the opposite of her shouting tone. "I can't throw the static I collect; actually, it doesn't even harm people, it was all just a show."

"I know it was all a show, Miss Faith; however, right now, I and everybody else on this planet are counting on you, and you are probably the only person who can save us right now," he said, unaware of cliches. "Just turn around, and we will take this monster down together."

The Man rested his right hand on her shoulder and helped her rotate. Her head was down, and her eyes were closed. She had no clue why the filthy man told her not to make eye contact with whatever she was about to face.

Why me? she thought, trying to remember how she ended up in the field in the first place; why couldn't she remember anything of importance? *Why do I even dislike this guy? He has done nothing to me. But now I'm here about to face something even the man who wasn't afraid of my static is afraid of. What do I do?* Her eyes started to tear up more. *Why did I decide to put my trust into him, when just a few minutes ago I claimed I wanted to kill him? I've never had those feelings before. I was going to attack him when he is clearly in pain. Why?*

"I am going to need you to open your eyes now, Miss Faith," The Man said with his hand still on her shoulder. "You are going to be alright, just don't make eye contact—DO NOT make eye contact." He made sure to emphasize that in order to remind her of the importance.

"What do I do?" she asked, the tears almost audible.

"Just follow my lead; you have all of my trust."

"Why?" She thought, *We only just met.* The Man's face still had concern painted all over it. He knew he was going to be in a world of hurt tomorrow morning after this event was over, and Miss Faith, he had to remember to protect her; she was priority number one. His right foot moved forward. His knee was obviously in pain, though he would never admit it. He forced his left foot forward and started to run forward. "Now open your eyes, Miss Faith!" he shouted behind him.

Faith's eyes opened suddenly, and her jaw dropped. "What the hell is that?" she whispered under her breath as she stared into what she thought was an abyss of nothingness. Her hand started to crackle once again, and the air grew thinner. *He said... he said I was supposed to aim for the chest, but how am I supposed to do that when I don't know where that is? And this thing doesn't have any eyes, so how would I make eye contact with it? This thing is just a giant black sludge monster. It is shapeless, and it doesn't have any features that would tell me what I am looking at,* she thought as she brushed her hair out of her face. It was now tangled and matted with dirt and tears, and her face was in similar shape.

CHAPTER 2

FAITH

All of this seems so familiar, thought Faith, as if she had gone through this sort of thing before. *Why? When?*

Once again, she closed her eyes, this time to think, to remember what she had forgotten. Air rushed into her nostrils, like a white water rapids river, as she inhaled to calm herself. Her index and middle fingers from her left hand were resting on the temples of her forehead, just above her eyebrows. The air rushed back out, this time slower; she had heard doing breathing exercises similar to this would clear her head and help her remember important information.

Was it two years ago? No, that can't be; perhaps a few months ago? No, it was definitely when I was younger. Was it when I had just turned sixteen? Yea, that's it, I had just turned sixteen, when something similar happened.

~~~

"We have breaking news tonight from the capital," exclaimed the female news reporter on the TV that sat in the corner of a bedroom that was just large enough to contain a twin-sized bed and desk. "There has been an official sighting of a UFO, just over the White House tonight. That means they do exist, and we are all here to experience history in the making, people."

A teenage girl looked up from her phone at the mention of

aliens and scoffed at the idea. "Yea, right, and I can read people's minds," she said sarcastically, returning to her phone.

"Faith? Sweetie, it's dinner time. Go wash your hands and get ready," a voice shouted from downstairs.

"I'm not hungry, Mom!" the girl returned to her mother, as her phone's screen started to glitch haphazardly; red and yellow lines started to appear vertically on the screen. "Dammit, they said this phone wouldn't pull this crap like the other ones did. Why is it always my phones and nobody else's? Actually, now that I think about it, why do my computers and mp3 players do the same damn thing? I am sick and fucking tired of it always happening. Maybe I should just give up on technology altogether," she muttered under her breath to avoid anyone outside her room from hearing her.

The sound of heavy, stressed footsteps came up the stairs and entered Faith's room. "I'm not going to make you eat if you don't want to, but did you at least finish your homework?" the middle aged lady said while leaning on the door frame, a ladle in one hand and her arms crossed across her chest. Her glasses were edging the tip of her nose, while her eyes almost dared them to jump, reminding Faith of her no-bullshit school librarian, Ms. Reinhardt.

"No, because this was my last week, remember? They gave me early graduation credits because I passed that test they made us all take. They're trying to kick the smart ones out, so they have more time to focus on the fucktards."

"Language, missy! I still don't understand the point of that test." Her motherly instincts kicked in, and she started to peer around the room, looking for something out of place, something that didn't belong; namely a boy. "But hey, you're a junior in high school and you are graduating on Saturday; not many people can say they did that. Any plans after you graduate? Are you going to stick around and live with your mama for a while or just roll with the flow?"

"No clue. Would you really let me do whatever I wanted after I graduate?" Her phone was now lying at the foot of her bed—to discourage her from throwing it at the wall on the other side of the room.

"We'll see."

"So that's a no."

"We'll see."

"AHH," she screamed, the temper in her voice audible. It was reminiscent of the old sitcoms, the ones where the teenage daughter always overreacted to their parent's answers in a semi-dramatic manner and would eventually storm off, leaving only an echo of a slammed bedroom door behind. "Why do you always fucking do that? You never give me a straight answer to my questions!"

"Language, and I'm not going to tell you again! I'm sorry, sweetie, but questions like the one you just asked, are difficult to answer and require me to think about them," she said as calmly as she could, without showing fear to her daughter. She needed to maintain her ground in the argument, in order to keep her daughter from getting the advantage. Though she was never the greatest at arguing, she did learn a thing or two throughout the years, and all the parenting books suggested she keep the high ground. Even if her daughter wasn't like most other children, she felt it was important to follow this suggestion. Faith was smart, and she never let her mother forget it too; the moment Faith saw an opening she would take it, without question, leaving her mother baffled and stuttering for counterpoints.

"Why suggest it?" asked the teenager while concealing a hint of contempt in her voice, her eyes squinted toward her mother's battle ready gaze. This question was more rhetorical than anything, and an answer was not expected. "My stupid phone is acting up again," she digressed and caught herself, not in the mood to argue. Her eyes shifted away and focused on a poster she had hanging next to her TV. "I think the warranty agency we keep getting the phones through is lying to us about the phones being new. I have gone through six phones in the last two months! That's ridiculous!"

Easing her battle stance, Faith's mother quickly decided that agreeing with her daughter's digression at this point would be good. "I'll go down there and see what they can do. Same issue as always, I suppose?"

"Yes, not as bad as last time but it is still pretty bad. It's like a magnet was used against it, or someone stuck it in a micro-wave."

"The guy said that those lines only happen if surplus electrici-ty flows through the system and fries a component on the touch screen. What did he say? Digi—digitimer, digitizer, something like that. When there is a crack in it or a static discharge against the surface of it, it just stops working. I'm not sure he knows what he was talking about, because what are the odds that you keep electrocuting your phone?" Proud of herself for remember-ing this information, the adult changed the topic one more time. "So, is that still a no on dinner?"

~~~

Faith had only closed her eyes for a moment, so she could think; however, in that short amount of time she had realized a lot had happened. The Man, who in her mind was the cause of all this bullshit, had disappeared, and she was left with summon-ing the static into her palm; she had no clue how she was sup-posed to do it and why the man had so much faith in her and her only, but if she was going to save some people, she had better do it properly. Time seemed as if it had slowed for her but sped up for everything else. She blinked. In an instant the monster in front of her had grown an arm, with a mountain-sized fist on the end of it.

An aura appeared around the void beast, similar to radiating heat waves from a grill on a hot summer evening, warping the background of the scene and pressurizing the air, making it dif-ficult to breathe. She could visibly tell that the thing was becom-ing more and more dense with every passing second.

Is this thing becoming a black hole? she thought, determined to stay a good distance back from it, as to not get sucked into it, if her theory became reality. "It sure is difficult to gather electric-ity from the air when this thing is making everything feel heavy. I can't focus."

The arm swung above what Faith assumed was the monster's head. She blinked once again. "Don't look into its eyes," she briefly remembered as the face of The Man popped into her head. Immediately her head dropped, placing her eyes at her feet. The ball of electricity she was palming had grown larger and brighter, but she knew it still wasn't big enough and the whole issue of throwing it was still very apparent.

An earth-shattering roar echoed out of the void monster; if Faith were any closer, she would have been deafened. As she processed that incredible sound and waited for her ears to stop ringing, it became apparent that her feet were no longer touching the ground, and she was in fact flying through the stiff, heavy air.

There is no possible way, in this goddamn world, that nobody in the city didn't just hear that. It could have made the earth shake, she thought, feeling the plastic-like air move around her.

~~~

Faith's graduation ceremony was typical: all students lined up in their gowns, single file, approached the stage, shook hands with the principal, and received their diploma. The difference between her ceremony and everyone else's was the fact that on this day something changed the lives of everyone who had attended the service for better or for worse, even if they were unaware of this fact.

Parents and their graduates were scattered throughout the school campus, getting the last-minute photo shoots out of the way before the ceremony began. The summer heat had started to create droplets of perspiration on the foreheads of the more heavily dressed individuals. Children could be heard screeching out of joy from playing tag with their older siblings, while people were still loading into the already packed, non-air-conditioned auditorium where the event was being held. The graduates stood next to their best friends, chatting, while anxious to get the ceremony started and to get out into the real world they had so wished they were a part of since they were children.

Faith didn't have any friends in this particular graduating class, not because the class was two years older than her, but because she didn't have any friends to begin with. Even in the class she once was a member of, she found herself to be the outcast, the one kid who always had a temper that showed itself at the most inconvenient times. On class field trips or at birthday parties, it didn't matter; she had always been a walking nuclear rage machine, and none of the other kids wanted to be in the meltdown zone.

"Faith, do you have your valedictorian speech ready?" asked the principal, Mr. Dewise, after he noticed she had been outcasted once again by her peers.

"Yes," Faith responded in a monotonous voice, growing bored with the wait and her surrounding peers' antics.

"Everything alright?"

"Yes."

"What are you going to do afterward?" His attempts to engage her in conversation were futile; it was obvious she didn't care to be there, and the longer she had to wait, the less she cared. After a minute of waiting for a response from the teenager, he decided it wasn't going to happen. "Good talk," he awkwardly said as he scratched his trimmed, bearded chin. "The ceremony will start in about ten minutes, and you're the first one up to give your valedictorian speech. Good luck!" Faith's mood did not improve as he walked off.

She was only there because her mother told her she had to; otherwise she would "regret it in the future and that was unacceptable." To the left of her, two upperclassmen were shoving each other playfully, trying to attract the attention of the girls to the right of her. She shot a disapproving glare in their direction and walked towards the PA room; she figured it would be quiet in there, and she would only have to deal with one adult, whom she could easily outwit and trick into letting her stay until it was time to go out and give her speech.

She approached the room and peered into the window to see who she was going to deal with; if they looked dimwitted, she wanted to know to see how easy it was going to be to outsmart them.

"Hmm, weird," she said with a hint of confusion in her voice. "Should the light be off at this time?" She opened the door with force, barely holding on to the brass handle.

"Hello?" the graduate called out, even though it was obvious no one was in the room with her—or so she thought. The mixing board that controlled the PA system was turned off and the window that overlooked the auditorium for the visual cues had its curtains nearly drawn. A narrow line of light cut through the darkness of the room, reflecting off of anything that had a chromed over surface. Three red lights, which she assumed were part of the sound board, blinked periodically.

Faith approached the mixing board and ran her fingers over it, and almost instantly everything turned on, like someone had flipped a switch that Faith was unaware of, somewhere hidden in the darkness of the room.

"Oh, shit! That scared me. What the hell just happened?" she asked herself as she took a step back to assess the situation. "Deep breaths, deep breaths. I did nothing wrong. Someone just flipped a switch in another room and everything came on, that's it, that's all that happened."

She opened the curtains and looked down into the audience; something didn't seem right. In fact, she knew something was off at first glance. It was the audience, or the lack of audience, rather. *This place should be packed by now*, she thought with immense concern.

Looking around the room, she noticed that the three blinking red lights were now gone. A feeling of overwhelming panic crept into her. Her hands started to shake, and she began to sweat profusely. In the corner of her eye, she detected something black move and run out the door.

She stiffened as she prepared herself to chase after whatever it was that had booked it out the door. *Maybe it isn't a great idea to go running after something that just sprinted out of the room when the lights came on. I mean, isn't that how people lose their lives in horror movies, they chase after something and eventually the table turns on them and the hunter becomes the hunted?*

15

She was looking for any reason not to chase after what she just saw. Good or bad, she just wanted a reason to stay.

"Nope, I've got to do this," she said as she pulled air into her nostrils to calm herself. "I guess this is more interesting than giving my speech to all those people out there who really don't care." Her eyes closed in preparation, to justify her actions, both of her hands approached her face and smacked their respective sides, to convince her she was still awake. "Okay, let's fucking start."

~~~

How did I get here? Why does the left side of my body hurt so much? These questions and many more flowed into Faith's mind in a matter of milliseconds. *Why do I hear a plane? No, wait a minute, that isn't a plane. What is that?*

"Miss Faith, I need you to keep your eyes open!" Faith recognized the voice; it was that of The Man, but though she was able to recognize it, she was uncertain of where it was coming from. "Are you alright? Can you stand?"

Slowly Faith started to realize that she wasn't flying through the air anymore, but instead was lodged into the side of the hill that stood adjacent to the field she was just in a couple of minutes previously. She assumed her thick hair must have protected her head when she collided with the terrain; otherwise, she might have been dead.

She lay dumbfounded, attempting to remember what in the world just happened, what it was she was doing, and what she needed to do. *Is this what being punch drunk feels like?* She lifted her head and started to come to. *I'm not lying on my back. I think I am lodged into the side of the hill, vertically.*

Only then did it dawn on her, she was no longer gathering electricity into the center of her palm. *Dammit, I knew this wasn't going to work. That man played me for a fool!*

"Miss Faith? Are you alright? Speak to me."

Where is his voice coming from? I don't see him at all, but he sounds like he is right next to me. Her thoughts were signifi-

16

cantly more clear now. She was calm now; still in pain, but calm. "I'm alright, jackass," she shouted. It was a lie—she didn't know if she could move much from her current position; however, she sure as hell wasn't going to let the man know that she may need help. And in her opinion, he didn't deserve the truth; it was he who got her into this mess, and it was he who seemingly disappeared on her while she faced the monster head on.

"Good, glad you're still alive," came the voice that seemed to be everywhere, and yet nowhere as well. "I could really use your help down here."

"Excuse me!" Faith couldn't believe her ears. "I was just helping you and you weren't there helping me!"

"Well, yes and no. I will explain later, but now we have to defeat this thing."

Looking down into the field, she saw the blackness of the monster in a stance similar to that of a sumo-wrestler about to start a match, minus the chonmage hairstyle. The beast was bent over (she assumed, as she was still unable to identify certain features of the beast), the fist swinging through the air demonstrating there wasn't much control over it. "I think I understand what happened now," she whispered to herself, to keep her thoughts localized and unmolested by what was happening down in the field. "That thing's appendage must have hit me at full force, sending me flying into this piece of land over here. But I still don't get how I can't see the man. At least from up here, he should be visible."

"If you want, I can handle the Voidtriss from down below, while you stay up there and gather the electricity; there should be plenty at that altitude."

Faith had completely forgotten that she still needed to gather the static. It didn't seem as important to her as it did to The Man. She dislodged her right arm from the soil and debris from the hillside and looked at her stiffened hand, grimacing from the tidal wave of pain emanating from her left. Her fingers relaxed and slightly collapsed into an arc that could perfectly fit a softball. The typical crackling and snapping started as a ball of light whirred into formation. The extra dirt, soil, and who knows what else that was still collected on top of her skin seemed to bounce viciously around inside of the sphere, forming a brighter ball than the previous iterations.

Faith was impressed. She had never been able to make a sphere so quickly, and on top of that, she was amazed at how bright it had gotten. *Maybe I should be on the high ground more often,* she thought while identifying more possible reasons as to why her ability had improved so rapidly. "There are just too many factors at this point," she said aloud while using her finely tuned reasoning and deduction skills that she was no stranger to than the back of her hand. *It is possible that the dirt is acting as a form of catalyst or something, or I guess it is possible that it has a large amount of iron in it. Not important right now, though. How does he expect me to throw this thing?*

The sphere had grown to the size of a basketball; Faith couldn't help but notice that the orb she was creating had gained some weight as well. *I'd better figure it out quick. I don't think I can hold it up much longer, not to mention throw it at something.* The brightness intensified, the snapping and crackling becoming louder, and the ball started to produce heat. *Well, figuring it out just became a little more fucking important, I guess, if I don't want to fry my fingerprints off.*

~~~

"You know, it's weird. I didn't hear whatever scampered off; I just saw it urgently leave the room, like I had disturbed it while it was in the middle of something that it didn't want me to find out about," Faith quizzically mumbled to herself while running down the hallway in the direction she thought she saw the little creature go.

"I wonder if this creature has anything to do with the disappearance of the people who were supposed to be waiting in the auditorium." Her hand entered her graduation gown and fumbled for her new phone. She was glad the gowns had pockets to store wallets or phones; otherwise, she wouldn't have had her phone on her. It would have been with her mother instead because of the pocket-less dress she was wearing (she usually only wore dresses with pockets).

She tapped the screen cautiously, hoping to prevent it from going into freak-out mode like the six previous phones. There was hope that her mother would pick up on the other side. The phone rang and rang again, but nobody picked up. *I guess it is possible that she has her phone turned off; however, if it were off, it would have gone straight to voicemail. Maybe she has it on silent?* She wanted some sort of excuse, anything, to understand why no one was in the auditorium. She tried calling once more, to make sure it wasn't a fluke or a network error. As she placed the phone up to her ear, she heard a sizzle and a high-pitched beep.

She stopped dead in her tracks, knowing exactly what those two sounds in succession meant. "Shit!" Any other day, she would have accepted it and told her mom, but not that day. She raised the phone above her head and threw it as hard as she possibly could against the floor, like a child who had a bouncy ball they wanted to launch into the sky. "God fucking dammit!" she shouted in anger, between her tears and worn down patience. "I hate technology! This is not what I need right now!"

Faith collapsed under her own weight, while practicing the stress management techniques she was taught when she was younger. She needed to take deep breaths while remembering something she enjoyed doing. She found that this worked okay, but if she really wanted results, she needed to clasp her hands together, start squeezing them, and rock in place for a minute or two, similar to how some kids on the autistic spectrum would do.

Stress attacked her suddenly; it was like it hit her all at once, and her phone dying on her was the straw that broke the camel's back. She hadn't felt this stressed since she was in junior high and discovered she needed to take a class that required her to interact with people, in order to learn acceptable social skills—the only class she got lower than a B in.

Her index finger found its way to her mouth, so her front teeth could work on trimming her barely there fingernails. *What do I do, what do I do?* She breathed slowly, in an attempt to relax.

Her eyes fixated on a wall as she rocked herself into calmness. *What do I do?*

~~~

What do I do? The ball of electricity had grown to three times the size of a beach ball. The brightness was nearing unbearable. It reminded Faith of the flame on top of the TIG welding torch her granddad used while working in his garage. She imagined herself tossing the sphere into the air and catching it in the palm of her other hand. *That could work. I think I just have to learn how to transfer it from one hand to the other first, and once I do that, I can learn to toss it. Baby steps first.*

The Voidtriss unleashed another gruesome, ear-piercing growl, one that should have made the earth shake.

Faith's right hand started to shake out of fatigue and fright. She lifted it slowly above her head and paused the flow of static she was forcing out of her palm. The static rondure dimmed slightly as energy stopped pouring into it. If an onlooker saw what she was doing, they would say her hand probably had some sort of Faraday cage glove on it to prevent the lady, who was now standing on her own two feet in a semi-torn dress, from getting electrocuted by what appeared to be a giant beach ball of electricity sitting in the crevasses of her petite hand. However, there were no onlookers and there was no Faraday cage glove separating her skin from the electricity, only Faith and Faith's ability to learn.

Her left hand worked its way to the ball for extra support. She breathed in the ever-thinning air and closed her eyes for a moment of concentration. *Deep breath, come on, I know I can do this.*

"Miss Faith, keep your eyes open please," the voice from everywhere shouted in her head.

Her eyelids opened viciously with malcontent. "Look, jackass, I can't concentrate if you keep shouting at me like that. Where the hell are you, anyway?"

"I am where I need to be," The Man's voice said, as calm as a hospice doctor waiting for one of his patients to cross over into the land of great wonder and relaxation.

"What the fuck is that supposed to mean?" Her makeup-thickened eyebrows wrinkled inwards towards her nose as she became a little more piqued. What little trust she had in this guy was shrinking rapidly with her patience, which was worn thin to begin with.

Dark clouds started to roll in and surround the field that was just south of outside the city limits. The monster swung its void-like arms around and smashed the hillside that was to the left of Faith, sending debris and boulders everywhere into the field of grass that it was currently standing in. *Fuck, that's some force. I definitely do not want to get hit by that.*

Faith dropped her right hand and let her left hand take the lead, to test her little theory on how her powers worked.

~~~

The hallway lights exploded with a force of a grenade, leaving a popping sound echoing throughout the building. It was dark. *Was that me? Did I do that?* Faith felt for the wall to brace herself from her panic attack. As she did, she noted the three red dots that were missing from the PA room were now sitting right in front of her, illuminating the room slightly. She reached out to grab them only to realize it was closer to her than she had originally expected. Her fingers brushed against something slimy. She pulled back her hand and started to gag, as she could only imagine what she had touched. Her fingers smelled of a mixture of sweat and rancid meat droppings.

One light went out, followed by another one, and then the first came back on. "Hello, I-I'm not here to hurt you, I just—wanted to know what was happening," Faith stuttered, choking over every other word.

A snore mixed with clicks answered back, and Faith realized the lights in front of her were not lights but red beady eyes, eyes that had built in bio-luminescence, giving off that red haze of light that she assumed were lights on a speaker system a few minutes ago.

"Fuck this!" she shouted with an about-face, set to run away. She started to sprint, the best she could in her laced-up high heels, in what she thought was a safe direction, her eyes still not fully adjusted to the pitch-black darkness.

Her heel caught the air between the floor beneath her and her graduation gown, snapped in two, and forced her to lose her balance. She tumbled to the floor, tearing her gown around her shins. Her anxiety was in full force at this point, and she thought she was going to die. As she fell forward, she headbutted a locker on the wall with a clang! Her eyes watered from the pain.

She felt closing her eyes might get her out of this mess; she needed to breathe and think. A slimy tentacle wrapped itself around the heel of her foot, climbing higher and higher until it reached her knees. It pulled her in towards whatever owned the red eyes. She kicked with her other foot, to encourage her slimy restraints to ease off and relax her imprisonment. "Get the fuck off of me," she screamed, underestimating the grip strength of the beast. Her heel connected and punctured the arm, producing a viscous fluid from the wound. The fluid oozed out with a steady stream, dripping onto the floor and sliding down Faith's heel. Everything the liquid touched began to hiss, sputter, and melt, like it had come in contact with hydrochloric acid.

Faith kicked her heel off and managed to wriggle her way free, before the monster's blood could make contact with her. She started to run again, her head pounding from her collision. "A little help would be nice right now. A nice little escape from this hell-hole is all I'm asking for." She breathed heavily as her uneven stride carried her forward.

Her palm tingled, as she slowed her pace. *Now my palm is going numb; did I accidentally get some of that monster's blood on me? I hope fucking not.* She could hear the vile creature maybe thirty or forty strides behind her, crashing into everything, like it didn't know exactly where it was going. *Was it lost?* she wondered. *I need to find a window or some light, so I can see what I am fighting with.*

She turned a corner, and there it was: a solution. Not the best solution to her current situation, but at least it was a solution. She couldn't believe she hadn't thought of it before; or at least it didn't appear to be an option until now. She was going to ask for help.

She was glad to see there was at least one other person still in the abandoned school, even if she didn't know where the rest of the graduating class's guests had disappeared off to. That would be a question to answer after she was out of danger.

"Hey!" she shouted at a shadowy figure, down the hall, "I need your help, and I would prefer you start running too."

The shadowy figure turned in the direction it had heard the girl shout. Faith's eyes were now adapted to the darkness, and she could see clear enough to be able to tell that the figure was a man, maybe in his early thirties. He looked like she had startled him as his face turned from surprise to relief.

"You can see me?" he asked, intrigued and shocked at the same time. "No one can see me, and even if they could, they aren't supposed to see me."

"What the hell are you talking about? Of course I can see you!" Faith retorted, more confused than she originally had been. "We don't have time to chit chat, dude, we need to run! Something is coming this way, and it sounds like it isn't happy!" She threw off her broken heel, to even her stride. She couldn't see the monster, but she definitely could hear its clicking snores down the hallway. It sounded like it was growing tired chasing after her, but she didn't want to stand around to find out if she was right.

She approached the man with speed, like she was trying to race the guy to the end of the thirty-meter dash. *Is this guy stupid or something? Why hasn't he started running?* "Fucking run, man!"

He stood in one place and grinned at her as she approached post-haste. He stared and watched as she passed him, only to see what she was running from come barreling around the corner. "Oh, is that what you're running from?" The Man asked in a lackadaisical tone.

Faith was done with him already; she had no patience for a guy who wasn't going to listen to her, or take her seriously, when it was apparent that he should. "Are you fucking kidding me?" she mumbled under her voice and briskly shouted, "Yes!" behind her as she continued to run like she was part of a Formula One race.

"This little guy," The Man said calmly as he bent down like he was trying to get a skittish cat to come to him, "is completely harmless, unless you hurt it first; however, which realm and universe are we in? I have a feeling this guy doesn't belong here."

"What gave that away, genius? The fact that I am running from it?" Faith shouted back, as she ran into another wall. *I only looked away for a second, dammit!*

The Man stood straight up, then looked around at the girl. His steady stride carried him to her as he asked, "Are you alright, miss? What do you need me to do?"

Faith's eyes were filled with tears. She was certain she was going to have a concussion after all of this was done, and she was exhausted from this day in general. "I want to be home, where none of this would have happened and I just want today to be over with," she said through her tears, now sliding down her cheekbones and collecting on her chin. She slowly collapsed to the ground, her bare feet sticking out of her gown, the inside portion of her legs touching the tiled floor.

"Hey, do me a favor," The Man said as he gently patted her head. "Don't be so hard on yourself, and be a little more positive. I'll see what I can do to fix this mess, okay? What's your name?"

She looked up at the man and tried to stop sobbing, but her head had taken too many blows, and it was causing the migraine from Hell. "Fai—"She sniffled a little to prevent snot from running down her face. "My name is Faith."

"Nice to meet you, Miss Faith. Now let's see what I can do to help." He lifted his hand off of Faith's head and walked towards the monster, which had slowed, more reminiscent of a Sunday stroll in the park than a charging boar. "This thing is called a Goobert," The Man said, trying to keep the teenager calm. "It usually lives on the sixth plane of existence in the third realm; however, this little guy is lost and frightened.

"Usually these things consume energy, which is why you currently have no electricity to light this building and why you probably feel so exhausted and drained at the moment, but don't worry, your life force will come back, though by the look of things the power to this building is not coming back anytime soon.

"The Goobert race typically have four eyes, but you probably noticed this one has three, which tells me that this one is special—sort of; it is probably an elder, about to die or evolve into something much, much worse than a Goobert, but that information is for some other day. Whatever you do, you never want to hurt them, as hurting them will send them into a fit of rage, and puncturing their skin will most definitely end in a cataclysmic event, not immediately, but years in the future."

Faith whimpered in the background as she heard this. She understood that she may have caused the end of the world by trying to run away from the monster. "I—I kicked it with my heel and broke the skin," she stuttered out as all the color in her face disappeared.

"You are marked for life now, unless—" The Man said, briefly interrupted by the monster lunging towards him in a final act of escape.

"Unless what?" Faith asked in her panicked tone she had been using for the last few minutes. She had a habit of speaking faster when her anxiety was acting out.

"Unless we save you, your world, and your universe."

Faith relaxed slightly at the sound of this, even though she knew she didn't have a reason to do so. As she did, she felt the color come back into her face and the overwhelming exhaustion she had been experiencing lift off her shoulders like cannonballs being dropped into a bed of water—the weight was still there but it was easier to carry them, and now that she was underwater, this man was her water, her light at the end of the tunnel.

She remembered that her palms were still numb from earlier; it felt like when she cut the blood circulation off in her arm when she fell asleep on it. She looked down at them, trying to see if they were wounded in any way. They weren't. *I think something is wrong with my hands.* She was disgruntled with her current situation, but she had to deal with it some way, somehow.

Her hands went to her waist, slid to the floor, and pushed the rest of her body to stand on her feet. She wobbled slightly as she stepped forward, her hand connected to the wall, to find some stability. The numbness in her palm grew into a sharp pain, and she noticed a spark fly off, brightening the surface of her skin. Her skin on her palm was a dark pink with a brownish hue, like it had cooked from the heat of the spark.

The spark caught her off guard as the man ahead of her said, "I've never seen that before, but I think it can come in handy. Can you do that again?" His voice was still calm and even, assuring Faith that everything was going to be all right.

Faith exhaled a sigh as she focused harder on her sparking hand. *I've never been able to visibly cause electricity to come out of my body before, but that shock would explain so much, so many bad things that have happened to my electronics.* She imagined the spark happening again, but this time stronger and more intense. She imagined holding on to it and carrying it in the palm of her hand, to the Goobert in front of her.

"Good," The Man said as he watched Faith's fingers start to glow. "Now, I am going to grab this little guy, and I want you to feed him as much of that power that you possibly can, charge him up and satisfy his hunger." The Man tackled the monster to the ground, wrapping his arms around its neck. The girthy squirming appendages bounced and fought, swinging and crashing into The Man's upper body. It was attracted to the energy Faith was producing, but it also wanted to breathe. The snoring clicks sounded more like gurgling than anything else. "Feed him, hurry!"

Faith approached the struggling beings, holding her hand flat, to encourage the spark to become even denser, even heavier, and even more pronounced. "What do I do with it?" she asked The Man, who was now on his back and entangling his legs around the creature.

"They can absorb energy from a distance. Just get close enough to this little guy, so it can drain the static out of your hand. If you need to, act like you are about to touch the static to one of its appendages, make contact with it, and I am confident it will help dissolve its lust for your electricity, sooner rather than later."

Faith caught one of the tentacles, which she could clearly see now was extruding out of the Goobert's mouth, and held it in the air, feigning a gag, as it tried to rip out of her grasp with immense force. She could smell the putrid stench emanating off the flesh of the Goobert. *Is this thing rotting to death!* It made the same motions a pouting cat's tail would make; the random wiggling motions. The hand that she had been incubating the spark in gripped the appendage, while releasing the stored energy into it. The monster started to become a little docile, slowing its frantic movements to a halt.

"Give it some more, Miss Faith, we are almost there." The Man loosened his grip, as it became easier to restrain the monster.

She strained for more electricity to come out of her hand, as she felt her skin start to bubble and fry on contact with the power she was summoning. She was certain she was going to have to tend to some major burns, later. Faith's hands started to shake and twitch as her limit was hit. She couldn't summon much more, aware of this even though this was her first time experiencing this level of power, but she already knew her limits well.

"We are going to save you, Miss Faith, but first we need you to finish satiating this thing."

"I know," Faith shouted as she summoned what little left she had.

As she converted her last little bit of power into electricity, The Man covered two of the Goobert's eyes; the left and middle ones. The third eye stood staring for a moment and then blinked out of existence, like the last little bit of power had just drained out of it, ironically. The Man released the Goobert from its choke hold, while looking at Faith in such a way that told her to release the monster as well. An aura of the Goobert lingered in the air, as the thing turned to stone, forever encased in a statuesque grave.

"Is it over, am I safe?" Faith asked The Man, who was back

to grinning.

"Yes and no; it is over and you are safe for now," he said as he hesitated to speak the next part. "However, you are still marked for life, with that little guy's curse. You and everyone else you know will be doomed for the rest of eternity if we don't do our best to save you."

"And how the fuck do we do that?" she asked as she was presented with the harshest truth she had ever heard, with regard to her own future.

The Man could hear the anger in her voice but chose not to answer her question. "How long have you been able to do that thing with your hand?"

"You know, jackass, it isn't polite to answer a question with a question," she said, changing her tone from agitated to relieved, welcoming the digression in her thoughts. "As far as I know, this was the first time I could visibly see the static, but I have been frying phones and computers since I was born. I just thought I was incompatible with tech."

"Hmm, interesting. You are an anomaly in all the realms I watch over," he said, stroking his chin, as if he were deep in thought. "I'm going to have to do some research on your kind. Which realm are we in?

Oh, great, he's a fucking looney. "You're on Earth, you know planet Earth, home to five trillion human beings, and apparently one alien as of a few days ago. That planet Earth."

"If you insist," The Man said, appearing disappointed by the information Faith just gave him, while maintaining his grin. "It is now time for you to sleep. I'll see you again shortly."

Faith's eyes grew heavy as she collapsed to the floor for the third time in one afternoon. She didn't understand what was happening as she fell, but she did understand that she was more exhausted than she had ever been in her life, and she just wanted to go to sleep. "Where did everyone go?" she asked as her head bumped against the floor in a final attempt to answer all of her questions she had been sitting on. Her eyes closed, as her exhausted consciousness took over and drove her into dreamland.

Chapter 3

Unfathomable Determination

Sweating and quietly screaming, Faith awoke in her bed, uncertain of her recent events. Her hands felt like they were asleep; numb and awkward. She was still wearing her torn graduation clothes, which was enough for her to understand that everything did happen as she remembered it, but how did she get home, and how long had she been home too?

Her bed creaked as she swung her bare feet off the side to position herself to be upright. "Faith!" she heard from downstairs. "Don't move, I'll be right there."

Faith placed one of her hands awkwardly on her forehead. The numbness was still apparent, but she didn't care; she just wanted the blurriness in her eyes and the vertigo in her head to go away.

"I'm glad you're finally awake, missy!" her mother excitedly announced as she entered her daughter's bedroom, nearly sprinting to wrap her arms around Faith. "You scared us. Your grandparents and I thought you had skipped the ceremony when your name was called and you didn't walk onto the stage to get your diploma, but then you were found in this condition by one of the student's parents, afterward—thank the heavens that he was an EMT—he checked your vitals and made sure you were alright, he said you were fine, just overly exhausted, and he said you had quite the goose egg on your forehead, but thankfully you weren't concussed or anything. Why didn't you tell me you were that stressed out? I would have—I should have noticed. I'm so, so sorry; it is all my fault that you were that stressed out."

Her mother's embrace was strong and sturdy as Faith returned the hug. "No, Mom, none of this was your fault," she whimpered, holding back tears. "Mom, you're going to think I'm crazy, but I might have done something fucking stupid without realizing it at the time. I almost don't believe it myself, but deep down, I am certain it is true." The floodgates opened, releasing the pent-up pressure behind Faith's eyelids. "Mom," her voice warbled as she spoke to her mother, "I think I am going to die soon, but that's not the worst of it. I think this planet is going to die too."

"Young lady, using humor and wit as a coping mechanism for overwhelming stress isn't good. You need to talk about it, get it off your shoulders." The woman broke the caring embrace and looked her daughter in the eyes, sternly, showing a smile that said she was happy that her daughter was trying to disarm the situation but disappointed that her daughter wouldn't be honest with her from the get-go.

Faith picked up the subtle nuances that her mother's smile held, realized she wasn't going to be able to explain what had happened to her without being sent to a therapist or a looney bin, and begrudgingly committed to a lie, with a fake grin, which she thought really sold it. She would from then on tell everyone, including herself, "I didn't want to stand in front of all those people, so I ran, I ran until I tripped and fell into a wall. I guess that is why I passed out." *But what about the lights; did they explode or not, and is that weirdo man a thing too? Ah, whatever, it doesn't matter anyway.* "I guess when I hit that wall, I metaphorically hit another wall—I hit my breaking point."

Faith's mother gently rested the temple of her forehead against her daughter's, reminding Faith that she would always be there for her.

~~~

Faith stood tall, with Hellfire in her eyes. She remembered

everything leading up to this point, where she had been, what she had been doing, why she was there. Her eyebrows were furrowed with concentration, and she understood now why the man was acting as queer as he was. She was in a literal life or death situation, and she had been so ignorant to it up until a few moments ago.

"I see you are starting to remember," The Man said vaguely in his omnipresent way. "That's good, avoid looking into the eyes this time and everything will go better for us."

"I know that now," Faith quietly said as if to avoid any extra unnecessary ill will from The Man.

The orb of lightning resting in Faith's hand glistened in the stale air, as she threw it around with ease, like it was a base-ball that she had had for years; one with subtle finger indents that told her which way was most comfortable to hold it. The orb went in the air a few times as she caught it with grace each time. Every time she caught it, she would slightly squeeze it, condensing the shape of the sphere from beach ball size all the way down to marble size. The denseness was outstanding.

"I see you remembered how to do that too," The Man stated with a strong sense of pride in his voice. "Welcome back. I am glad to see you have recovered."

"I thought you said I would only forget for a few minutes. I guess we are ahead of schedule then," Faith declared through her toothy smirk, aware that at any second she was destined to kill the giant monster in front of her, with the slightest flick of her wrist. She seemed like a completely different person, and for all intents and purposes, she was. Her memory had regrown, reminding her of everything she had ever forgotten.

"You were always an anomaly, so why would this occasion be any different? I just wish you would have been yourself a little sooner."

"You can't get your way all the time. Even a monkey knows how to bet against the house every once in a while." The marble she was holding sparked as she rolled it around in her palm, as if it were a fidget toy the kids were so fascinated by nowadays. She paid no attention to the Voidtriss in front of her, only caring about rolling the marble around with her thumb. "Let me know when you're ready for me to do my thing."

"Anytime would be good, just remember to aim for its chest; we don't want any repeats of the last hour."

"Yeah, yeah, I know, I learned from my mistake the first time." You could almost hear Faith roll her eyes as she spoke to The Man with exasperation.

Faith shut her left eye as she aimed her dense marble of electricity in the direction of the black figure. "Why do I always have to do the hard part?" she asked as she flicked the marble with her middle finger across the field of wheat and grass. Her demeanor exuded confidence as the makeshift bullet shot across the open field, blasting a dime-sized hole in the middle of the Voidtriss's chest.

The caw of the monster's cry of agony shook the earth and split the land into two separate pieces, forming a ravine between them. The enormous figure stumbled backward dramatically.

"Open the gate, before in regains its composure," Faith shouted at The Man, whom she could see clearly now, standing at the base of the monster's feet.

"No can do," he said calmly.

"Why the fuck not!" she blurted out. She didn't spend the last couple minutes remembering what she had stolen from her, only to let the asshole punk several yards in front of her tell her she was going to lose this fight. She knew she was going to die, but it certainly wasn't going to be today, of all days, and she sure as shit wasn't going to be told that the plan, his plan, changed right before the most crucial of moments.

"You missed your mark."

"I didn't fucking miss." Her voice stung the surrounding air, as if her words were a viper striking on its prey. "I hit it square in the chest, just like you told me to. Can you not see through to the other side of that thing from where you stand?"

"Let me rephrase: you hit the Voidtriss, yes; but, unfortunately, you killed it too. We weren't trying to kill it, only maim it. Killing these things always makes things so much worse."

"I don't see the big deal. If it's dead, it's dead, so how could it be worse?"

"Can you tell me why we call them Voidtriss?" The Man didn't wait for an answer; he continued his thought while maintaining a steady, back and forth, balanced gait along the edge of the ravine. "They are essentially sentient black holes, and when you kill one, you know what you have left? A black hole with no consciousness. It turns itself into a cannon; it just spits out thousands of pin-sized gravity disruptions that will either cannibalize themselves or nurture each other into full-blown black holes. Miss Faith, I am sorry to say, but our situation just got leagues bigger."

Is this how it happens? Is this the end of the world as I know it? Faith felt the world's pressure upon her shoulders; it was enough to knock the wind out of her in a single blow. She could tell her anxiety was approaching critical levels. The confidence she was showing previously was no longer apparent, even though a glint of optimism was attempting to break through. "Can we move the Voidtriss to a different realm?" she asked, already knowing the answer.

"We cannot. You know how dense a single black hole is right? A single spoon full of neutron star would weigh more than everyone on Earth. I don't think that is a single spoonful," The Man said, pointing at the massive, black carcass lying in front of him.

Faith incoherently mumbled to herself as she thought through her predicament. Her mental health had grown in strides over the last couple years, but in this second of weakness, one of the banes of her existence, aside from her looming destiny, poked its weary head through the door to her mind and waved a neighborly, hello; anxiety. She wanted nothing less than to run over to that door, slam it, lock it behind her, and throw the key into the ocean, cutting that bitch anxiety out of her life.

The weather changed from overcast to downpour in a matter of a few seconds. Edges of the ravine started to slide into the canyon, forcing The Man down its throat.

~~~

The ambulance's siren cried out, as Ron sped through the evening rush traffic, weaving and avoiding all vehicles that ignored the call of the siren. "At this rate we are about two minutes out from the hospital. Why don't people move out of the way anymore, Kev?" he said in a frustrated tone to his younger cohort, in the back, who was attempting the best he could to wake the unconscious man.

The man still had a pulse, and he was still breathing, but something seemed off about him to Kev.

"My generation has an issue where we think the world belongs to us, and by all means should work around us too," Kev said as he felt around the abdomen. He had noticed a swollen spot he wanted to check out. He applied pressure to the spot, to feel for shifting under the skin, and there was none. He lifted his hand off the man and tried again to wake him, but his results were the same as always, no response.

Ron turned the vehicle at an alarming rate; Kev could have sworn the passenger side of the ambulance lifted as the centripetal force carried them around the corner. "Warn a guy next time!" Kev shouted toward the front half of the bus, while holding on to anything he could. *Thank God for those restraints on the cot, or that guy would have gone flying.* A small side glance out the windshield let him know they were almost to their destination; the ER. Meanwhile, a cold clammy hand reached out to grab the man, begging for answers from the closest person it could touch. Kev jumped as the man who was previously unconscious brushed against his arm. He looked in the direction of contact. "Jesus Christ!" he shouted, making sure to emphasize every unique syllable.

The sheer loudness of Kev's fright sent shivers down Ron's back. "What? Why are you yelling?" Ron swiveled in his seat to see what all the commotion was, and his jaw dropped as his eyes became fixated on the set of full size arms, protruding out of the man-in-the-cot's belly button. In all his time as an EMT, he had never seen anything like it, not once.

The two arms wiggled and waved as the two men watched in awe. The hospital was less than a block away, but the ambulance had stopped traveling forward. "Check for a pulse," Ron managed to push out, half-jokingly.

"On the arms or the man?"

"Both, I guess," Ron said hesitantly. He wasn't even sure if they should; it felt like they were re-enacting the famous chest-burster scene from *Alien*, a movie he'd seen at least thirty times as a child. *What would Ripley do?* he thought, trying to change his perspective on the situation.

Kev reached for the wrist of the man lying in front of him, his hands trembling the entire way. Gently, his index and middle fingers rested on the man's wrist vein. *BA-DUMP, BA-DUMP.*

"That has to be the strongest pulse I've ever felt; it's even stronger than before."

"Good, the guy's not dead yet, What about his house guests?" He spoke as if it were completely normal to witness a couple of voracious limbs trying to climb their way out of another human being.

Kev's hand trembled harder as he repeated his test on one of the arms flailing about. Nothing. He reached out, calmer this time, for the other one; the paramedic wasn't sure the two arms were connected in any way, but he felt compelled to check. As his fingers touched the surface of the clammy skin, the arm jumped from what Kev could only imagine was being startled. "When did we enter a godforsaken horror film!" he shouted as he pulled his hand back violently.

The older paramedic could see tiny hairs standing up on the forearm of the stomach-bursters. "Well, you definitely scared whatever that thing is."

"Yeah, well, it scared me too!" Kev stated loudly and out of breath. "You know, I'm not the biggest fan of jump scares in movies, and I'm now aware of the fact that I hate them in reality too." He leaned against the side wall, in an attempt to calm himself.

HONK!

Coming to the same conclusion, the pair of paramedics realized they were blocking traffic, and commuters were becoming antsy to get home. "Let's get this guy to the ER before we are arrested for inciting a riot," the older of the two said, managing to bring Kev down from his adrenaline rush simultaneously.

~~~

The Man held on to a small jut of stones, while he watched more mud slide into the ravine. He was more worried about Faith than he was about anything going on around him; in fact, he was never really worried about anything, except for the occasional scuffle with anomalies in all the realms he watched over, but even then, everything around him was inconsequential and would eventually work to his favor, conveniently. If a vehicle he was riding in ended up crashing, before anyone got hurt, all parties involved would conveniently be flung to safety. If a pandemic broke out, with death counts in the millions, his blood would conveniently hold the key to eradicate it. When The Man moved through rain, he stayed completely dry, like he was made out of some hydrophobic material; the rain conveniently dropped around him. Everything worked to his favor, without a doubt, sort of like a nice little convenient superpower. He could tell his fingers were becoming fatigued from holding his weight against the mud-covered cliff side, but he knew somehow the universe would give him something to work with before he fell to his death or before the black holes from the Voidtriss ate the entirety of the globe like it was part of an All-You-Can-Eat buffet that was having a half price Tuesday.

Heavy stones broke loose and dropped to the bottom of the pit, catalyzed by The Man accidentally becoming too greedy on how much weight he could distribute to his toe holds. From his estimate, the bottom of the ravine was maybe twenty-five feet down, and if he was lucky (which he sort of was) he would be able to survive that fall with minor damage, spare a broken bone or two. With a quick analysis of the possible outcomes, the benefits seemed to outweigh the drawbacks. For one, he'd be able to save his fatigued fingers from cramping more than they had already; that was the big one, the one he would rather fix before anything else. The cramping sensation throughout his fingers, wrists, and forearms disgruntled him, making it increasingly more difficult to think clearly. His laissez-faire demeanor perpetuated the longevity of his life, but sometimes he had his doubts; it was quite clear to him that the universe, realm deities or whomever else was in charge, was paving his destiny with bricks of gold, but in order to get to the end of the road he would have to jump through some hoops (or fall off some cliffs) and take his lumps while he was at it.

The Man released his grip, flooding his poor tensed hands with bliss, a feeling he was excited to feel but feared all the same. His hands might feel better, but he knew the impact from his fall would erase any bliss and would replace the agony in a new stronghold, fortifying and barricading it with any chance of the bliss brigade returning equal to zero.

Rocks pierced the side surface of the precipice, shredding The Man's skin on contact as he fell. Though he was not indestructible, and he had expected to take less damage, his destiny was set. The bottom of the ravine grew closer and closer, and in a few short seconds he would be crash landing into boulders and mud; there was no external force that was going to slow his descent from plummet to float. He just had to brace himself for the impact, something easier said than done. He prayed that his date with destiny did not lead up to a foolish way to die; he still had important inquiries that he felt to be a better use of his time than death would be. Miss Faith's untimely demise, due to her unfortunate history with the Goobert, still loomed in the future— he had to make time for that too, but he would not be able to if his gilded path led to a sudden brick wall and cut his adventure short.

He expected to be in a fair bit of pain, after he collided with the ground; however, he did not expect the numbing and tingling sensations in the lower half of his body. His neck attempted to lift the weight of his small head, so he could see just how bad the damage was. "It could be worse," he slurred out, noticing that his left arm had taken the shape of a lightning bolt. His legs were nowhere to be felt, but that did not prevent his pitiful endeavor to stand up. He needed to stand up, as that was the only way he knew he was going to be able to save Miss Faith and her world; sheer determination and stubbornness. He could be more paralyzed than one of Medusa's stone statues, and that still would not prevent him from helping her; he had promised her that her life would be saved, and by all means he meant to keep that promise, one awkward and goofy roll at a time; for however long it took.

It was irrefutable to deny The Man was trying his best to stand up, but with one working arm and no feeling in his legs, erecting himself proved to be the greatest challenge he had ever faced. Every jerk, every twitch, and every subtle breeze agitated his jagged arm, and if he weren't so hellbent on saving Miss Faith, he might have given up the moment he landed. Eventually someone would come along and help him, and he'd still be able to walk down his gilded course. *I just have to manage the pain better,* he thought, mentally preparing himself for every ounce of pain he was about to endure. He twisted his back like he was rolling around in bed, allowing the forward momentum to carry his broken arm around his body and land next to the working one. The dense sound that came from the impact forced The Man to grimace as it only reminded him of what did not need reminding; the loudest discouragement that his body could throw out, shrieking in agony to let him know that it did not condone his reckless behavior. His body, folded in half now, needed a moment of rest. The Man could feel his blood pumping through the broken arm, every heartbeat wrenching his poor arm with unfathomable pain. He imagined it was worse, too; of course he had endorphins flowing through his body to ease the pain, but what would happen after his fight or flight response dissipated?

The Man exhaled, then bit his lower lip as he forced the hand at the end of the broken arm into a fist, repeating this action on the good arm afterward. He thrust his unbroken arm into the muddy soil and pushed against the ground, his broken arm swinging like a pendulum as he lifted himself into what he could only describe as a yoga position gone wrong; downward facing dog, but the dog had one broken leg and two limp legs. When his appendage slowed its pendulation, he forced it, too, into the dirt, to prevent any unnecessary, unbalanced tipping. Of course it hurt, but he pressed on; his determination would not waver, especially when he had important things to do. He only realized his futile attempts were not going to work after maintaining his position for the longest thirty seconds of his life.

The nerve ends surrounding the split bone in his arm wept for The Man to cease his inconsiderate actions—they wanted to lash out and retaliate to deter him from doing any further damage, but in order to do so, they would have to be in the driver's seat, a seat they would not occupy if The Man had anything to say about it.

The Man threw his broken arm around the adjacent hindquarter, hoping his fingers would respond the proper way and catch his pant leg, so he could push his thigh in a position to better perch himself on. He just needed to bend his knees at a ninety-degree angle, and that would be enough to get him upright at least. His fingers missed their cue when they brushed against the underside of his buttocks; the pain was too much to muster. Throwing his splintered arm around all willy-nilly like he had been had severed what skin he had covering and protecting the broken bone. Now it peeked out, pretending to be the neighborhood recluse, trying to spy on its neighbors from behind closed blinds. The jagged ends of the bone were a pinkish color, dyed in The Man's blood, as if it were some sort of cheap, plastic Halloween decoration, designed to give the holiday a humorous shock value.

Well...that is not great, he thought. It was pretty apparent he was at peace with his situation, even though most people walking in his shoes would be hysterical—then again, not everyone would fight monsters or anomalies on a regular basis either. The Man attempted to throw his arm behind himself again. It flopped and waved, similar to a screen door on a house that had children who couldn't decide if they wanted to play in the yard or in the living room. This time he caught his pant leg, not with his fingertips, unfortunately, but with the bone protruding out of his skin. The denim of his jeans wedged itself between the crimson-colored skin and bone of his arm, and when it had occurred to him what had happened, it was already too late to halt his actions and reverse them. For all intents and purposes, his arm was tied behind his back; in his mind there was no recovery of it. It was stuck there until someone came along and greased it up or until he felt brave enough to separate the connection with a hard, swift tug. If he had a choice, he wanted to avoid the latter option, as he felt it would be the straw that breaks the camel's back, his pain threshold would shatter into a million pieces, and he knew he wasn't ready for that, considering he could barely tolerate everything he had already been through, and he hadn't even hit the pinnacle yet.

The Man managed to use his unfortunate predicament to his advantage. As his good arm held his weight against the earth's gravitational pull, his bad and feeble arm supplied enough make-shift leverage to wrestle his leg into the correct position. Though his leg did not have any feeling in it, he could tell it had enough strength to hold him up as he contorted his body to repeat the motion with the other leg, this one more of a balancing act; since he couldn't use an arm for support, he had to trust in his ability to hold still, only for mere seconds, but to him it felt like an eternity.

Finally, The Man was on his two feet, gruntled by the fact that he could stand, or rather lean, using the ravine wall for stability. The first challenge was done and over with (just as long as he did not tumble to the ground for being unbalanced or ungraceful). His legs did not move on their own, putting his problem-solving skills to the test once again. The solution was simple in concept but difficult in practice; however, it would require his second arm—a brutal solution, but indeed the only one that came to him. He would essentially pull his legs to wherever he was going, a challenge of its own and to be dealt with after he had practiced his leg dragging technique. He set every motion in his head, just to ease what little concerns he had about the method. *It is going to be tricky, but it is going to have to do.* He initiated his tactics like a computer running a main function in a piece of Python code, but before he could fully begin, he had to define some key elements; the disconnect method.

The dark blue denim attached to the splintered end of The

Man's bone had settled into its new cozy home and was acting as the gatekeeper, holding back the inevitable flood of blood that lay waiting patiently for The Man, for whenever he felt brave enough to open the gate and fight that battle. The anticipation of the immense amount of pain he was about to feel strongly persuaded him not to go through with his plan. He could give up right now and maybe he would spare some agony, but he had already come too far, only to quit when the end was in sight (he assumed), and he did not play that game. He wanted to count to three, to mentally psych himself up, but he knew that was a delay tactic. He was only procrastinating because he did not want to deal with the pain any more than a child wanted to clean their room or do their homework; everything was more important than the one thing he actually needed to do.

The Man took one final deep inhale and gritted his teeth as he ripped apart the connection between his jeans and his arm. He could feel the fibrous bone fragments break apart in his arm and the trickle of a blood droplet flow down the outside of his forearm, sliding to the tip of his pinkie. The blood had clotted and welded the connection together, making the separation far worse than it had to be. He pulled with gusto, building a layer of tears behind his eyes. The connection reminded him of when hands get dirty and dry, then touch a sweater or microfiber cloth; the fibers of the cloth seem to hook into the skin like little striking vipers. The amount of force required to separate the two objects amazed The Man. He figured he was in a weakened state but not as frail of a state as the connection was making him seem; it was so sturdy he was starting to become slightly exasperated at the thought of never splitting them.

"Come on, already!" He groaned, applying more strength. He felt if he applied too much strength, he would become unbalanced and topple over, only to be right back where he started in his forsaken position. "What in the realm are these pants made out of, Elven Ridgeworth leather?"

KKKRRIITT! A ripping sound, audible enough to anyone within the ravine, echoed throughout the walls as The Man had an epiphany, brightening his eyes with glee and optimism. His arm was free from the clutches of the evil denim, but he did not care—he did not even care about walking anymore, as his mind was on a new path of thought, forged on a whim, but he felt he'd travel it with grace and efficiency compared to his old path.

"Miss Faith, are you still there? Where are you? I have an idea, and I need your help." The Man communicated via the telepathy he used earlier. He'd rather not let her see him in his current condition, but he knew his new plan was going to work; she just needed to let him know she was still alive.

~~~

Faith was in the middle of the worst anxiety attack she had had in years. Her breathing was fast and heavy, leaving her light-headed. She was locked away in her own head, hiding from reality when she heard The Man's voice in her ear. Her head turned in the direction she last saw him, expecting to see his shining outline bursting through her mind's fog. To her surprise, he wasn't standing there, and the opening of the pit had grown in width. She hadn't even realized he was missing. As far as she was concerned he was still pacing on the edge of the ravine trying to plot out what to do next. She was just fine letting him come up with the plan, though, because she couldn't even hide from her own thoughts, let alone think rationally enough in a stressful situation. Besides she had no reason to not trust The Man anymore. She had known him for years now and every convoluted and vacuous plan he had ever come up with had somehow worked out, even the odds that went against all odds. She was convinced he had some sort of superpower that bent the will of the universe around his thumb, but no way to prove it.

"I'm here, where are you?" she said aloud, knowing The Man would be able to hear her, as if they were talking through two-way radios. Her anxiety slithered away, defogging and clearing her brain as she started to speak.

"I am in the ravine. Are you able to get down here relatively easy?"

"I don't know but I don't see why I wouldn't be able to." Her eyes shifted from left to right as she remembered something she hadn't done in years.

When she was just out of high school, she had experimented with her static and learned she could walk up and down certain material; stone was a no go, it provided no conduction, but mud and dirt were easy, and all it took was a little confidence with her foot placements. The water in mud made a great conductor when you were trying to send static electricity through your feet to walk in. When she was learning to walk vertical walls, she imagined herself as a balloon, excited to connect to any small bit of hair willing to provide the slightest amount of static so it could take a ride and go on an adventure; she no longer needed to run this simulation through her mind, however. The process had become as natural to her as riding a bike, and she only needed a few seconds to allow her muscle memory to take hold.

When she approached the hole in the ground, she looked around to make sure the Voidtriss was still in the same spot she had killed it in; she didn't like the idea of being anywhere near it, sort of how when most people are uneasy in a graveyard—everyone knew the dead were dead, but what if the one time we step on that field of grass and gravestones is the same exact moment the zombie virus takes hold, and they decide it's eating time? The Voidtriss could rise up and start the Erasure Apocalypse; she just didn't like it. The shadowy body of the monster still lay in its final resting position, comforting the woman minutely, but she still had questions that needed to be answered about the monster before she felt she would be completely comfortable, like why hadn't the black holes started?

She walked down the vertical slope with ease, only slipping when the mud was extra watery. The pointed high heels she was wearing gave her extra stability, and the heels dug at the surface of the wall, preventing her from sliding any more than she should. As Faith reached the bottom of the crevasse, she extended her dirt-covered leg, creating a smooth transition between the vertical and horizontal planes she was moving between. As she took her last step, a small, rocky pop sounded beneath her shoes, like they had been strapped to a pair of suction cups. Her instincts told her to double step when she heard it, out of fear that she might be stepping on something that didn't want to be stepped on, but she fought her instincts, knowing it was just her static ceasing its flow through the soles of her feet.

"Miss Faith!"

Faith turned towards the ecstatic voice as she saw The Man, pinned against the wall, blood running everywhere, his arm broken in three spots with a portion of the bone sticking out. The woman gagged and covered her mouth, in case her body wanted to get rid of some extra nutrients, as she saw the protrusion. She had a weak stomach for that kind of thing and wasn't afraid to show it. The ravine smelt like it had been filled with blood, but she quickly became used to the smell, having smelled worse in her past. "What in the hell happened to you?" she asked, noticing The Man wasn't moving toward her. She figured he was in an exorbitant amount of pain from the looks of his arm, so he was probably resting and conserving his energy to hopefully heal faster.

"I fell, it hurt," The Man responded briskly, wearing a smile that displayed his exhaustion. She did not need to know that he was in more pain than he appeared to be; he would rather her not worry about his health or well-being, as it would only cause unnecessary coddling and really slow down their misadventure. He would worry about his own health later, when he had more time to think. "Hold your left arm out, away from your body, ball your hand into a fist, stand on your right leg, and repeat after me."

She was confused and didn't understand why The Man told her to do all the things that he did, but she did exactly as she was told. She looked like a cheerleader rooting for her team, while she waited for The Man.

"Aperi Portam, Lacus Domum Realm, Amici Accipiat."

"What?" Faith remarked, while squinting her eyes, understanding The Man was speaking in broken Latin. Her tone suggested she was becoming a loose cannon and would explode out of aggravation at any second, presenting the problem she was blessed with from childhood; rage. Faith was smart, however; if she didn't understand something or something made sense to other people, but not her, she'd get a little upset and show it through a barrage of verbal assault towards all parties involved. Her face paused in a moment of disgust, then immediately continued, "Why are you speaking fucking Latin?"

"Repeat it, please, it just means open the gate to the home realm, and transport us too. I would do it myself, but you know." His head rotated around in a bobble head fashion, implying he was too hurt to do anything, even a simple transportation.

"A-Aperi Portam," she said, stuttering, attempting to remember what exactly The Man had said. A circle with characters outlining the edge that Faith was unfamiliar with appeared below her fist. The circle descended downward, increasing its circumference as it went. The moment it was level to the ground, it lit up, and every character radiated a blue color.

"Good, keep going, do not forget to enunciate."

"Lacus Domum Realm." The circle changed from blue to green and deepened its hue. The sudden change alarmed Faith. She almost thought The Man was pulling some sort of charade. "Amici Accipiat." The circle split into two, one encompassing herself and the other locking in on The Man, who was no longer leaning against the wall, only standing in one position, his broken arm hung off to his side. Faith noted that it looked heavy for him, like he was carrying all the hefty stuff from a grocery trip on that one side. The pair stood still as energy surged through the air, fabricating a turquoise cylinder around each of them. Within an instant the two people then disappeared, leaving no trace that they had been there, except for the blood The Man had lost, which now stained the muddy surface of the ravine floor.

NEW HORIZONS

Chapter 4

Home Realm

A blurring light, followed by an obnoxious silence, announced the arrival of the pair. It had only been a tenth of a second, but to them it felt longer, much, much longer. Faith felt as if she was going to throw up. Her stomach was churning from the instant transportation and wanted to crawl out of her body. An arm swung down to support her belly, to fight off the urge, but it was a feeble action, leaving her overwhelmed with stress she didn't quite care for.

The place where the two people were transported to was the embodiment of nothingness. Pure white extended out as far as the eye could see. The place was somehow lit with nothing lighting it, and all sounds instantly died out but felt like they carried on forever. It was cold but hot, but not neutral. The place was filled with contradiction, sending all the mixed messages, but somehow revealed nothing from its dulcet tones. The place was both pleasing and uncomfortable to be in at the same time.

"Where are we?" Faith asked in utter shock. She had never been anywhere like it, and she didn't know if she'd like to.

"My birth place," The Man said through the widest grin Faith had ever seen him put on. "This place is home and I sure did miss it."

"What? You were born here? How?" These questions and many more fell out of Faith's mouth uncontrollably; she was confused, intrigued, fascinated, and longing for answers. The Man never really talked about his life. She didn't even know his name (if he had one), but being in his home released every question she had ever thought of while being in the presence; she needed to know everything.

"Well, actually, I would not say birth; it is more *appeared*. You see, Miss Faith, I came to existence at the same point in time that everything else did, all of us did." The Man "stood" still, his legs, still unable to feel anything, held his weight, and he had enough control over them to at least prevent himself from collapsing. His arm still dangled to the side, while he used the good one to talk with. His arm pushed through the air in a broad motion to gesture at the vastness of his home as he continued, "All of us watchers were brought into this realm for a single purpose; our job, per se. We were tasked with the incredible responsibility of watching over our universes; not to meddle with them unless an anomaly arises. You, Miss Faith, are an anomaly. You should not exist, but the Great Powers Be willed you into existence for some reason or another. Out of all of my four hundred trillion universes I preside over, you are the only Faith and the only electrokinesis in existence."

Faith had been told several times in the past that she was an anomaly, but she always just assumed The Man meant she was weird or different in his own awkward way. Her brain started to swim with thoughts and questions. "What? Are we talking about many-worlds interpretation; every decision creates a new universe?"

"No, it is more like every universe has the same timeline, with inevitable anomalies to shift it off course. It is my responsibility to nudge it back on course if I find it to be on a bad path. It is easy enough. Good, honest work. In my realm's hub I can see and track every fold. Which is when the universes shift or divert along their paths, and actually the day I met you, I was standing in this very spot watching a large spike happen because of you and that Goobert—you remember that thing, right?"

The woman side-stepped back in shock, her eyes widened in disbelief. Of course she remembered the thing that marked her with the worst curse imaginable. She may have been under the

Voidtriss's trance a half an hour previous, but it was mostly worn off by now, she felt, and besides, it wasn't like she was going to forget her own pending death to begin with.

"Miss Faith, you would not be able to tell me, off the top of your head, which universe hosts the Rymuth Elves, by chance, would you?" The Man contemplated aloud in a slight digression. He already knew she did not but felt it was an appropriate question to ask. His index finger poked at the air as if he was using a touchscreen computer. Faith could tell that The Man's mind was trying to figure something out, but she would rather not ask him, just in case he needed to focus harder. "Let us see here. The RorNor Entanglement—no, that cannot be it, there are not enough spikes in there... I really should have organized these better."

A look of puzzlement surfaced on Faith. "What are you doing?" she stuttered, reminding The Man that she was unable to see what he was doing.

"My sincerest apologies, Miss Faith." He waved his hand and flicked his wrist in her direction, providing her with a myriad of new information. Directly in front of The Man lay a semi-transparent board at his eye level. She could tell it was essentially the equivalent to the futuristic computer screens from movies. She watched The Man poke at the screen, causing it to manifest an entirely new visual as he continued to mumble to himself. "Perhaps the Theon Group? Oh jeez, I hope not, I never want to step foot in that group again. Oh! That is right, it is the Kalolo Embassy! How could I have forgotten the Kalolo Embassy!"

The monitor changed visuals once more, displaying a circle with a mess of color even Jackson Pollock would have scoffed at. Above the circle lay five squiggles in cuneiform fashion, which Faith could only assume spelled out Kalolo or Kalolo Embassy. She wanted to ask The Man what they meant, but she figured they didn't have the time to go over God's Alphabet. *Is this guy a God, some sort of deity? If he was, he took quite the amount of damage from a fall!* She thought, internally brawling with herself in a half-assed attempt to find out the origin of The Man she had known, in a sense, for years.

"I know what you are thinking, and no, I am not a God, or at least not one by my definition." The Man kept his eyes fixated on the invisible monitor as he spoke in his normal calm tone. "I will tell you anything and everything you want to know, so take a knee, Miss Faith, we have the time now that we are in my realm. Besides, it is going to take a few minutes to find the correct planet in this universe that we need to go to anyway."

"I don't know where to start."

"Start wherever you want. Time flows differently from the constraints you humans put on it. If I need to, I could be watching the end of time and then the beginning of time a few nanoseconds later."

"Are you in pain?" She noticed The Man had stopped embracing himself.

"No," he lied, still avoiding Faith's concern for his health. He knew she had bigger questions, more important questions than his well-being.

Faith immediately knew The Man had lied to her; short answers were never his thing, but she figured if he didn't want to tell her, he didn't have to—that was his right. "If we all run the same timeline, what's the point?"

"I am sorry, Miss Faith, please allow me to clarify. The universes run parallel to each other, that is what I meant by the same timeline. Think of it as one of those thirty-meter dashes you humans have on Earth; the runners run even if one of them trips. Their only goal is to get to the finish line. However, if one runner veers off her path after tripping and collides with another runner, that second runner is now off their chosen path as well. Basically, I have to watch over my universes for anomalies so no one veers off course. A good anomaly will not veer off the course destiny has chosen for them, but a bad one trips and collides, causing more to trip and collide."

"I think I understand," she said, processing the information. "Am I a good or bad anomaly?"

"I do not know, Miss Faith. Every time I check the analysis is inconclusive."

"What is that supposed to mean?"

"That means the realm does not even have a plan for you. As far as I have found, you and all of us Watchers are the only life forms capable of free will. You could personally be the harbinger of chaos to multiple universes or your life could be so important that the universe would rather not disclose what its plan for you is; that is how I personally interpreted the results."

"We already know I'm destined to die of that Goobert bastard's curse, right? So how can the universe be so uncertain about my destiny?"

"Easy, you may be marked with the curse of death, but every decision you make up until that point could change your destiny; you do not have to die, if you will it. You have an aura about you, Miss Faith, that bends the fabric of reality."

"When you promised to help me all those years ago, did you know I could will myself to live through the curse?"

"Yes and no. I could see a hint of the surrounding aura; your body radiates this purple light that at the time I assumed was the veil of the Goobert, which is usually a dark, wispy black, but this light was different. I had never come across something like it before. That is the real reason why I had to leave you, so I could do my research. Come to find out, when mixed with the white aura of free will, the veil turns a purple color. I call it the 'Veil of Hope.'"

"Wait, has a Watcher been draped in the veil of the Goobert before? If they have, can we go talk to them? I want to ask them how they survived."

"No. I looked into your past and extrapolated that information. You are the first to have the two cloaks around you, which just makes you all the more unique in the eyes of the realm's overlords."

"Realm's overlords? Are those even a real thing?"

"Possibly, I am not certain for sure, but logically speaking, someone or something had to create me and the other Watchers, why else would we all be here? There has to be a greater being that rules over us." The Man was now making direct eye contact with Faith, his face a deadpan, revealing to her that he really did believe in something greater than himself; a god of gods.

Faith finally felt she could ask the one question she probably should have asked years ago. "What is your name?"

The Man's head fell as he moved his eyes away from hers, looking depleted. He digressed the conversation to avoid that one question. "Have you ever met an elf, Miss Faith?"

His head came back up, his face covered in a grin so big that Faith thought he was hiding something. *Why didn't he want her to know his name?* she thought. "Okay, if you are not going to answer my question, what can I call you?"

"You have been doing just fine in that regard, Miss Faith, no need to worry about that." His eyes darted around, like a liar's eyes, being hard-pressed into an unfortunate corner. "Now, we should really get going; those elves are not going to be waiting around for us forever," he said sarcastically, knowing all too well that, one: those elves were not expecting them at all; and two: they could wait in his realm for literally ever and time in the universes would have passed by only a fraction of a second.

Faith could see a green, oblong spherical object on the screen. She assumed it was the planet that housed the Rymuth Elves that The Man had been so enamored with. "Why do we need to visit this planet?" she asked as The Man waved his hand once more, summoning what looked like a mirror out of the sky. It sank to where they stood and morphed into a one-way portal, from the realm to a lush, green forest.

"We need some technology that only they have." The Man bumped the portal and passed through, leaving Faith in severe silence, amplified by the intensity of the white from the realm. She hurriedly sprinted to the gate and bumped into it, following The Man's example, and disappeared. The silence grew even greater as the two life forms were nowhere to be found outside of all time and space. The portal extinguished itself with a hiss, like water putting out the weekend flames of a campfire.

Chapter 5

Rymuth Elves

The wind rustling the green forest leaves was a welcome change to the eardrum-shattering silence of the realm. Faith could feel a mild breeze against her face while the smell of petrichor lingered in the air. The birds in the background chirped in a harmonious choir, treating the ears of anyone who would listen to their song. Every tree was full of leaves with colors ranging from dark, emerald green to cherry blossom pink; a complete feast for the eyes.

"I already love this place," Faith said, taking in all the scenery, as she felt more relaxed than she had ever before.

"Welcome to the Kalolo Embassy's, Planet Quii, home of the Rymuth Elves, a race of beings that are one and the same with nature, but who have progressed much further than the people of your Earth regarding technology. They are leading in ingenuity across all of my universes," The Man announced, raising his good arm into the sky, revealing how excited he was to be standing there. "I personally have never had to come here, any anomaly that happens here is good, and I cannot for the life of me figure out why, but thankfully I now have a reason to introduce myself to them." If he could sprint forward, he would have, like a kid in a toy store. His level of excitement rivaled that of a prepubescent girl at her first boy band concert.

"Do you know where we are headed? Which direction do we need to travel in to find these elves?"

"We are not going anywhere. We are going to sit right here and wait for them to come to us. It should not take more than an hour for them to find us."

Faith would have been distraught with the idea of waiting an hour if it weren't for how relaxed she felt. "An hour, but what if I start to get cold or you start bleeding again?"

"We will just have to cross those bridges if we come to them, Miss Faith."

The lady sat where she stood, collapsing dramatically to show she was displeased with The Man's words. Her eyes glared up at him as she bent her knees to cross her legs. Her dress was still quite dirty from the events in the field, so she didn't mind it getting even grubbier. Every motion she made indicated she would rather be exploring the forest than sitting and waiting for unknown help to show up and escort them to a city of tree houses. "I will sit here and wait, but the moment I get bored I am hightailing it out of here, and I have no problem leaving you in the dust too," she remarked, squinting her eyes at him the entire time.

~~~

"The trees in the north have just informed us of a couple intruders, sir!" a deep and booming voice shouted across the rustling foliage. Voices from nearby pedestrians could be heard quieting as the youthful-looking elf could be seen sprinting down a well-worn pathway made of sticks, stones, and other particulates that had been mushed into the forest floor over the centuries. The elf may have looked young to any untrained eye but was the second oldest civilian in the city. His hair was a white blonde with black highlight and ran the length of his back, nearly touching the backside of his knees, covering his pointed ear tips.

"Calm down, Siel, don't forget about the prophecy," a feminine charged voice answered from behind a sequoia throne, slowing the man named Siel to a halt. "Was it two men? Or two women?" she asked in an overwhelming confidence, brightening the tone of the room. Her people trusted her not because they had to out of respect for royalty, but because she filled the room with positivity and lightheartedness; she earned every heart in her domain with earnest and well-mannered respect to every constituent, even to those who showed they were willing to back-stab her at any moment. She felt everyone deserved respect because if it weren't for her people, she wouldn't have the position she humbly and graciously maintained.

"Both a man and a woman, ma'am. The man looks as if he has been in a battle with death for a while now, and the woman looks like she agitates at a gnat's breath."

"The prophecy foretold of a pair of travelers, two men or two women but not one of each. We must be weary of these two, for they may bring misfortune to our civilization."

"I am aware and understand, my liege. Shall we go greet them or watch from a distance?"

"Welcome them as guests and support their endeavors for now. If they get anywhere near the Orb of Blood Disdain, shun their existence."

"Sir? With the utmost respect, I highly doubt two outsiders have ever heard of the orb, and there is no way they will know where to look for it."

"You are probably correct, Siel, but take no chances when presented with obstacles. Do what you think will protect the paradigm we have grown with since the beginning of time. Understood?"

"I understand. How many should I take with me to greet the pair?"

"Include no more than four of your adventurers. You and I will accompany them as well. The party shall leave in no more than fifteen rhonts."

"Fifteen rhonts, sir? That is hardly enough time to establish a party of decent caliber."

"Remember, Siel, we are not looking for a fight, volunteers will be sufficient, preferably anyone who has a low intimidation trait. We just need to outnumber them, so they don't get the jump on us. If they are here to wipe us off this planet, so be it, but I would rather we try to find out why they are here and prioritize companionship over war."

~~~

"Miss Faith, stop climbing that tree!" The Man hollered at the woman who was hanging from a large tree branch above where he sat. "When the locals get here, they are going to besmirch our names, and then we will be out of luck if you do not stop marring the appearance of that poor tree with your heels."

"You of all people should know that when I get bored, I have to find ways to fight it, otherwise I get a little shocky," she asserted exploding a round of electricity out of her hands to demonstrate she wasn't joking around. As she dangled from her natural jungle gym, her sundress, which was torn in more places than one, crept up her hips and waist, revealing more than her pasty white, inner thighs.

"Could you at least show a little dignity and pull down your dress? Your undergarments are showing."

"Fuck you and the horse you rode in on. If my panties bother you that much, look away, asshole!"

"Yes, my humblest apologies, Miss Faith." The Man redirected his eyes, continuing to patiently wait for the elves to arrive. He hoped that they were not as overbearing as the lady in the tree, but he knew better than to think that way; in fact, he endeared that trait of Faith's, he just wished she was not so blatant in her demeanor even if she had always been like that.

"How long have we been waiting?" Faith shouted down, her eyes still blazing from The Man's comments about her clothing.

"I would say maybe seventeen or eighteen rhonts; it is hard to tell without my sundial, but my internal clock is usually within a few with little error," The Man said nonchalantly, forgetting Faith had never heard of the rhonts system of time before.

"What the hell are rhonts?"

"They are the minutes of this world. Fifteen rhonts here is about ten minutes your time."

"So what you're saying is, we've only been waiting for maybe twelve minutes, and you think they are going to show up within the hour? Those were the longest twelve minutes I've ever had to wait and I have to wait forty-eight more of them! I don't know if I can wait that long. It is going to feel like a century before it is all said and done." Another burst of electricity exploded through her hands and surfaced like a lightning bolt in the middle of a summer storm.

The electricity singed the tree where her hands connected to it, perturbing The Man. He did not want the forest to burn down, especially at the hands of Miss Thor-God-of-Thunder over there. The last thing they needed was a catastrophic fire in the lush wilderness of Planet Quii. He knew nothing was going to happen, but he still preferred to be on the safe side of things.

~~~

In the allotted fifteen rhonts, Siel had gathered his volunteers, all of which seemed to be less intimidating than a fly to a fly swatter. The elf had lined his volunteers up, shoulder to shoulder in front of their leader's throne, which happened to be vacant at the moment, while he conceptualized a contingency plan in the unlikely event that their mission went awry and the intruders decided to take up arms against them. The party consisted of four men, who looked no older than their mid-twenties but were probably closer to their mid-two hundreds, and two women, who looked even younger yet. All of them had the straightest rose gold hair imaginable; not a hair out of place.

Siel patiently stood in front of them, his arms tied behind his back, chest puffed out with pride; he felt his team was a good one, for fifteen rhonts, that is; if he had more time he might have sought out a more versatile team, but he would have to commend those who volunteered off the street for their bravery. They were going in blind, and for all they knew the two strangers could be decoys, hiding the presence of an entire army beneath a perception blanket. They would have no way of knowing until they showed up on the scene, even if the trees were listening and watching for them.

The Rymuth Elves had a symbiotic relationship with the nature that surrounded them. The elves received extra eyes and ears to protect them in exchange for nutrients and nurturing; the sentience that every tree and shrub held helped establish a form of telepathic communication between the two different organisms, growing the link even stronger.

"Already then, Siel?" a voice said, enthusiastically approaching from behind where the people were lined up; it was the party leader, the one, the only queen. She had entered the room without anyone noticing, excited to go on an adventure, even if it was only to the northern sector of her kingdom. She hardly found reasons to leave the city gates but was enthralled with the idea every chance she got. Her charcoal black hair danced with every step of her thick soled boots, clapping against her calves, straddling the silver blue ribbon that it was tied up with. She had changed from her appropriate royal garb to an outfit fitter for a midday stroll up a mountain; a tight smock over a frilly, short sleeved blouse and a pair of fitted utility pants that hugged every curve. She couldn't contain the mile-long grin, ending at craters, she was creating, influencing everyone in a thirty-mile radius to be just as rambunctious.

"Yes, sir!" he shouted, turning his head towards the entrance of the room.

"You don't have to be so formal; we're going on an adventure, and I am just another party member right now."

"Of course, my apologies, my queen."

"Siel." She blasted a scornful warning gaze at him through her bubbly mien to persuade him from his formalities. The way she saw it, if she wasn't in her throne, she wasn't going to ask for respect, even from her second in command. Out of her gussied up chair she was just a normal Quii-ite, like everyone else in the room; they breathed the same, they ate the same, and they disposed of waste the same, so what made her the gift of god when the people standing in front of her were more worthy of that title? The difference between her and her constituents: nothing, other than who birthed her, the same people who gave her the birth right to call herself queen. "Call me Hope, while I am standing here with you guys."

"Sure thing, si—Hope." He had to bite his tongue, as his knee-jerk reaction was to dignify Hope to her position, he had always called her some synonym of queen or liege and it unsettled him deeply to call her by her birth given name.

"Who did you get to volunteer for us today?" Hope stood next to Siel now, soaking in the group of people in front of her.

Her second in command had lined the people up in two groups, from shortest to tallest in each one. An outsider wouldn't have picked up on the two separate groups, maybe just thought the people lined up wanted to stand next to their own gender and subconsciously chose to stand in a raising-the-bar forma-tion. Siel started with the male group, all of which were told to stand at attention, like they were soldiers; a stern but approach-able smile and a glazed over stare was what he expected from them. "From left to right you have: Bramish, one of the first to signify that he wanted to volunteer. Rein, he is going to be our navigator. Kithor, Rein's assistant. Qunor, the last one to join our party."

Siel moved on to the second group without missing a beat. "Joena, she volunteered first after hearing that you were going to be joining us, and finally this one with the hair covering her eyes is Marn; if need be, she'll be the member to carry every-thing we find on this excursion." He despised the fact that Marn had let a strand of hair fall into her eyes while in the presence of the queen, and his tone become more aggressive while intro-ducing her. Before he had noticed it he was going to explain to his leader that Marn was top of her class in Quii Tech but instead felt compelled to punish her by turning her into a pack mule.

Picking up on his aggressive tone towards Marn, Hope stat-ed with sternness shadowing her smiling face, "That won't be necessary, Siel." It was obvious to everyone in the room that Siel had struck a nerve with his queen. She was too polite to bluntly say it, and he was too bullheaded to understand that he had screwed up. She knew he had some annoying hangups but instinctually looked past them, for the most part. However, for some reason his control issues really irked her to the ends of her benevolence, especially when it was directed at a younger member of their civilization. "If we do happen to find anything on this journey, you, Siel, will be appointed pack mule, not one of the young ones, do you understand?"

Siel refused to make eye contact with her as he said in the most sardonic tone he could muster without any further consequences, "Yes, Hope."

The bubbly persona returned without hesitation. Hope glanced at Marn and noticed she was a bit lanky for an elf but personable enough. Her hair reached her shoulders, cluing Hope in that Marn was still relatively young, probably even the youngest in the room. Her ears peeked out from behind the curtains her thick locks were fabricating, which allowed Hope a little peek at the points—one was there and fully grown, while the other one was missing and outlined the tip of her ear with a serrated edge like something had bitten or torn it off. Hope walked over to her graciously, nearly floating with a balanced gait, perched one hand on the girl's shoulder, and swiped away the hair in her face, tucking it neatly behind the deformed ear. This bestowed the queen with the secret she had been holding back on; the corners of her eyes were flooded. "It's alright, we won't make you pack our stuff; that is a job dedicated for those who are full of themselves."

"Thank you," Marn said, lifting her head to an angle that encouraged direct eye contact with her leader. She wasn't grateful for Hope preventing Siel from being a bully; she was thankful for being allowed to volunteer in one of the rare quests that the queen sometimes found herself on. Just like everyone else in the kingdom, Marn idolized the ruling class for the exceptional leading skills and transparency it was known for, causing a mass following and engraving a trust into them that would be difficult to falter.

"It is my honor," the queen stated, slightly confused by what exactly the girl was thanking her for.

Hope returned to the spot next to her second in command. She stood straight and looked forward, trying to look into everyone's eyes. "You may all know that today we are going on an adventure. Though it may be short, I would like to prematurely thank you for volunteering and would like to wish us all safe travels. The dangers of this journey are not apparent at this time and if you feel you would no longer like to join us, let it be known that we understand and will not hold you accountable. That being said, if you choose to leave right this moment, I will gladly have one of the guards escort you safely home. Let it be known that we are traveling north, to welcome a couple strangers to our land and will not be enacting any violence towards them, with no exceptions. Failure to abide by these laws I have set forth will call for immediate disciplinary actions against you and any accomplices. Siel, do you have the signature capture?"

"I do, Hope." He tapped at a rectangular object he had pulled from his pocket, walked over to the volunteers, and held it out in front of them.

"Please sign this form stating that you understand these terms and conditions." One by one the elves placed the palm of their hands onto the top of the rectangular object. The object scanned each hand, beeping after every scan was complete. "Welcome to the party; let's carry forth unto the unknown that awaits our presence."

Hope couldn't stand it any longer. She was antsy to get going, nearly deriving the potty dance into a "come on, let's go already" dance. She told herself she would boot anybody out of the party if they started to slow down progress, but she knew she wasn't going to—she just wished she would.

~~~

Everyone in Hope's party seemed to keep her pace, except for Siel, who decided he would walk at his own sluggish pace. He didn't quite care about the journey and was still under the impression that once they got to where they were going, they were going to be jumped and brutally attacked by an army of strangers. There was no way he was going to be the first one they attacked, and if he could help it, he would be the saving grace by showing up later and surprising them. He also didn't care to admit to himself that he was way too out of shape for the hike to the north, especially since the trek started with a near vertical climb and led through rugged terrain afterward; of course there was an obvious path they could have taken, and if it were any other party leader they would have taken it, but Hope had her mind set for adventure, and it was cranked all the way up to eleven. Why take the boring old path, when you could potentially see something you'd never seen before? The hard path was the fun path, so that was the road they were going to take.

If Siel had his way, he would have broken away from the group and strolled down the groomed path instead of climbing the sheer rock face that his queen forced him to. He didn't even understand why he had to go on this expedition to begin with; after all, someone needed to look out for the city while their queen was absent. He was the second in command, so it was undeniable that it was his duty to fill in when she couldn't...or wouldn't in this case, but no, he had to go too, and he wasn't even allowed to lead the charge.

He was certain the party had already reached their destination but figured he was still four or five rhonts out still, when he heard a loud female voice he wasn't familiar with above his eye line shout, "Hey, jackass! Are you awake over there?" Siel crouched where he stood, in hopes he wasn't noticed. The sudden voice had set him alert and on guard. "The elves are finally here!"

CHAPTER 6

HOPE AND FAITH

The Man opened his eyes from the short meditation spell he figured he needed, in an attempt to start the healing process. Daylight blotted out his retinas and with a large exhale of breath, his vision became clear and focused, and he was greeted with an onslaught of eyes as he realized he was surrounded by seven of what he presumed were Quii's finest, Rymuth Elves.

In his best Julia Child impersonation, The Man said "Hello." This intrigued the elves, who whispered to each other, trying to coax out what they had just listened to, unsure of what to do next. When The Man had opened his mouth and talked in their tongue, they felt he was one of them, but something was off, and it wasn't apparent to them. "I am glad you guys finally showed up; my partner over there,"—he pointed at the tree Faith had been climbing a few minutes earlier—"she is getting obnoxiously bored."

The group of elves rotated their heads in synchronization toward the way he pointed. *This stranger had to be one of them. He was saying he was friends with that tree over there,* they all thought, not realizing Faith was crouching in the tree leaves, watching the interaction. "Why are you here?" one of the female elves asked; her hair was the longest out of all the onlookers and there was something about her eyes that said she was the wisest of the group.

"We are here because we were looking for help, and the only

place I could think of that might be able to supply it is here on Planet Quii."

"Who is we?" the woman asked briskly. She already knew the answer, but she was worried about the positioning of his partner.

"My friend over there and me." The Man pointed over at the tree again and hoped that Faith would come out of hiding. *I am surprised they did not hear Faith when approaching; she is not the quietest of people, especially in this forest.* "I would love to talk to whomever is in charge. Please, it is very important."

"Your desires will be met in time, as long as you walk with us back to our home."

"That is one of the reasons why we are here actually; in case you did not notice, I am a little worse for wear. My arm is broken in several places, and do not get me started on my legs."

"What happened to your ears?" the shortest of the men inquired, almost pleading for a good story, refusing to listen to what the male stranger was trying to tell them.

"Not now, Bramish, you'll get your chance for questions later, but right now I am the one who gets to ask them," the woman said while placing one of her hands atop his sloping shoulder, her dark hair fluttering with the wind as it strove to free itself from the ribbon it was entangled with.

The Man turned and faced the one named Bramish. He was short and stocky, and if he had facial hair, he might have been confused with a dwarf, which The Man thought was rather peculiar. He, like the rest of them, looked young. His skin was porcelain white, which bounced the sun's rays in such a way that made the eyes want to feast on the delicacy that was presented to them on a platinum platter. "Your name is Bramish, right? I will tell you what, Bramish: I will tell you what I think you may be referring to, about my ears, but you have to tell me who is in charge here first." The Man had turned into the smoothest speaker and negotiator, directing the group of elves to spill the information he was asking for.

"It is obvious, asshole!" Faith dropped out of the tree she was in, startling everyone in their welcome party, except for the dark-haired lady, who was grinning ear to ear, overly excited about the situation. *I don't like her,* Faith thought, glaring at the woman as she brought herself to her feet. Instantly, she regretted dropping from the height she did, and her knees felt like someone had jammed a screwdriver into them.

~~~

The screams of the elves penetrated the wind's ominous presence, carrying the fear they felt across several acres of green forest, assuring Siel he was correct about the strangers. *They were definitely there to hurt them. Thank the overbearing presence that I decided I would stick behind the group and pounce when the time was right.* Siel grabbed a stone off the ground, one large enough that it had some heft to it but small enough for it to fit neatly in the crook of his hand. He raced toward his party members, to protect them from the ensuing danger they were facing, and when he was within range, he lobbed the stone haphazardly, determined to be the hero, without taking a single second to assess the situation.

The stone flew through the air in slow motion, forming a parabola too subtle for the eye to detect. It flitted to its destination; the temple of one of the stranger's faces. "WHAT THE fuck WAS THAT!" the stranger screamed, the rage fully apparent in her voice, but more intensely through her pupils. She was wearing a torn drape that matched her eyes, which looked red and puffy like she had been crying recently. Her thick eyebrows folded in such a way that reminded him of how his queen looked when she was frustrated with something or in severe states of focus.

"Oh ho," the second stranger uttered with a hint of melancholy in his voice. Siel could tell he had awoken something inside the female stranger, but whether it would wreak havoc or not was his biggest question, his only question really. "Miss Faith, are you alright?"

"Of course I'm not alright, I just got blasted in the fucking head by a rock! A fucking rock!" She glared at all the elves surrounding them, while holding the tips of her fingers against the temple of her forehead. "Which one of you did it? Was it you,

Bug Eyes?" She looked at Qunor, who was avoiding direct eye contact with her while leaning back to circumvent collision with possible retaliating fists.

"N-No, S-s-sir. 'Twas not I. The stone came from yonder." Qunor fumbled for his words while he looked in the direction the stone had been hurled from, in the direction Siel had set up his hideaway among the bushes.

The lady the second stranger had called Miss Faith got closer to the trembling Qunor to intimidate him into being docile. Her face was directly adjacent to his, almost close enough for her to bite the tip of his nose. "If I find out that it was you and you're lying to me, I'm not going to be very nice when I come knocking on doors for you. Do you fucking understand, Bug Eyes?

Siel readjusted his positioning; he wanted to be able to watch and listen in a more comfortable manor, something that persuaded his aging body to continue to keep moving if the time came and he had to launch another assault on the enemy strangers. The rustling of the bushes seemed loud to him, louder than they should have been, like when sneaking into the food storage in the middle of the night and every deafening creak in the floorboards traced your whereabouts through echoes and reverbs, straight to the ears of the people who didn't need to know you were gallivanting across the kitchen, in search of that midnight sweet-tooth soother. *If I'm not careful, I'm going to draw too much attention to myself, and then who is going to save me? We'll be done for if I get myself caught, doomed to forever be enslaved by those strangers,* he thought, dramatizing the situation in his head for no other reason but to ham it up. Between the razor sharp edge of exaggeration and reality, he realized the air started to feel thinner, something he only perceived during storms of astronomical proportion.

~~~

The pain in Faith's head had increased in magnitude, and her fingers slipped across her now blood-soaked forehead, while applying pressure to where the stone had struck her. Never in her life had she experienced anything so painful. Whoever threw it at her was going to pay wholeheartedly with their life. Subconsciously she had started to gather static in her unmolested hand. Her body had spent years fighting, or rather hiding from, anxiety, and no external force was going to beat her where she stood, while she was just getting a handle on this thing called life free of crippling depression and panic attacks. She didn't quite buy the bug-eyed elf's story; he seemed too innocent, like he was trying to play her through a loop. *Maybe he is an anomaly too, able to throw stones with some sort of telekinesis or something.* She refused to turn her head to see where the bug-eyed creep was looking. He might try to plant another stone on her face, this time right square on her nose, and if she was going to take another rock to the head, she was going to have to wipe out a race of elves off this planet, without hesitation, too.

"Take it easy, Miss Faith, I am sure it was just an accident, a misunderstanding, right?" The Man watched six of the elves nod their heads in unison, in agreement. The only one who did not seem to be afraid of the furious Faith was the one lady who also decided she was the speaker of the group. "Ah... I see," he said, watching the lady close enough to rival a lion's gaze towards a herd of prancing gazelle, to see what she might do.

"I guarantee, Qunor didn't hurl anything at you... Miss Faith, was it? The rogue stone came from the direction he had already pointed out. I trust him, and he is fully aware of the consequences of harming our guests. He didn't do it, so leave him be."

"Listen, bitch," Faith barked out, entering the personal space of the lady she was talking to as if she were about to get free coupons from the store manager at the local retail establishment. "If your little posse here knows the ramifications of harming guests, then you have a snake amongst your ranks, a snake that likes to throw rocks and slither away to a hiding spot."

"I'm sorry, I don't understand, your filler words, you have a weird accent, I think," the speaker of the group said, her face perplexed and twisted, denoting that she was more curious about the linguistics of the strangers than what was going on in reality. "Could you explain the meaning of the words 'fuck' and 'bitch'?"

Faith was flabbergasted; she had never heard of someone being ignorant to profanities. *She's joking, right? There is no way; those words are universal.* She relaxed a bit from the shock, enough to make her fighting stance, a single finger parallel with her eyes and her shoulders at a right angle, resemble the posture of a brooding teenager, who cared more about their cell phone than the world around them. She had unwound enough to realize the elves were being honest about the direction of where the stone had come from and unbeknownst to her conscious mind, her subconscious had already released the spare static it had been gathering, dispatching a minute, nearly invisible ball of static in the direction they were all currently thinking about.

"I am curious about those filler words too," a quiet, squeaky voice cut through the un-stimulating silence Faith had left in her bafflement. It was the tall lady, the one who looked like she got pushed through a taffy puller when she was younger, and got stuck right at the end of her ear.

"Me too," said the one named Bramish, as he raised his hand in the air.

"Same here," the bug-eyed Qunor included, in his best shaky-purse-dog impression.

Faith came to the conclusion that they were not screwing with her, no matter how shocking it seemed to be. "Don't you guys have profanities?" Her rage began to peter out; she couldn't justify being one hundred percent committed to her rage mode if the people in front of her were innocent enough to not have curse words. *If one of the elves did throw a rock at me, it was probably more an accident than anything.* She was comparing an entire race of mature and seasoned elves to children, because in her mind the only people who didn't curse were prepubescent preteens pretending to know what life was all about, and The Man, of course. She had never heard The Man utter a single profanity in the eight or so years she had known him. No profanities, and he enunciated every word with conviction, avoiding contractions or slang like it was the plague. "Do you have any bad words?"

The tallest man chimed in, "Bad words like evil and demon?"

"What? No." The wholesomeness in these people piqued her interest. "Not synonyms of the word bad, but... You know what, I don't have fucking time to explain this to you guys. Why are we here, jackass? Certainly it isn't to get bashed in the head with stones or explain the preciousness of curse words?"

The group of curious elves cooed with glee as they learned another way to use the new word. "That time the mean stranger used it as an adjective, how interesting," Qunor said with less tremble now as he could see Faith was losing her temper and replacing it with something else, something less threatening.

"We are here—" The Man started to speak but was interrupted by a new voice, of which the duo had never heard before, but their welcome party was all too familiar with.

"My queen!" the voice shouted, deafened by the diminishing echoes that wandered through the forest. It was loud and demanded attention, booming into the skulls of anyone nearby, listening or not.

The Man turned to see who had interrupted him, something he thought was easier said than done. His back had started to cramp and stiffen up as the adrenaline from his mishap with the ravine trickled out of his veins, disintegrating into a void much more vast than the Voidtriss had ever been.

"Hope!" the new voice called out again in overwhelming panic. "I've been shot. I told you these strangers weren't to be messed with and guess what, I was right!" The ocean of trees surfaced a face to match the voice. It was thin and sunken in, his eyes were being carried by thick bags, and the bridge of his nose looked as if he had taken one too many dukes to the face. The rest of his body emerged while he stammered for help. He had his fist clenched above his right hip, dragging his leg behind him.

"Siel, I demand to know the meaning of this!" the speaker proclaimed across the field of Ent cousins. Her tone told anecdotes of frustration as the man named Siel limped his way closer to the throng of people.

"I need help, I've been shot!" Siel repeated with heavy breaths.

"Kithor, Rein, if you would be so kind as to help Siel over here to join the rest of us?" The two men who had been quiet this whole time took off sprinting towards Siel. In a flash the two of them wrapped their arms around the limping man and carried him to the rest of the group, without uttering a single groan of exhaustion. "Marn, sweetie, do you know how to work a medical extrapolator? If not, it is pretty easy. I have faith in you figuring it out."

Marn nodded her head, indicating that she had at least dabbled with medical extrapolation before. "Do we have a Terune around here?" she quietly asked.

"Siel usually keeps one in his back pocket; it should be loaded up with whatever you need."

Marn rummaged through Siel's back pocket before the two voiceless elves allowed him to sit down. She pulled out the device, realizing it was the same one from earlier, the one that they all had to sign on. She fingered through files and pages to reach the destination she wanted, held it above the spot Siel had been grasping at, and proceeded to scan for any medical issues or dire health concerns.

The Terune chirped as it finished its analysis. Marn looked up in a librarian fashion; if she wore glasses they would be at the edge of her nose. "You know how if you cut off circulation to your foot after sitting on it for a while, it becomes numb and feels like there is white noise all throughout the entire limb?" She was trying to stifle a giggle because she knew after everything was said and done, Siel was not going to be happy about the results. "His leg just fell asleep. It looks like he may have been slightly electrocuted, not enough for him to believe he was on his death bed, though."

"Miss Faith," The Man whispered, before being nudged in the rib by Faith. The welcome party was already wary of them. They didn't need to know she had the ability to create electricity and project it across great distances.

"What is that?" Faith immediately said, in an attempt to cover up The Man's quiet tones. "Can you use it on my friend?"

The confidence Marn had been feeling while playing with the extrapolator quickly evaporated as she mumbled shyly, "It's a Terune. It has immense versatility."

"What can it do?"

"Anything you need it to."

"My friend is pretty injured; could you scan him with it?"

"Hope?" Marn turned to look at her leader, asking for permission to use the device on the strangers. She was aware that Terunes were rare, and only those with wealth or fame had them. When she was still in the academy, every class had one, sort of like a class pet in a primary school. She was lucky to have played with one to begin with, but two in a lifetime was unheard of, especially one belonging to the royal family.

Hope nodded her head in agreement; she didn't see a reason not to scan the stranger, and besides, if he was really in that much pain, he hid it pretty well. It was important to her to show as much hospitality towards the guests as possible, more out of common courtesy than anything.

The Terune was brought over to where The Man sat. No one, including Faith, had noticed that he had not moved an inch since arriving. The chaos of everything had conveniently covered up his lack of motion, and that was the way he wanted it. "Please, you do not need to do that." He persuaded Hope, as he had come to understand she was definitely the one in charge. "We are here for something else, not to heal my wounds."

"Something else?" Hope cautiously asked, worried about what exactly the strange people had come to Quii for, praying that they weren't there for a specific item she had warned everyone to keep away from.

Disregarding The Man's plea to prevent the scan of his biometrics, Marn giddily held the Terune above The Man's broken arm, in preparation of a complete scan. She moved it around his entire body, pausing any motion whenever it vibrated in her hand or chirped. When she got to the portion of the scan that included his legs, a single tear ran down her cheek. "This man needs our help, Hope," she cried out as the machine in her hand chirped a final time to conclude the analysis. "I honestly have no idea how he made it this far without a wheelchair. He has no feeling in both of his legs, from what looks like a recent spinal injury. The more visual injuries are obviously his arm and his ears. His arm alone is broken in four locations, fractured in three, and the part that confuses me the most is two of his ribs are penetrating vital organs, but here he is, as calm as can be and smiling at us."

"My ears? What is wrong with my ears?" The Man asked, ignoring everything else Marn had just relayed to him.

"The Terune wasn't sure, it said the scan was inconclusive, but it is blatantly obvious to us that you and your partner are missing chunks of your ears. I can't even begin to comprehend how unhealthy that must be!"

"There is nothing wrong with our ears, lady!" Faith, who had fought self-esteem issues for years, took the observation the elf had made as a personal attack. She swiped hair over both of them, to cover them and avoid any extra unwanted attention to them. It had been funny to her when they were picking on The Man's ears, but as soon as she was included, she no longer found it humorous. "Where I come from, this is normal, and you guys would be the freaks!"

Marn hurried over to where Faith stood, understanding that time was of the essence if they were going to seek out medical attention for The Man. She wanted to see if the emotional lady in front of her would yield different results from the Terune about their ears first, however. It hadn't occurred to her that Faith might be telling the truth about her origin, but it did to her queen.

As Marn started the scan, Hope asked with a face that resembled a scornful glare, peeking through her bubbly facade, "Where do you come from? We realized you people weren't from around here, that was obvious, but nowhere in our solar system has the technology to travel via immediate transport, which I assume you did, since you lack the necessary tools to get here. Also, I demand to know what you came here for?"

"Then I fucking demand that if you guys are capable of fixing this man, you will," Faith snapped back; she didn't like the idea of someone telling her what she could or could not do, especially when the two groups had only come in contact with each other no more than five minutes previously.

The Man placed his firm, pleading hand on Faith's shoulder as a gesture to convince her to step down from the war she was about to wage. He would rather be truthful and honest with the elves, as it would be easier to get to his overall goal; nabbing that technology he thought he might need. "Faith comes from a planet called Earth, of the Garf Universe, and I am a Watcher of universes just here to help her save the day."

The group of curious folk displayed a range of faces, from perplexed to surprise. None of them quite understood what The Man was telling them, but all of them seemed to understand that he was being one hundred percent sincere with the words he just spoke.

"Okay, let me start again," he said as he rephrased what he told them, placing his thumb and middle finger on the outermost points of his eyebrows; his thinking pose. He wanted to clarify any details that might have been misconstrued. "You have seen the edge of space or at least know of it, right?"

They all understood, and nodded their heads in unison; that was one of the first things they taught you in school. "The vastness of space is limitless, until you come to the end," was an old metaphor the ancients would teach the younger elves, but of course it meant live your dreams to the fullest, and don't settle for the first step when you could attain something greater, until the end of time.

"So you understand that the edge of space is always growing outward? It is true, sort of. Think of the universe as a sphere being bounced along a hard floor. When it makes impact with the floor, as it inevitably will, the sides push outward, and then in a millirhont, it snaps back to its original spherical shape. The edge of space is the inner circumference of the sphere, and your world is right in the middle of it. Now imagine several trillion of those spheres bouncing in harmony with each other. If you were to envelop all of them into a net, you would have a realm. I am from a realm and Faith is from another one of those bouncing spheres."

"How did you get here?" Bramish innocently asked, his inner scientist curious about how they traveled through that much space and time to get to Quii without aging.

"When I enter my realm, I can instantly broadcast myself and others across all time and space. I can also bridge universes while there too." The Man's voice had become exhausted and dry from the pain he was feeling. Now that everyone knew he was in so much pain, he did not have to hide it but felt it was more important to stick with the original plan than fixing himself.

"Why here, out of all time and space, you come here, why?" the leader of the elf party inquired. She was becoming annoyed with The Man, only answering the questions she cared about.

"We are here," he initiated, only to be interrupted by Faith and her well-meaning frustration.

"We are here so you guys will fix him! He told me you guys are the most technologically advanced race in all of his universes, but all I have seen are thousands of green fucking trees and that tablet thing! Where is all this tech, I want to see it, I want you to fix him!" She was in the dark of The Man's actual reason for bringing them there but decided it was best to continue pounding in the nail, so the picture would stick; she was compelled to get The Man healthy again, like it was some greater purpose she was meant to fulfill. Besides, she could at least help him out once to balance out the few times he had saved her butt.

Hope wore an agitated grin. Her lips were pressed together and her eyes let out what her mind was really thinking. She knew from the moment Faith started speaking over The Man that her intentions were to be dishonest with her hosts; however, being the benevolent leader she aspired to be, she graciously accepted the dishonesty that the woman was trying to feed her. "Before we help your friend, please answer one final question," she said, staring directly into the faceted sapphire abyss Faith called her pupils. "I have never, in all my three hundred years, seen a purple aura around someone before; what does it mean?"

"You are the anomaly?" The Man shouted in disbelief. His eyes grew large and his jaw slacked, sending a tingle of pain down the center of his back as he gasped with surprise. He was aware that there was a near constant anomaly since the beginning of Quii's timeline, always working themselves out over centuries or sometimes over millennia, but it had never occurred to him that it could be a single person. "Let me guess, you received the visual prowess to see auras from one of your parents?" he asked when he realized one single person could not account for such a large timeline, going back for nearly one hundred tera-seconds.

"So I've been informed," Hope answered. "We as a people never meet our parents. When it is time to die, or it is time to procreate, we have to rely on stories from the ancients to learn about our familia, and I have been told that my ability to see what isn't there, my visual prowess as you called it, has been in every female in my bloodline since the beginning of time."

"Hmm, interesting. Are there any of these ancients still around?"

"There are only two left, Siel and..." Her voice trailed off and became distant for a moment as she thought about the lack of answers to her questions; the bridge of her nose rumpled, decreasing the distance between both of her eyebrows. "Don't you dare goad me; answer my questions, please. What does the purple aura that you radiate mean? I have seen a dark blue, which from my understanding is the presence of immeasurable strength. It only covers those who need it immediately, like if you are pinned between two giant boulders during a landslide. And I've seen crimson red, denoting an overwhelming hatred or grudge toward the world, but not once have I seen a plum purple so perfectly pristine; perhaps it is a polymerization of the pair?

"It is the Veil of Hope. The perfect ratio of the embodiment of freewill and the Goobert curse," The Man slowly revealed.

"Flattery will not be tolerated, Mister Man, and naming an un-known aura after me will not get us moving faster to your recovery."

"You vain bitch, the universe doesn't revolve around you. He named it before we got here, and I am pretty fucking positive that he had no clue we would run across a lady who would rather hear herself talk than help someone in dire need of medical attention."

Hope didn't understand why, but she felt offended by the words Faith allowed to tumble out of her mouth. The sharp sounds that Faith uttered sliced at her eardrums with a dull serrated blade, causing the queen to wince at the resonance the consonants were creating.

"Please calm down, Miss Faith... She did not know," he pleaded with the spitfire hell raiser. The pain was really getting to him, building up, making it difficult for him to speak. "Faith has an unwritten destiny, and the universe has no plans for her yet... so as of right now, she is the only non-watcher to be able to choose her own path. Her future is not determined; however, the weird and contradicting thing is: it is. You see, Miss Hope... Miss Faith had a little accident with a Goobert when she was younger, meaning her fate and her universe's fate are in grave danger. She was marked for death because she accidentally killed a member of the Goobert race without knowing the consequences, and now...and now she bears the mark; a wispy black haze covers her body, like Death's cloak, larruping about on a windless evening, excited to clock in. But through the haze, a bright white light radiates from her, from the deepest part of her soul and from the farthest corners of her heart...this light shines and penetrates through the fog of this curse, this light is her free will, her ability to choose her own destiny and her ability to choose life over death when the time eventually comes."

The amount of questions that flooded Hope's head was comparable to the amount of atoms in the human body; trillions if not septillians. The ability to articulate every last one would last the rest of her lifetime plus that of her offspring's offspring. She wanted to know what a Goobert was, what a Watcher was, and she still wanted to know why in heaven's grace did they come to Quii; the real reason, not the fabricated reason Faith had obviously lied to her about.

In the way only she knew how, Hope conveyed a multitude of reactions; concerns for The Man's health, confusion on all the foreign concepts she was just presented with, and distrust of the people standing in front of her, all at once. Her seasoned ability to display all the emotions she felt came from years of practice. She felt her constituents needed to know what she was feeling at all times, a vital part of her full disclosure and transparency policy as a leader. "Kithor, Rein." She motioned the two silent men to support The Man, to catch him if he collapsed from the overwhelming pain he was feeling. "Carry this man gently back to the city. He needs our help, so treat him as if he is a frail ancient. And you,"—her daggers for eyes rested upon Faith with unsettling judgement, while the two elves transported The Man away from the group— "this is my predicament: If I let you come with us, back to the city, I feel you may extort ill-will from the people who live there, just with your mannerisms alone. There is something about you that just brings out offensive hatred toward you. My best guess is people can't see the aura like I can, but they can feel its presence, like a tightness in their stomach; however, if we don't bring you along, I fear you might disagree with my actions and come a long anyway to protect your friend. I will assure you right this rhont that your friend will be protected and cared for to the fullest of our skills. We mean him no harm and would love to see him recover. That being said, I hope that you stay put, right here."

"No," Faith briskly responded without hesitation, slightly agitated about Hope's honesty, "I'm coming with you guys whether you like it or not. I don't fucking care that you guys don't fucking trust me or whatever bullshit you aggregate together to prevent me from going with you. If you are worried about the Goobert's curse being transmitted to your people like the common cold, don't fret about it; it isn't contagious or anything like that, and it also is of no concern to you. It is my problem and I will deal with it when the time comes, but for now, let me go with my friend!"

"Faith, I don't trust you around my people. There, I said it. I don't trust you not to go volatile. In the last few rhonts, you have changed your mood more times than a schizophrenic with bipolarism." Hope hated conflict, primarily in front of other people, and if those other people were part of her kingdom, it was a huge faux pas. Breaking unjust news to people was to be done behind closed doors, sparing any audience, but she suffered through the brutality she had to force-feed to Faith.

"I appreciate your honesty," Faith said, eerily calm. Her demeanor changed so suddenly it should have set off red alert alarms in the heads of the elven party but didn't. Her head tilted and displayed her eyes at a squint, matching her long gaping grin that curled up her cheeks. Behind her eyelids, the gate to her soul was vacant and dark, unprotected by the hollowness that bounced Hope's words around, flinging them about hazardously. "I have a lot to mull over, so if you wouldn't mind, I would like to be left alone now." She felt as if someone had just nailed her in the gut with an iron fist—she was short of breath and became excessively fatigued, feeling as if the world was out to get her, to drown her in a pit of sorrows and then forget that her cold, dead body was still there, lying in wait for the decaying process to begin. She was coherent enough to understand why the unforeseen anxiety attack happened, though. Hope's words had reminded her that she didn't have many friends, only one really, and he was being taken to an unknown area, where she wasn't allowed to follow him. It hadn't occurred to her that the aura she was draped in might actually dissuade other people to spend time with her; she hated that might be a thing, knowing all too well that it was already difficult to connect with other people.

CHIRP CHIRP! Faith had forgotten Marn was scanning her with the Terune, and the final chirps grounded her to reality and fought off the devastating anxiety attack she was about to conform to. "Well, that is interesting," the squeaky voice said, unaware of the little skiff the two women just had. "I don't have any idea why it took so long to scan you, but it says right here that you have an innate ability to 'listen' to metal." She applied air quotes to add emphasis to the word "listen." "But nothing about your ears either, unfortunately."

"Marn, what do you mean by 'listen' to metal?" Hope mimicked the same gestures the lanky lady used. She was a little shaky from the verbal abuse she had let Faith have and prayed she would calm down in a timely manner.

"I don't know, her biometrics read out as metal listening. I've never seen that before. I mean, I haven't seen a lot of diagnostics from Terune medical extrapolation before, but something tells me that is a rare report case, and we need to take her to the city so we can run more tests on her."

"Absolutely not!" It was Siel, who had been sitting with his back to a tree, perfectly content watching the conversations unfold, munching on some imaginary popcorn. His brash tone made the depressive Faith want to shove a lightning rod up his butt and take potshots at him. "I will not stand idly by while this insolent brat tries to weasel her way into our city, especially when a few millirhonts ago you said she was not welcome because she is untrustworthy."

Hearing Siel, Marn immediately reverted to her quiet, timid nature. She thought she was in trouble for suggesting they take the poor little stranger home with them; she wasn't quite accustomed to his atmosphere-shattering voice and thought she was getting yelled at, even though that was just how the second in command spoke to people around him. "I'm sorry, Hope, I didn't know you didn't want the lady to come with us. I didn't mean to contradict your ruling on the subject."

Faith was almost positive the scrawny girl was going to start bawling, but she didn't, and the lack of tears upset Faith; she wanted to see someone else start to cry instead of being the lone ranger when it came to emotions.

"It's okay, sweetie," the queen cheerfully said, displaying a small warming beam across her face, patting Marn's small head in reassurance. Her touch was warm, enough to bring a small glimmer of ease to the girl. "You know what, Siel, I have changed my mind, Faith, you're coming with us. You'll be under supervision for as long as you are in the city, though. Faith will be your responsibility. Marn and Joena, do not allow her to rampage through the city, and she is to be calm the entire time she is there. Do you understand, Faith?" One of Hope's eyebrows lifted higher than the other as she asked her question.

"I'm a test subject? Just a rodent to be watched and cared for? I'm not sure if I want to go with you if all I am to you people is an experiment waiting to happen, but if this is the only way I get to go with my friend, then I guess I have no choice in the matter, do I?" Faith asked with morose clogging her attitude.

"You do have a choice," Siel uttered before being smacked across the face by Hope's open hand.

She was fed up with him and felt she needed to take the

proper means to quiet his relentless snipes at her guests. She looked across the gaping mouths and wide eyes, while neatly tucking a strand of hair that had come loose behind her ear as she said, "I apologize to you all that you had to witness that. I'm not prone to anger outbursts like Faith, with all due respect, but Siel has been wearing me down for the last forty-seven years, and that seemed to be my last straw."

Faith began to hysterically giggle at what she just witnessed. Her attitude seemed to return to its normal position on her wide spectrum of emotions, and she rapidly clapped her hands together. "You don't need to fucking justify your motives, lady, we all wanted to hurt him, and you're just the one who acted on it." She took a deep drag on Quii's air and continued. "I'm just surprised it took you so long; you have way more patience than I do! You know you're not half bad actually?"

"Thanks, I think," Hope mumbled. It was written across her face in permanent marker, she felt bad for hitting Siel, but something in her snapped and compelled her to lash out against him. "We should probably get going back to the city. Our adventure has been going on for too long, I think. Bramish, keep Siel by your side, support him as we go back; he strayed too far away from us last time and I almost thought we had lost him." The more she spoke, the more she rebuilt her bubbly facade. By the end of her statement, her facade was completely rebuilt, and she wore it proudly like a knight in freshly forged armor. "Let's get going!" She clapped her hands and pointed in the direction home was. The group of people marched forward, eager to get home and tell the stories of what they witnessed on their little adventure with the queen.

CHAPTER 7

MEGALOPOLIS ENIGMA

Through the deciduous landscape the group of exploring adventurers emerged, taking in the scenery and scents of the wilderness. The topsoil was soft and compacted when the group of people stepped on it, leaving pronounced footprints of roughly the same size along the path, so when the squishy feeling underfoot changed to firm, dense concrete, Faith couldn't help but notice her heels made a hollow thud, in rhythm to her quick stride, compared to the suppressed footstep sounds they had been making the entire way there. She noted that the line between the thick forest of trees and the cement extended well past her line of sight. The trees thinned out a minuscule amount, breaking the cement's dull, flat appearance apart; every tree was surrounded by circles of cement at the base of their trunks and appeared to be well groomed so that the branches only grew upward on the higher portion of the bodies. *It is rather peculiar,* Faith thought while observing her new surroundings. *Why are a group of people, who are so engrossed in nature, according to the jackass, barricading it over with thick plateaus of cement?*

As Faith raised her head, to see if she could see the sky, she saw a skyline off into the distance, of towering buildings in varying shades of gray, black, and white, and to her surprise, there was a building that stood several stories taller than the tallest of buildings, right in the middle of the dullness. The building looked as if it touched the sky, penetrated it and the clouds, and then flew high into the atmosphere, maybe into space, maybe farther. "What the hell is that?" she asked Marn and the one name Joena in awe, pointing in the direction of the tall structure.

Joena ignored the stranger's curiosity with her nose pointed to the sky and a faster pace. However, Marn squeaked out, "It is the Orbital Elevator; it goes from the core of Quii, to the edge of the planet's atmosphere, following the radius of the orb the entire time. Go to the top if you want to observe space, without atmospheric blurring, and go to the bottom if you are interested in thermodynamics or geology. Only important people are allowed to travel it, and you need permission from the High Council of Engineers. They guard it better than the queen, right, Hope?"

"Information is very crucial to us, so I prioritized the safety of the Orbi-vator over my own, not to mention it took years to build it, and millions of lives spent buckets of blood, sweat, and tears engineering it. So to honor those who built it and lost their lives while building it, only those who have the right credentials and proper training are allowed to ascend or descend it."

The way she shortened and combined Orbital Elevator endeared Faith to her; she thought it was cute that she gave a massive project and undertaking a little pet name. "How did you guys do it? I know that the higher you build things, the more unstable it becomes, so why hasn't that thing toppled over?"

"You just have to account for the structural integrity, the base, or at least the middle of the structure is significantly wider than the pinnacle, and it even widens farther the deeper into the planet it goes. I would have to estimate that the surface area it covers, above Quii's crust, that is, is roughly forty-two percent of the planet's surface."

"But it looks so small!"

"We are still a good distance away from it, and the city," Bramish joined in; he enjoyed talking about the Orbi-vator, like it was his own child.

"I thought we were close, because the path became solid; we aren't walking on the dirt path anymore."

"You must be talking about the cement structure underneath our feet." Bramish stomped his foot after pausing for a moment to indicate they were speaking about the same thing. "This is a relic, a gift from the ancient's past. Even Siel wasn't even conceived when this thing was built. They didn't pass the information on before they all disappeared, so we are left in the dark. No one knows what it is for, or why it's here, or even how to gain access to it."

"How far out does it extend?"

"The Orbi-vator sits right at the edge of it; of course there is a little bit of space between the two, so that the Orbi-vator can flare out when it goes beneath the planet's surface, but for all intents and purposes they sit next to each other, with little to no interaction between the two."

"I've heard rumors," Qunor chimed in, dropping his medieval accent Faith was accustomed to. He whispered to avoid unnecessary attention from Hope or Siel but was intrigued by the conversation. His ears drooped in the same way a cat tries to show that they are angry. "I've heard that when you descend the elevator, the relic is visible most of the time, and the queen built it so she could see what exactly it was. Why do you think only a certain few are allowed to go down, while a lot more are allowed to go up?"

Hope heard every word come out of Qunor's mouth, but knew if she denied anything for the reason she built it, it would almost guarantee the solidification in the minds of her constituents of that rumor. Rumors in the city spread like wildfire, perhaps even worse—the population was only seventy million, but everyone enjoyed a little take in the rumor mill and the gossip would be in everyone's ears by the time lunch rolled around. She would rather that her people spend their time more effectively than spreading lies to anyone who would listen.

"That is not true," Siel boomed. "We have more astronomers than we have geologists, and that is why more people go up than down, not because we are trying to cover up the existence of something that everyone is already aware of."

"Right? And there is nothing wrong with our guest's ears," Qunor exclaimed, in a joking manner, unaware that his volume had picked up unwanted attention from Faith's fist. It clenched as she mustered the strength to stay calm. She wasn't a big fan of being picked on, not by her friend, not by her family, and most definitely not by the freak whose skull couldn't even contain his own eyes. She had to remember, staying calm was the only way she was going to stay in the good graces of those who were watching.

"Now you are just being a bully, Qunor; as far as we know, there is nothing wrong with Faith's or her friend's ears. Remember the Terune said so." Marn squeaked in frustration, doing her best to draw the teasing away from the one she was responsible for.

The closer to the city the group got, the fewer trees there were; however, the ones that were there had shifted their hues from bright green to golden brown to crimson red. It was a pleasant shading effect that added a nice aesthetic to the terrain, which Faith had observed there were no more ups and downs, no hills or little ditches to climb through, but only flat, smooth floor, almost exhausting to look at, but even more boring to walk across. *It's so weird how quiet it is,* Faith thought, realizing she hadn't heard a song from the birds or even the slightest crunch of a twig from a scampering rabbit or deer. *This fucking planet has animals, right?* "Why is the silence in this forest so deafening?"

"Wildlife haven't been to these parts of Quii in nearly a millennium; we think the relic has something to do with it, but we aren't entirely sure," Joena finally said, putting away her snobbish attitude. Her voice sounded more masculine than the feminine wiles she exuded, her voice did not match her face or her dainty body, and this unsettled Faith.

She wanted to hear Joena speak more, to get used to the idea that she might be able to wrestle a bear, by speaking to it. *I wonder if that is the reason she doesn't talk much.*

"As soon as the birds fly within proximity of the line back there,"—she turned to look behind her, to indicate which direction she was talking about—"they retreat or turn the other way. Some have heard rumors of a bird shield, or some sort of anti-aviary technology that cancels out their need to travel in our air space; of course these are just subjective assumptions that mean nothing, because other wildlife can't stand to be near that line either. The small river that runs into another side of the city always has a clog of fish, right on the line, which makes the fishing industry pretty easy, but still, that doesn't change the fact that the fish are trying to swim upstream after carelessly floating downstream for whoever knows how long, as soon as they get to that area. You'll also notice the lack of insects flying around. Most people in the city have never even seen one, which I personally find hilarious, because most people in the city are over two hundred years old."

Wow, when she starts she doesn't stop, does she? Faith contemplated while taking in the information she was being fed by the spoonful. Her eyes started to glaze over, doing her best to not sound annoyed as she asked, "Why do you know about all of these things?"

"It is my job to watch animals and their habits; however, I can't do that when I am stuck in the city, so I spend most of my time outside the relic's line. I am the one and only zoologist for the city."

"We don't have any need for an official zoologist in the city," Siel interrupted with heavy gasps, incredibly winded from the excursion so far, an interruption Faith was actually grateful for, assuming Joena would go for another long-winded lesson. "She is a self-proclaimed enthusiast of animals, who has an uncontrolled obsession for anything outside the city. To me, she is just a glorified conspiracy nut, who ignores any form of information obtained in any way other than her own 'research,' which are not backed up by authoritative sources or cited in any legit documentation."

No, I was wrong, naysayers are why she doesn't talk much. Faith's level of frustration rose; she hated something about Siel's voice and wanted to end the frequency genocide he was committing as he spoke. She wanted to break off a branch from one of the trees, pull off every leaf, and shove them straight into his mouth so that there was a glimmer of aspiration that he might choke on them, but she resorted to name-calling instead. "Did she provide me with any false information, dickhead?"

"Ma'am, my name is Siel, not 'Dickhead,' and if you'd prefer to, I would gladly accept Sir or Lord, whatever would fit your fancy at the time."

"Sure thing, dickhead. Now answer my question."

He mumbled something under his breath in his exasperation, pouted for a few minutes as they walked along the trail that wasn't really there, and then aloud said, "No." It was out of context and no one remembered what the conversation he was a part of had been about, as the subject had changed too many times to remember the transgressions that had been applied to him, forcing those in the adventure party to pass his single word off as the ramblings of a crazed person, one of which almost everyone in the group had to respect due to the significant age gap. He returned to his sulking like nothing had ever happened and remained silent the rest of the trip back to the city.

~~~

The group approached the edge of the city's limits, which was lined with the grayest of metals. *Probably some sort of steel,* Faith thought, blown away by how protective the elves were. The city border extended a few hundred feet in the air, like it was some sort of skyscraper from a big city. It expanded in both directions, indicating to Faith that it wrapped around whatever it was protecting and constricted it from the outside world. From the base of the expanse, it was hard to see the Orbi-vator, unless one were to really crane their neck. When the trees and other flora had finally disappeared completely, it left a light shade of gray nestled up against a darker slab of gray. The two grays clashed into each other, forming an optical illusion that confused the eyes of whomever laid rest upon them. The darker of the two cancelled out the lighter, jumping into a barrage of hurdles Faith's mind was never going to be prepared for, no matter the distance she ran to pick up speed.

"Well?" Hope asked, glancing at her guest, looking for an answer that no one asked.

"Well what?"

"What are our walls saying? Are they speaking to you?" Hope was incredibly intrigued by what secrets the walls were willing to give up. She wanted to put Faith's "metal listening" to the test but was unsure if she really wanted to know what the walls were willing to reveal about their long history standing watch over the ancient city.

"Uh." Faith paused, convinced she was going to be caught in a lie, something she didn't ask for, but was willing to keep it going as long as it served her purpose. Her eyes shifted from left to right and back to left as she met all the elves' prying peepers waiting for some sort of confirmation that she could indeed listen to what the metal was saying. "They aren't saying anything," she lied, praying to some great deity watching over planet Quii that there would be no follow-up questions. "Well, we tried; might as well keep moving. We are almost there, right?"

She began to move forward, but her stride was cut short when Marn said, "I bet it doesn't trust you yet."

"Yeah, she is probably right," Bramish seconded. "You're just making them nervous. They've never had someone listening to them before, and now they have stage fright or glossophobia."

You have got to be fucking kidding me! Are they screwing with me? When did they have time to set up this hoax?

"Try speaking to it first," Qunor said, wanting to be part of the conversation, but failed to understand how to add to it. "Maybe if you show it that you're willing to have a heart-to-heart with it, it will answer back? Try it."

Faith closed her eyes to hide her annoyance with the group of ignorant fools, pressed her hand against the cool, hard exterior, while tracing a hardly there dimple in its surface with her fingers. She exhaled and then awkwardly spoke to the sheet of processed ore in front of her, "Hi, wall...is it alright if I call you that? Do you prefer metal instead?" She despised the interaction she was creating; to her it felt clunky and forced, but the elves were soaking up every word, buying into the little fib they had unknowingly created themselves. "My friends here seem to think you want to share some information with them, and I was talked into helping them. Would you please throw me a bone, so we can move forward and I can see my other friend?"

Silence came back, not to Faith's surprise. She held her hand against the surface for a short little bit afterward, just in case the metal did actually want to speak to her. As she pulled her hand away, the oblique silence ended as she heard someone or something shout, "Help me!" The sudden unexpected voice rowing across the folds of her brain startled her. She jumped and retracted her hand with voracity, leading to a wave of gasps from her onlookers.

With a moment to look around and to figure out if she was the only one to have heard those words, Faith nonchalantly said, "The wall shocked me a little, but still no response. I guess it just doesn't want to talk to me." She couldn't believe that a single lie, forced upon her, was snowballing, but the thing that was even more unbelievable was that she heard a voice and it said "help me." It sounded vaguely familiar, like she'd heard it before at one point in time, but she couldn't place it; she was never really great at distinguishing voices without a matching face, though.

"Weird, I could have sworn the wall was grounded, so no one would be shocked. It has never zapped anyone before," Hope said as plainly as she could, still interested in if the metal in the wall could speak. Her pupils were attached to the farthest portion of the structure—they were unblinking and empty. She seemed like her mind was vacant of thought but somehow still seemed to be functioning in a totally normal, non-robotic fashion.

"It happens to me all the time, more than I would care to admit," the trans-dimensional lady promised, allowing for the smallest hint of honesty to peek through her cloak of lies, to enhance it and make her tall-tale more believable. She followed her statement with a sarcastic jovial laugh, which she forced from her diaphragm, to encourage the leader of the group to stop pressing into the subject. "Since I was a little brat, really."

"Hmm, interesting. Just to be safe, Siel, send a couple engineers out to do a routine maintenance on the outer wall's wiring; we don't need anybody getting electrocuted on my watch."

"Why does it have wires? It is just a metal slab, right?"

"Yes and no," Marn quickly said, willing to discuss something she had learned in a lecture at the academy. "It is a metal slab with a few holes bored through it to allow for the wiring harness to slip through, but the wiring harness is a gigantic network of cables and cameras, going to and from the information hubs of the city. Everything you say or do in the city is recorded and then uploaded to a vast database that consists of speech patterns, DNA results, facial recognition, and other things like that. The odds of the city knowing your work schedule better than you are highly probable and extremely likely."

"And you're okay with that? That sounds horrible."

"We are; we wouldn't have known about it unless the queen came out and said it directly, so we are grateful that she is so honest."

Faith was in disbelief. She couldn't wrap her head around being constantly surveilled one hundred percent of the time. "But why does she need that much information on you guys?" She turned to look at Hope. "Why do you need that information?"

"On our quest for knowledge, it occurred to me that if we were going to know everything we possibly could about our world and universe, we needed to know the people who work for me and with me too. One hundred percent of my constituents, that is over seventy million people, voted to install the wiring harness. Since inserting this technology into our everyday lives, our crime rate has dropped to lower than one percent, there are more jobs, and my people feel less stress from the strain of a possible violent outburst. I am not the only person who has access to this information—the information we collect, that is. Everyone has complete access on their own files, plus that of their significant other's. So, to answer your rather rude-sounding question, I need all of that information to increase the longevity of my kingdom. It is for the people of Quii."

That sounds like a typical politician's bullshit response to me. Faith picked up on the slight subtleties of Hope's jargon; the words that didn't align with the previous set forth words. "Oh, I see, interesting response... Wait a moment. Marn literally just said you came out and told them, but then you said the vote was unanimous. Which is it? It can't be fucking both, now can it?"

Hope observed Faith's cunning, and saw she was eager to catch the queen in a lie; a game she was used to and had been playing with every new person she had ever met since setting out her political agenda centuries ago. "It can. Marn was just stating that I came out with the information that we had the technology and then my people voted for if it should be ingrained into the fibers of our city." She was incredibly circumspect with the phrasing of her words, understanding that a word out of place would proposition her guest to follow up with questions. Questions were great as long as they didn't force a perception of ineptitude in the way of those answering them, but follow-up questions were never just one question; there were always three or four more that would unravel the entire argument or set up mass confusion, a vicious cycle Hope would rather not indulge in. She briskly digressed the conversation, to persuade Faith from creating more political uncertainty amongst the party members, "We should press forward, before it gets dark; we don't want to be outside the city walls when the sun sets."

Why? Faith asked herself before seeing the giant metal slab, slicked up with some sort of lubricant, slide across the cement ground with ease.

~~~

The Man sat motionless and unresponsive in a brightly lit room, surrounded by a stale shade of white. The lights sat above his head and intensified when he moved the slightest bit; every muscle in his aching body tensed and cried out in agony for even the smallest of twitches. His head felt heavy and swollen, manipulating his vision into seeing double between the blurred focus it was creating. It was hard for him to process any information he was taking in, his head ached in pangs, but he was unaware of the reason why and could not care less about it, for it was the least of his worries.

His vision cleared as he felt his consciousness pour into his head. The room he was in resembled a sterile room. There was nothing on the walls and nothing really to look at. His befuddlement was written across his face, as he took in the mild appearance of his cage. "Where am I?" he asked aloud, hoping someone would answer. He knew he was the only entity in the room, but that did not mean he was alone.

A solemn, masculine voice sounded from every corner of the room. "Great to see you're awake."

What? The Man was confident that the last thing he remembered was entering the city. The buildings were stacked on top of each other. It felt cramped and crowded but in a conspicuous sort of way, it felt open and unmolested by the outside world. "Where am I?" he asked once again, evaluating the environment; he wanted to examine the possibility of him being watched. "How did I get so honored to be treated to this colorless room?"

"We brought you here."

"Who is 'we'?"

"You were severely injured, to the point of paralysis. We brought you here to fix you."

"I remember being brought into the city, but how did I get here?" The Man threw up his arms to indicate he meant the room, not the city.

"We brought you here." The voice remained at its monotone cadence, confirming to The Man that he was speaking to a robot.

"Where is Faith?"

"Faith: a complete trust or confidence in someone or something."

"Where is the person I came here with?" The Man was being pushed to the brink of being annoyed. He hated having to ask the same question over and over but figured it was necessary in order to figure out what information the system had on him.

"The people Rein and Kithor arrived here at approximately twenty rhonts past seven, with one unnamed stranger. Rein and Kithor are now located in subsection four point three two."

I guess it did answer my question, but that is definitely not what I meant. A single brick of frustration planted itself amongst the wall that had been forming. "Where is Hope?"

"Hope: a feeling of expectation and desire for a certain thing to happen."

The Man released a sigh of agitation and asked, "Where is the queen?"

"The queen exited the city at approximately five rhonts and thirteen millirhonts, with the people Bramish, Joena, Kithor, Marn, Qunor, Rein, and Siel, none of which have an official criminal record and are currently safe to travel with. No further information is available. Would you like to make an appointment with the queen, when she arrives back in the city?"

"That would be wonderful."

"Appointment successfully set; would you like an alert when she is ready to see you?"

"Yes."

"Alert successfully set."

"How did you fix me?" The Man said without missing a beat, relieved to hear that Faith had not made a name for herself yet. No record was probably a good thing with regard to Faith and her exuberant shock.

"We determined you had paraplegia, affecting the lower half of your body. All we did was encourage your body to remember that your lower half still existed by exposing your nerve endings to a highly controversial procedure that stimulates several sessions of physical therapy all at once. Your entire body will feel like your muscles are going to explode, but do not worry, you will feel better in approximately thirty rhonts and twenty-four millirhonts.

"As for your arm, our procedure did not go as planned. We had difficulty fusing the bone back together and drawing out all the shrapnel from the bits of bone that essentially disintegrated. We did the best we could to repair your limb, but the fusing process had to be replaced. Fortunately for you, we were able to obtain donor ulna and radius bones, from one of our farms. There may be unwarranted and undocumented side effects from the replacements; however, there is no way of knowing, until they happen.

"We were unable to fix your ears. The cartilage in the upper portion of your ears, the helix, refused the stimulation process and denied growing any higher than its current position, even after multiple attempts."

"There was nothing wrong with my ears, so I am glad the process did not work; that being said, what do you mean I have two new bones from a farm?"

"That information is behind quite a bit of redaction. Please present your credentials before I obtain that information for you."

"I do not have any credentials, but I was under the impression that you guys were overwhelmingly transparent on your policies. Does that not apply to this information?"

"Access denied, please present your credentials to proceed."

"Could I at least get the abridged version, you know the version without the redaction? Is that alright?"

The voice took a moment to respond. The Man figured it was processing his request, potentially removing the words or information that was redacted. When it finally responded, the information it could not give out was censored with high-pitched screeches. "The Bone Farms were developed in a preventive motion to aid in the queen's contingency against the likely odds of a {SCREEECH} in year two-zero-six-eight-nine. After the {SCREEECH} in year two-zero-six-nine-nine the farms were hidden away and shut down under the {SCREEECH}. In year two-zero-nine-zero-four the farms were re-found and re-opened to reduce cases of severe outbreaks of {SCREEECH}, this greatly reduced the population by one tenth, but genetically enhanced those who did survive. The bone farms were then re-shut down and closed off to the public in year two-zero-nine-nine-two because of {SCREEECH}, only to be reopened again on {SCREEEEECH} year two-zero-nine-nine-two, for an unknown reason by unknown personnel."

There was a tenacious ringing in The Man's ears after listening to the intermittent screech barrage the voice made him suffer through. The silence was a nice, welcomed consequence afterward, as it allowed The Man to think of more questions he felt were important to ask. "What is today's date? Specifically the year."

"The current year is two-zero-nine-nine-two, the fifth of Rown." The words, as natural as they were, rolling out of the corners of the room, hit The Man hard, as if they were a bag of bricks, enough to knock the wind out of him. He had a sneaking suspicion the reason the Bone Farms were reopened recently were because of him; he was the unknown reason, but who was the unknown personnel that was so willing to break the laws for him? He did not enjoy being left in the dark of this detail; someone needed him for something and that fact scared him to no end.

"Who did my surgeries?"

"We did, we fixed you."

"Define who 'we' is, please."

The Man attempted this question, once again expecting a definition of the word "we," but instead was greeted with an ear-piercing redaction screech. This one seemed louder than the rest of them, placing The Man on edge, like he had just carelessly walked into the epicenter of a nuclear explosion.

~~~

When the heavy metal doors slid across the eggshell-colored cement, in the slowest way possible, they unveiled behind them a drab copy and paste of buildings, which looked as if they were precariously leaning into one another, stacked like Legos but built like Jenga towers. A dark moss green color lined the edges of most of the building with a few exceptions, to really make those that didn't appear important. The architecture of the buildings were finely detailed to the smallest of bricks, which broke up the gray into several shades. In the sky were countless machines jittering across the light blue background, at a steady pace. The machines resembled that of vehicles Faith was already used to but appeared to be using a very different fuel system, one that Faith did not understand.

The metal tainted terrain of the metropolis expanded far into the distance, well into the vanishing point of Faith's vision. Buildings were clustered together, forcing a claustrophobic feeling, mixed with a bout of dizziness and nausea. The Orbi-vator was now in plain sight and Faith could feel its overbearing presence cast over the city. The tallest building in the area stood next to the Orbi-vator; it was comparable to an ant next to a human, barely even registering that it, too, cast a shadow on the rest of the surrounding structures.

Faith could see cloud formations around the middle of the visible portion of the Space Elevator, causing her to assume it controlled the surrounding weather patterns. There was what looked like a river flowing down one of the sides, and along the embankments were greenery and shrubbery, to make the entire area more lively. The river curved and slithered around the city in a random path, ending at one corner of the interior wall.

After following the level concrete flooring to the city, Faith was surprised to see the urban expanse had pits and divots, along with hills and bumps, all of which added character to the boring display of the Quii lifestyle.

"This is our home, the city of Quii," Hope said, raising her hands above her head to show the pride she felt from being its keeper. "Home to so many unique individuals and characters that singling out a few would be absurd and impossible. A place so unlike any other place in our solar system that it is hard to say we stand by ourselves. A melding of personalities, and divine and exquisite thought processes that leap bounds to strive for greatness only we can muster. All of that in a neat little package, wrapped by our finest architects and engineers."

Faith ignored most of everything Hope was saying; she was in awe, reveling from the breathtaking scenery she could only imagine was straight out of one of those sci-fi movies she enjoyed so much as a kid. She wanted to take a picture but was in between cell phones; an ongoing battle of hers with the universe. Knowing more about her electric abilities was great but that did not correlate to her understanding that electronics hated being bathed in pure electricity. "Do you guys have a picture of this that I can have? I want to show it to people from my world."

The surrounding elves passed her off as talking to herself and ignored every word she said. They were excited themselves to be home. Their adventure would be coming to an end very soon, and they wanted to tell their family and friends what they had witnessed on their journey. The stories they would tell were brewing in their heads and blocking out any outside distractions, including that of a crazed madwoman, rambling to herself.

An elf, the same caliber of attractiveness of the rest of the group, approached from the side. He wore a long robe that dragged along the ground and walked with a fluid motion to make him be perceived as floating. Siel turned and spoke to him, away from everyone else, so they couldn't be heard. The new elf nodded his head a few times in agreement and then disappeared faster than the wind could carry him, causing anyone who had seen him to ask themselves if he really had been there. Siel returned to the group and approached Hope, whispering into her ear, as if he were attempting to keep something secret from the rest of his party members. Hope pushed her second in command away from her ear and finally said in the most professional way she could, "Would you look at the time? I think it is about time for me to retire to my chambers, but first my attention is needed elsewhere."

"Your liege would like to extend her gratitude to you, for joining her on this adventure. Compensation will be sent to your homes," Siel stated in a monotonous voice, which clearly implied this was routine for him, before turning and steadily treading away.

"Marn, Joena, you two are responsible for Faith, remember. Don't let your kingdom down, okay?" Hope said, before following in Siel's footsteps.

As Faith watched the royals foot-slog away, something stretched into her mind, a little ping she couldn't articulate, but which would seed itself into a stalk that eventually planned to hold a feeling of doubt and uncertainty. Something in her head just refused to make sense, but she was unaware of the connections her synapses struggled to make.

Chapter 8

Bone Farms

"{*SCREEECH*} This is your automated reminder for your appointment with the queen, set two-zero-nine-nine-two, the fifth of Rown."

That was fast. If I had known she would be in the city within a few minutes, I would not have set that alarm, especially if I knew I would have to listen to another ice pick to the ear, The Man thought as he cupped his hands over his ears to block out the horrifyingly loud appeal from the room's speakers. "Great, take me to her, please."

He sat in the room, patiently, for what seemed like an eternity, but no one came to escort him to Hope. "Look, I am growing rather bored here; please take me to the queen," he would eventually say, understanding that it was a waste of his time, but felt it was a good effort at least. "If you are not going to take me to your leader, at least give me something to entertain myself with. How long have I been in this room?"

A slow clicking sound was audible throughout the room, emerging from the corners. It sounded like a phone sitting in its own silence, the random tick of an engine cooldown, a sound companioned with an embarrassing amount of second guessing and self-doubt. The clicks dissipated and quiet instrumental music, probably played in elevators, began, drowned out by the voice that The Man was familiar with. "You have sat in this room for one hundred rhonts."

Not as long as I thought, but longer than I would have liked. The Man sat still, his newly recovered muscles stiff and tense from not moving "How do I get to the queen? Since, you know, you are not going to escort me to her location."

"We cannot allow you to visit the queen at the moment; the system has flagged you as dangerous and has prevented any further contact with her."

"I am not dangerous. What system? What did I do?" Rattling off these questions allowed The Man to ease the stress he was feeling, even though he was technically in captivity.

"The system has analyzed several million possibilities and scenarios, of which you become accountable for the queen's death in approximately ninety-eight percent of them. We cannot allow you to be in her presence, to further prolong the health and longevity of our city."

"So I am being confined to this room for a crime I have not committed, because your system seems to think I am going to go directly to her and kill her? I am not a judge, but I feel as if you guys are prosecuting me, without substantial evidence against me. Sure, ninety-eight percent of your analyses tell you I am a bad guy, but what causes do I have to kill the queen? She graciously allowed me to use your technology to heal me and has been nothing but nice to me and my partner, and for me to kill her would go against my morals as a Watcher. I kill unstable anomalies that push the equilibrium the wrong way. I do not kill innocent people, who happen to be an anomaly and shift the balance to the good side. As far as I can tell, your queen does not create absolute mayhem in this universe and I do not foresee her causing a dimensional collision, so why do you guys think I am going to kill her?"

There was a heavier silence, filled with hesitation from the system. The music halted, without The Man noticing, leaving the room stale as he was left fuming from his rude host's implications. He was never one to get heated over something as trivial as a computer's over-extrapolated conclusion of the future, but something in him told him that it would be convenient for this situation. He heard the ponderous sound of a thick deadbolt unlatching from his left side, turned his head toward the noise, and watched as a sliver of darkness wedged itself between two panels of bright white. "You are free to go," a new voice announced; it sounded more unresistant and anthropoid-like. "You will find the queen in her chambers, located in the tallest building in the city. We apologize for the unruly restraints we applied to you. Please exit out this door."

The Man sat, discombobulated. He was surprised his little tantrum, of sorts, worked in his favor. *No wonder Faith is always angry, it moves things along,* he thought, as his arms pushed him off of his perching position. The tightness in his muscles that was left over from his surgery scurried away, leaving a refreshing coolness as blood flowed into its proper channels. The ligaments in his legs sputtered momentarily as they remembered that they could hold his weight. His first steps were pain-inducing and caused little uncomfortable twinges fly up his spine but steadily became natural to him. "Thanks for the help," he politely said in the doorway before following a dimly lit corridor. The few fluorescent lights that were floating above his head buzzed with curiosity and intrigue. They flickered periodically, leaving an unscrupulous perception. *Something is going on; otherwise, they would not have changed the tune they were singing so rapidly. I guess I will cross that bridge when I come to it.*

He ran down the hallway, making sure to keep his right hand pressed firmly against the wall, just in case he was in a labyrinth to prevent him from escaping. The texture of the wall reminded him of those rubber mats people used in their kitchens; a firm feeling that would prevent fatigue if they were to stand on them for too long, but also a soft, cushioned feeling, with a thin dusting of dirt across it, that would be easier to rinse off with water than sweep away.

As he progressed through the seemingly never-ending passageway, it started to occur to him that it felt like something was keeping an eye on him, watching his every move, observing every choice he made, including the subtle instances when he felt it was pertinent to blink; ironically the Watcher was being watched by prying eyes, and there was nothing he could really do about it. However, he did not care to begin with, because he knew there had to be a catch for his release. A fair trade amongst the parties involved. An equal and opposite reaction to every action he was the center of; the universally consistent Newton's Third Law.

He knew that when motives changed in every sentient being, there was a good reason for their behaviors to change too. In his particular situation, the elves were holding him as a prisoner, but then strategized some unique ploy, which sent his approval to be released from their custody into motion. Of course, they were going to watch him—they were still under the impression that he was going to murder the queen, and why would they trust a stranger over their computer system, which simulated millions of possible outcomes in a matter of minutes? A system they finely tuned for an effective and reliable fortune.

~~~

"Where are we going?" Faith asked as she begrudgingly followed Marn and Joena around the urban streets. It seemed to her the two were parading her around town, like they were showing off a prize they had won at the local carnival. Up and down the roads they went, speaking to anyone and everyone who crossed their vision. Faith despised every second of the questioning glances that followed them wherever they went but remained as calm as she could allow herself to be, an act she thought was literally killing her. She would snap if the wrong person said something to her or about her that she thought was inappropriate; just the slightest nudge of her restraint and she'd most likely end up incarcerated for manslaughter.

"We are going to the academy, so we can research your intriguing ability. You'll have accommodations and a living space all your own," the squeakier of the two responded. Even though Marn was a skittish character when first interacting with new people, as she got to know them, she would warm up to the idea of being friendly and become a motor mouth. She was overly excited, a characteristic new people rarely saw from her, for being somewhat of a social recluse.

"Why do we have to talk to everyone that so much as passes gas in our general direction? Can't we just go straight there? Isn't it almost dark anyway?" Faith whined, extending the end of the questions with meagerness, a coat not befitting of her at all.

"We can't just show up; we need to give them time to set your room up, and get the machines ready. Don't worry, we'll be there in no time."

"How does this academy even know we are on the way? I don't recall you guys communicating something like that to anyone we have stopped and gossiped with."

"They'll know, they always do," Marn said, making sure to display her cheerful smile, her cheeks proudly wearing dimples as if they were a coat of arms.

"It is a certified information hub and all the information they gather goes into a network of computer systems that analyzes and predicts the future, with a very small margin of error. They run several million simulations to enlighten themselves on possible outcomes, but unfortunately they won't release the research and technology to the public. The queen herself can't even get her hands on it, from what I've heard," Joena replied with disinterest, leaving a conspiracy feeling in the back of Faith's mind, tangling itself with her amygdala's receptors. "They try to keep it under wraps. No one is supposed to know about it, but everyone does, which in my opinion."

Faith cut the speaker of too many words off, intentionally, "Why don't they want anybody to know about it, or using it? I would think they would allow the queen of all people to use it. I mean, who in their right mind would deny the queen the privilege to interpret her future?"

"We have checks and balances, so she doesn't become a tyrant," Joena said, upset about being interrupted, her eyebrows rippled to show her dislike, forcing the skin around her eyes to compress and give her the appearance of someone who was squinting at the blinding rudeness that ensued. "The council is always controlling her actions and thoughts. She has the ability to make new laws, but if they swing in favor of her own personal agenda too far, one way or the other, the Council of Ancients can veto her authority. She always can appeal, though, and random jury members, selected from the cities' pool of trusted constituents, are the deciding factors; however, it never really makes it that far along. She usually sees the error of her ways and retracts the law.

"If the Academy has access to this Psychohistory technology, why don't they share it? I would think it would be beneficial in many factors of your lifestyle."

Once again, entering the conversation, Marn peeped, "The Council of Ancients restricts who can use it, for unknown reasons, Faith. All we know about it is they use their algorithm to detect who will commit a crime before it even happens."

"That is so messed up," Faith said as they approached the Academy's steel, engraved doors. The building shot into the sky, showing off a steeple in every visible corner. The wall's support beams were carved out to resemble Hope's likeness, in several standing positions. Tinted windows painted the building, alternating the gray pattern, enough to make variants of the color stand out, especially against the similarly shaded background of the cityscape.

Marn was excited; she loved the Academy with all of her heart and then some, due to her long history with it. She enjoyed learning as much as the next elf, probably more, and the best place to learn anything was towering right in front of them. Her exuberance radiated from her posture, warming the area with positivity; passersby couldn't help but smile back at her. "Welcome to the Academy! I think you're going to enjoy it here!"

A short, succinct response fell out of Joena's mouth. "Doubt it."

"Is this where my friend is? Was he brought here too?"

"No, probably not."

"Then I agree with Joe-na here." The way Faith pronounced Joena's name implied malicious intent, at the elf's expense. A ridicule subtle enough to go unnoticed by the person it was meant for. "You're going to take me to him the next chance we get, do you understand?" she demanded, nearly throwing a tem-

103

per tantrum.

"We can't do that; we don't know his whereabouts," Marn said. Her innocence would have worked on anybody else, but Faith considered these words as the wrong words to say, and she considered Marn was being ignorant on purpose.

"Then we'll ask Hope where we can find him. Or we will make these people, at this school, tell us. They are an information hub, are they not?"

"They aren't going to let you waltz into their building and demand the whereabouts to your friend," Joena stated with cynicism. She appeared bored and uninterested in the subject matter, and still held on to her snooty attitude, while metaphorically sticking her nose up to the sky.

Faith was becoming sick of Joena's pessimistic outlook on everything, Joena's words birthed an uncharacteristic trait in her, causing her to tread swiftly to the entrance of the building; every step she took was heavy and with meaning. A determination cloaked her body. She was going to find her friend, and she was going to get the people inside this building to tell her where he was.

She was unaware of the barely tangible static she was emitting throughout her body. To her it felt like hype and endorphins, mixed with tenacity. She marched her way to the doors of the Academy, a journey only taking a few moments but which lasted forever in Faith's head. If anyone had bumped into her or accidentally touched her, she would have zapped them to the end of their life, revealing to her captors that she was hiding more than she let on. As she shoved her feet into the cobble flooring, her demeanor demanded anyone in her path to move out of the way, for their own protection. She ran up the steps leading to the narthex of the building, grasped the metal doors, and flung them open, shouting, "Hey, fuckers! Are you ready to tell me where my friend is?" Her silhouette disappeared through the doorway as she took off in whatever direction her head was guiding her, like a ravenous Tasmanian devil.

Marn was shocked by this show of egregious rage Faith decided to put on for everyone. Her first thought, since she was responsible for the heated lady, was that she was going to get shunned from the city and every academic circle she was ever a functioning member of, especially since Faith was raiding the most prestigious and most grandiose society Quii had to offer.

"Aren't those doors usually locked?" Joena asked, as something finally intrigued her enough to pull her snooty facade away.

Marn's eyes widened as she realized the pessimistic, sulking elf was correct. The doors, which Faith launched open with ease, required a six-digit pass code to be entered before entry, before the doors would unlock themselves and permission to enter was granted. There was no possible way she threw the hunk of metal slabs so easily, unless the Council wanted her to do so or someone had muddled with the pin pad and broke it. She ran up to where the keypad was, followed by Joena in more of a leisurely stroll, looked it over, and observed nothing unusual about it. She popped the front cover off, revealing a semi-transparent acrylic that encased several rigid yellow lines, none of which intersected but all led to a single point on the board. "Nothing looks tampered with, Joena. I think the Council knew she was going to pull this sort of attack; she might be walking into a trap. We need to go help her!"

"Of course they knew. They know everything that happens in the city; they probably knew she was going to want in the building, so to prevent any damage to the structure, they opened the doors for her. I don't know why you think she is running into a trap. There is no possible way she can be. The city wouldn't do that, especially to someone of great research potential." Joena rolled her eyes out of exasperation towards Marn's heigh-ho attitude. "Even if it is a trap, we can't be running after her so enthusiastically; otherwise, the city will think we are on her side, and renounce us both as citizens. You don't want to live outside the city walls, do you? I know I don't, and I love it out there, but that place is scary after the sun goes down!"

"You're right, Joena." The duo gracefully walked to the doors. Marn brushed against one of the panels with her elbow and felt a sudden pinching feeling as she did. "I think the door just shocked me a little bit. I think the Academy is experimenting with electromagnetism again." *That would make sense as to why the door just opened; there is no other explanation.*

Upon entering the building, an ominous voice broadcast itself into the ears of the two women. "Welcome, Joena Rightmer and Marniple Clourn; what brings you to the Academy's campus?"

"Hi, Cline," Marn said as if she were familiar with the voice.

"Our ward just came blasting through here. In which direction did she go?"

The voice spoke once again, holding a steady cadence and speaking efficiently, "You two are the first guests the Academy has had in thirty rhonts. Would you like me to contact the Royal Guard, to help you find your missing person?"

"No, Cline, she entered this building just a few millirhonts ago," Marn said, attempting to clarify Joena's request. "She was the one who opened the door, didn't you see her?"

"Our records indicate that you should have one other counterpart this evening. Would you like me to contact the Royal Guard, to help you find your missing person?"

"You're not listening to us," Joena stated, becoming annoyed by the cheerful-sounding, robot voice speaking into her ears. "Our ward, she is here, where is she? She has to be close, she literally ran through that doorway." Her head spun to direct her eye to the metal doors, to point to what she was referring to, only to retract back immediately. "Who entered this building before us? Who opened the door? Where is she?"

"Brimy Werthms is the last person on record to enter the main hall of the Academy's campus, prior to Joena Rightmer and Marniple Clourn's entrance at approximately thirteen rhonts past eight, year two-zero-nine-nine-two, the fifth of Rown. The last person on record to open the door to the Academy's main hall was Brimy Werthms, conflicting with the current information we have." The voice groaned in a way that resembled human pain. The woman had introduced an error into the system, which triggered an audit to the entire security network that was in the works.

"Cline, we are trying to help you; please just listen to us." Marn spoke to the voice as if it were a pet of hers, her speech gentle, warm, and understanding. She understood that the robotic voice couldn't comprehend the information the ladies were relaying to it, even though it should have a very detailed report of Faith entering the building. "Joena, I am starting to think the Council was unaware of this attack. Cline has no data on ever seeing Faith, and it would be the first to know about her. I definitely believe there is something happening here that we don't know how to answer. Why doesn't Cline know about Faith?"

"It does know. It knows we have someone in our watch, but it just can't grasp the concept of her being in this building already. Is there a possibility the Council is behind a conspiracy, and they really know where she is but figure we don't need to know?"

"Why would that be? The city wouldn't hide someone the queen specifically decreed to be watched and guarded."

"I mean, you saw Faith's face when we were telling her about our city. By the look of things, how we live our life is completely different from the way she lives hers, which means there are other types of government styles, and I think our politicians are aware of that. I don't want to believe it, since I love the queen so much, but I think there is corruption in the government."

~~~

Faith wasn't far from the confusion and befuddlement she had left in her wake; only hiding behind a corner, observing the interaction between the two women and the menacing voice. She found it interesting that she could blow past the security so easily, sure anything that requires electricity was her never-ending nemesis, but a camera system so vast should be able to track her with ease, like it was second nature to it. *Does this mean I can walk into anything I want, since their technology can't see me? I have to sneak past Squeakers and Bitch over there, but I might be able to find The Man myself. Should I explore this building first, just in case he is really here?... That would be a good idea, wait out the two women by the door, and circumvent them any chance I get.*

Faith ran down a hallway that seemingly led to nowhere in

particular but branched out in every direction. She preferred to stay on the main trunk but discovered it was more difficult to do that. In a short time she found the first dead end, or rather split in the road. There were no signs to indicate where she was, or where she was going; she just had to rely on her instincts to lead her to an exit of some sort, one that wasn't being blocked by her keepers.

Her heart told her to follow the path that branched to her left, which followed a long stretch of staircase downward to six or more landings, all preceded by their own eternally long staircases; Faith was unsure of how many floors she had actually descended, since she had lost count closer to the top. She reached the final landing and noticed it had brought her to a large empty room, in the shape of a pentagon, with three options to wander down attached to each of the surrounding walls and a single orange buzzing light in the center of the last wall. *Are they trying to get me lost? This place looked a lot smaller on the outside, but I guess you can't fucking tell how far down a building goes just by looking at it.*

She chose the path that appealed to her the most, which was a hard decision, given every single one of them looked identical, down to the grain on the inch-wide traction strips that lined every tread leading to the nosers of the steps. The density of the walls dampened her hurrying footsteps to a mild knocking sound, which bounced off of every angle the noise could find in the narrowing corridor. She was surrounded by a dense slathering of solidified concrete, and above her was a sibling light fixture to the one she saw in the hub of hallways at the end of the staircases, about every fifteen feet or so. There was no good way of telling how long she had been traversing the entanglement of passageways; for all Faith knew, it had only been a couple of minutes, but in reality it had been much longer than that. She was aware of her internal clock rivaling a dumpster fire but still tried to estimate the time anyway.

After the thirteenth, or was it thirtieth, bifurcate, Faith was genuinely lost. She couldn't remember how she had gotten to where she was, and the lack of people definitely concerned her.

It seemed to her that the walls were pressing in on her, condensing the oxygen in the tunnel to tiny, heavy cottony balls, instead of the smooth fluid ocean she was used to breathing from. Her desire to have a panic attack out of claustrophobia was greatly present, but she resisted its call by grounding herself to the situation; she listed three things she could see, and as she trudged past them, she would caress them in her trembling hand to remind her she wasn't dreaming, then two things she could smell, the must of crumbling infrastructure, and the molding of ancient pipes, and one thing she could taste, though she didn't want to lick any portion of corridor or its offshoots, out of fear of contracting a disease from it.

She wished she could sense the presence of her friend, The Man, or hear his omnipresent voice in her ears, but all she felt was a vertigo feeling, and all she heard were intermittent plops of dripping water from the pipes overhead, nothing really to be concerned about, just the condensation sweat breaking away from the group of molecules keeping it tied to the pipes.

Her free will had led her into a spiraling labyrinth that she was certain she wasn't going to be able to traverse her way out of before her untimely expiration. *At least if I die in these tunnels, Earth won't perish, right? I technically didn't die of that damned Goobert curse the jackass was going on about. So I guess that is nice,* she thought, including a melodramatic flair for her own playback later on.

She continued to stumble through the mess of hallways before it occurred to her that the smells in the air had changed. It had gone from the staleness of years past and morphed into a more pungent, horrendous odor; one that would peel the paint from the driest of canvas and would put the local Surfeit of skunks to shame. Faith gagged as the smell glided across her taste buds, and she couldn't resist putting her hand over her nose and mouth as she caught a concentrated whiff of it, before hurling the little remains of food particles previously resting in her stomach. Chunks of her last meal coated the palm of her hand and insides of her nose with a viscous, rank layer of vomit. Her eyes started tearing up from the acidic feeling that doused her esophagus and sinuses.

"What the fuck was that?" she asked herself audibly, applying emphasis to her profanity, knowing she wouldn't be able to process many thoughts as her mind was screaming from the agonizing stench. She tried to sponge up the layer of mucilaginous fluid covering the lower half of her chin with the arc of her wrist. When she thought she had wiped most of it off, she ran her hand along the surface of the rough concrete, to smear her bile onto the walls, in a half-assed attempt to clean the smell of her own vomit from her skin. She left a streak of chunky, greenish yellow viscid goop as she walked closer to the smell, against her better judgement. She brought the upper hem of her dress to her nose, placing her smeller-teller right where her cleavage previously sat, to filter some sickly smell that was flowing through the passageway. It was obvious the closer she got to the gut-churning stench, the more her eyes blurred as if the mucus membrane protecting her optic nerve was melting away, distorting any chances of her ever having perfect vision again.

Another bout of nausea came over her, as she rounded one final corner in the labyrinth of concrete walls. The hallway finally led to something, a locked metal door, with the first sign she had seen since arriving on Quii that read "Bone Farms." Faith could tell the smell was coming from behind the door, and she deduced that if it was bad on the side she was on, it was going to be far worse on the other side.

Her hand moved on its own toward the door's latch, like something was remotely controlling it. She needed to know what was behind the door and what was causing the stink that slapped her in the face so viciously. She knew it was locked, but she tugged on it anyway, out of pure curiosity. Nothing, as to be expected, happened, but that didn't ease her compulsion. Faith sent a small amount of electricity through her fingers and shocked the door, assuming it wasn't going to work, but to her surprise, it did. She heard a heavy, metallic clunk dissipate into the walls of the labyrinth. *These stupid fucks.* She smirked to herself. *I don't talk to metal, but my static conducts through it.* She pushed against the door, as it slowly swung on its hinges, creaking the entire way, and sending spasms up her spine; she hated the perpetual grind of metal against metal, especially when the rest of the surrounding environment was already setting her on edge.

To her disbelief, she had discovered an area that opened into a room the size of a standard football league stadium. The periodic lights cast a reddish orange haze across the entire room, in spurts, giving a nice strobe effect to hide what was in the chamber. Faith was glad she wasn't epileptic; otherwise, she would have been harshly convulsing on the ground the moment she opened the door.

She stepped into the room and heard a wet scraping sound, similar to that of a bleeding deer dragging its near dead body through thick bramble. The sound made her uncomfortable and the awful smell made her discomfit. Together they were tag-teaming her into an awkward, and unwanted, threesome, where she was about to pass out, and the other two were willing to continue until they were satisfied, but unfortunately they wouldn't be. Her stomach irked, as she willingly went farther into the room, disregarding every warning sign hanging right in front of her eyes and nose. Her feet squished against the floor, persuading her forward foot to retract momentarily, before she decided to press onward.

It took a moment in between the flashing frenzy of lights, but she finally understood where all the unwanted sensations were coming from. She saw what had squished under her foot and another load of bile charged through her throat, at a pace quicker than her muscles could counteract. Underneath her heels lay a grotesque glob of rotting human flesh, including a small bit of bone sticking out to cap the entire experience off with insanity. Faith took in her surroundings, carelessly ignoring them before, only to realize that the tiny glob of flesh she was stepping on was part of something bigger.

In the nick of time, Faith was able to pull her nose and mouth out of her imitation face mask, preventing the soiling of it with a layer of stomach waste. She felt weak, as most people do after tossing their lunch on multiple occasions. Her movements, though limited, stuttered with grievance and exhaustion.

She pivoted on her heels and saw thousands of hills of similar-looking piles of rotting flesh and bones covering the entire floor of the room. Every one of the stacks had a retching limb sticking out of the side of it, spinning and churning the vile mess below it, creating the sound that was making her so uncomfortable. The limbs were skinny from lack of muscles and looked closer to their skeletal make-up than an actual leg or arm that they were supposed to be.

The muscles in Faith's stomach tightened, preparing itself to hurl once more, but she found it to be impossible, dry heaving instead. Without thought, Faith screamed, a blood-curdling sound she herself was unaware that she could produce.

The individual limbs halted their rummaging and rotated slowly toward the sound's epicenter, terrifying the woman into silence and stillness. Faith could feel her heart pump blood into every major artery; her neck received the worst of it, releasing pain into her head, right behind her right ear. Her eyes grew wide, and she hadn't realized that she had also stopped breathing as well, a discovery she wasn't savvy on, until her head became light and fogged up.

Her muscles refused to listen to her brain shouting at her to run and opted to stay stiff and unmoving, out of fear that the limbs might start moving towards her; she had no clue how to handle that kind of stress, if it were to happen, and she didn't want to find out. The fingernails on one of her hands began to cut into the meaty portion of her palm, drawing blood from her clenching it with enough thew to crush a fully pressurized aerosol can. She could feel the ligaments in her forearm becoming fatigued from the Hulk fist she had formed and was tightly maintaining.

Why do the elves have fucking sentient limbs? Faith thought, watching the anthropomorphic limbs return to their rummaging, a sight that did not ease Faith's tensions one bit. She felt for the wall behind her, to catch herself in the likely case of her losing her balance. She never thought she was going to come across something so drastically traumatizing in her lifetime, but here she was, witnessing the most disturbing and unsettling thing someone could imagine, an orgy of scrawny, muscle-less legs and arms morbidly sifting through decomposing remnants in a cannibalistic manner.

Faith's hand touched the wall, but to her, it did not feel like the concrete she had seen the entire way down to the room. She was expecting the roughness of cinder blocks; however, what her fingertips brushed against felt closer to a wet slime than a hard porous stone. She noticed, as she closely examined the wall visually, that it was secreting a sticky fluid that coated the entire room.

The fluid had created a carbon copy molding of her brief but firm interaction with it. A few seconds later, the fingertip indents she had left in the muck had disappeared and were replaced by three red nubs that protruded in a menacing way. They grew outward until they were bona fide replicas of Faith's dainty index, middle, and thumb fingers, wriggling and trying to free themselves from their confinement they grew into. They looked as if they were going to rip themselves off the wall, by over-stretching their ligaments and pulling out their roots from the base of what typically would have been the knuckles.

The finger replicas showed no sign of mouths; however, Faith could hear them scream with joy, as the first finger, her duplicated index finger, finally detached itself from its shackles. It fell to the floor with a light but dense clunk, shortly followed by the remaining two fingers, producing similar sounds. They inched their way toward Faith, causing her to recoil, taking a step back. Her foot created the wet squishing sound it had when she first entered the room, but this time it was different: it was preceded by a hollow cracking noise that sent a shiver of panic up Faith's neck. Her initial reaction was to kick her leg out from beneath her, out of fear that she had just stepped on something she didn't want to; a force habit she had developed as a child when she discovered her love of heels. The secondary reaction was to stumble backward, to try to keep her balance.

Her legs pushed her backward at an awkward speed, persuading her center of gravity to climb to her throat and shoot back down to her waist, as if it were a catapult ride at Six Flags.

Her back hit the floor, as her body decided that it couldn't handle the extreme changes of perpetuation. Faith heard a goopy splat when her butt hit the floor, a sound she would rather not replay in her head, due to the nausea she felt from hearing it the first time. Her attention stayed focused on the fingers crawling toward her; it hadn't even occurred to her that behind her was something worse.

The replicated thumb lunged at her, hissing as it did. She kicked it away while pushing herself to her feet in an uncontrolled scramble of endorphins. She decided it would be best if she could run, if she needed to; an option she wanted to use as soon as she physically possible. "Get the fuck away from me," Faith shouted, forgetting the sentient limbs were sensitive to over-zealous sound.

Behind her, every limb rotated in the direction the unwelcome sound came from, her direction, and though she had only heard the noise of them rotating once before, she felt she was too familiar with it and rotated herself to see what careless damage she had done. It was a slow turn; first her feet, then her torso, and finally her head all stood within direct eye contact with something she hadn't seen before, something far worse than a few individual arms or legs sticking out of fleshy hills.

In front of her was a conglomerate of flesh tones, in the shape of a human; spikes dripped from its skin in random directions, and its body seemed to melt but was solid at the same time. The thing's body didn't hold a candle to its head in deformity, though; it had a drooping, gaping mouth and a surplus of glowering eyes, all of which pointed in different directions and reflected what it saw. Underneath every single eye was a carpet of bumps that made the skin look more like scales, but on closer inspection the little bumps were actually micro tentacles wiggling to free themselves from the monster, just as the replicated fingers had, from their birth place on the wall.

Faith, frozen in terror, stood and stared at the monster in front of her. Her legs quivered in an attempt to run from the room, but the message her brain was sending and the message her legs received couldn't have been further from complete opposites.

The thing steadily approached her, bobbing its hunched back in a half limp stride, dragging one of its forearms along the ground as it did, like it was carrying several hundred pounds of extra weight in it, to support it posture. It stood a good three or four feet above Faith, leaving it naturally intimidating; however, the closer it got to the terrified woman, the more grotesque and tyrannical it became.

When it felt it was close enough to her, it bent down to make sure its eyes drew a perfectly straight line to hers; she could see her distorted silhouette in the reflection of its pitch-black marbles. She saw that, to the monster, she looked like an awkward fun house attraction, from a traveling circus that was about to be in tears.

In the background the scavenging protuberances followed the sludgy growling noise the bastard creature was pushing through its ever-open mouth. All of them acted like sunflowers following the sun in the middle of the summer.

Faith stood as motionless as her muscles would let her, shaking in her heels, as the monster snarled and wheezed in her face. She couldn't smell the stench it was producing in its mouth, but she could tell that it wasn't much worse than the room in general; it gave off a nauseating aroma, one she could feel in the pores of her skin and the tips of her nerve endings.

It watched as Faith stood pinned against the wall (without touching it). It heavily breathed on her, waiting patiently for her to move even the smallest amount of air with minor sound waves. After leaning over its voyeuristic intrigue for a moment, it huffed in her face and growled, "You don't belong here."

Though she was frightened to her core and it showed from her trembling body, she unthinkingly stuttered with a pailful of sass, "Who the fuck cares." A mistake she only realized after the act of doing it.

The creature leaned in closer to her, an attempt to intimidate her into submission, and spittle shot from its mouth as it roared in her face, "Leave or die!"

Faith wanted to revert to her fragile teenage state of mind, a state she typically hated and would do anything to avoid, but this situation seemed to not call for an anxiety ridden conscious-ness; she needed to think clearly and prevent the monster from killing her right on the spot. *What would the asshole do? Would he attack it or flee for his life?* Her body moved on its own, be-fore she had come to an apparent decision.

Her foot shot into the air and kicked the creature with the force of a thousand cannon blasts, with the point of her shoe, in its stomach. It stumbled backward, as the shock of what she just did to it hit its nerves and the realization that the woman wasn't playing around sunk into the crevasses of its mind. "Get the fuck away from me," she shouted once more through the fire of her temper and the shade of her unrequited fear. She took off running towards the door she had entered from, her heels slip-ping and sliding across the surface of the floor as she did; she was used to running in heels and wasn't afraid of twisting her ankle, but the fleshy, viscous feeling the floor produced, had her worried she was going to do the splits and prevent her escape.

She stole a second to glance back at the monster before it dove at her with surprising speed. The boney spike protruding out of its forearm caught the fabric of her dress, tearing it, along with a few layers of Faith's epidermis, leaving a spiteful gash above her left hip. The pain was enough to knock her to her hands and knees and create an overwhelming sense of help-lessness, a feeling she despised more than being left in the dark. She felt compelled, because of the pain, to check to see if viscera was leaking out of her wound, but fortunately the slash only flowed heavy crimson fluid instead of vital organs.

The blood pooled on the floor around her stomach, staining the blue of her dress a more maroon color, as she tried muster-ing the strength to push herself to her feet again. The cut stung like it had salt, lemon juice, and hand sanitizer rubbed into it by a cactus; it created a numbness in her upper thigh and hip that willingly fought the stimulus she was sending to it subconscious-ly to encourage it to move. Her abdominal muscles spasmed in multiple quick bursts, inducing her desire to vomit again, but was counteracted by the realization that the monster lay in wait, hovering above her, giving up on its "leave" option and only allowing for the "die" choice.

Faith could feel the monster's presence lingering above her; it felt far superior to her than facing it directly. The looming sensation it presented stood the hairs on the back of her neck up, straighter that a steel beam sustaining the weight of a skyscraper. It shoved its foot into her back, forcefully, to prevent her from standing up. It wasn't going to allow her to kick it back the first time angered it; if she hit it a second time, it was going to have to kill her, without regrets. The monster applied as much force as it could to the woman's back to keep her pressed to the floor in the gooey substance that covered every plane in the room.

She could feel her body being cloned beneath her, a feeling she could have lived without; it tickled and stung but also felt like it was trying to suck her into the sticky mess, like it was vacuuming her skin, so that she would only consist of her skeleton. She was worried she was going to have a whole-body hickey that she would have to explain to her friends and family, and she was willing to bet money that they weren't going to believe her honest story either.

Faith discovered it was hard to breathe while the thing's foot was pushing her into the floor, being assisted by gravity and the sheer weight of the creature. She thought her ribs were going to crack under the pressure and the weight on her spinal cord was worrying her too; the last thing she needed was to be paralyzed, especially since she was unsure that The Man would recover from his paralysis. As the monster acted as a newly graduated chiropractor, for the woman on the floor, it squeezed out an idea from the deep pits of her memory.

In the chaos of everything that was happening to her, she'd forgotten her not so latent ability to stun—it was second nature to her, so thinking of it never occurred to her, even if she had used it a few minutes previously.

She channeled all the static she could gather in the room, including what little she could feel flying around in the monster's body, and guided the particles to the spot of her back the monster was stepping on.

She was aware of her ability to transfer the electricity she gathered from the room to any spot on her body, when a creep tried to touch her backside when she younger; a quick zap kept the pervs at bay, and a quick jolt prevented floor play, she had always said since this discovery. Her life had given her tasing powers, and she might as well put them to good use, she figured; the best situations to do so were those that protected her and her innocence from extra gropey hands.

She hadn't realized how much static she had gained in the short amount of time. To her it felt like a minimal amount, but in reality, her perception must have been off. She felt the ease of the lack of resistance from the creature's foot. It was refreshing, and she could finally breathe again. Her hands pushed her up, off the floor, so she could see where exactly the thing disappeared to. It was lying on its back, on a hill of skin and sentient limbs, about half a football stadium length away, a distance that still seemed entirely too close for Faith's comfort.

"I said get the fuck away from me!" she demanded, as she limped towards the door, placing her hand on the laceration above her hip, to coax it into coagulating. She grimaced from the pain her fingers dancing around the wound caused.

Her movement had significantly slowed since the creature tackled her to the floor, but she wasn't going to allow that to deter her from escaping the worst place on Quii. She felt exhausted and wanted to take a nap, but the only way she was going to get to do that was if she found her way out of the labyrinth of tunnels and hallways she had wandered down in the first place, and into a bed the elves were willing to part with for a few hours. She exited the Chamber of Hell the locals called the "Bone Farms" and slowly hobbled down the passageway, refusing to look back out of fear that the Thing might be right behind her, bulldozing its way down the same tiled path.

ESCAPE

Chapter 9

Rekindled Friendship

Faith had no semblance of an idea on where she needed to go. She was hoping just to dumb luck her way back to the surface, like she had dumb lucked into finding the awful room that was now behind her, forever to be solidified into her nightmares. The idea of never returning to the surface was perfectly fine to her, and dying in the corridors she was currently stumbling around in was okay as well, just as long as she never had to return to that room.

Faith had to fight off the constant waxing and waning of her drowsy eyes while her vision was waterlogged. The tears sat in the corners of her eyes, drowning her corneas in an attempt to push out the lingering smell and taste the stench from the room had left behind, which had been burned into her mind, causing a baby barf every time her thinker found itself dancing around the memory of it.

She had managed to ease the bleeding above her hip; however, one wrong move and the sneeze of a gnat would reopen the wound. It was obvious to her, from the inflammation and pus around it, it was going to be infected if she didn't get it checked out soon. The gash traveled a good one to two inches and felt much deeper; she wouldn't be surprised if it was down to the bone but knew it wasn't. With every step she could feel the throbbing of her nerves, screaming out, so they could remind her that they were in pain and she needed to take a break for a while. She didn't have time to stop, though, not when there was distance to be made and jackasses to be found.

Faith was worried about what else she might find behind closed doors, leading to her overall decision to not open more. She might not have remembered how she got to where she was in the first place, but she did remember only opening one door, hanging on the hinges of her regrets. She finally found her way to a staircase—she didn't know if it was the same one she came down, but in her head, it was going to get her closer to the surface and that's all that mattered to her.

Her body moved a few steps up the stairs before giving in to her exhaustion and collapsing face first onto the rigid flooring. Her nose took the brunt of the impact, but her forehead took a beating too, as they caught the edges of the risers. Her nasal passages began to flow with crimson rivers, and a final thought rushed into her mind before she slipped into her narcoleptic-like coma: *I might have shocked that fucker a little too hard.*

~~~

The Man felt as if he was finally getting somewhere; of course his sense of direction was screwed up, but following the labyrinth of hallways lulled him into an optimistic mindset for some reason. He enjoyed mind-numbingly boring tasks; they gave him a break from his stressful job. On the plus side of his wanderings, he got to stretch his legs, which even for being paralyzed for a couple of hours was nice.

He was convinced that if his hand left the wall's surface, the entire maze would change. He had no explanation on why he thought that, other than a small feeling in the pit of his gut.

Occasionally he thought he heard other footsteps, and once thought he heard someone screaming, but the sounds would always cease to exist before he could explore them, an occurrence that sent needles of adrenaline down his back every time. If there were people nearby, they may know how to exit this building, and if he could exit the building, he could get to the queen and ask her a few questions.

In the distance of one of the hallways, he could see a pile of blue and a glimmer that was reflecting off the lights above. He could not quite tell what the glimmer was, not from the distance he stood at least. It caught his eye, drawing his attention, due to everything else looking the same in the hallways. The unfortunate thing was that there was another hallway branching off, perpendicular to the wall he held his hand on, separating him and the thing lying on the floor. And only the deities themselves knew how many branches that hallway would branch into. He needed to make a choice: stick with the wall or remove his hand and walk towards the glimmering object.

Why are they making it so hard to get out of this place, he wondered. *I have come across maybe four doors, and they were all locked.*

He got closer to the object on the floor, and as he did it became more and more apparent that it wasn't an object on the floor, but a collapsed body. *Do they need help? Is it a trap of some sort?* His head raced with questions, but what made him act was the realization that the glimmer was blood.

His hand left the wall without him even realizing it. He had forgotten his fear of shifting walls and ran towards the body without thinking. He did not care if it was a trap—there was someone lying in a pool of blood and the likelihood of them needing help was high.

The closer The Man got to the body on the floor, the faster he ran. His legs tripping over his feet periodically forced him to stumble a majority of the distance. The pile of blue and blood began to grow legs and arms, as it became blatantly clear to him that the body on the floor belonged to the person he vowed to protect. "Miss Faith!" he shouted, fearing she was dead or dying. "What happened to you? Are you alright?"

There was no response, and he did not expect one either. She was lying face down in a pool of blood, at the bottom of a set of stairs, with no elves in sight. His first thought was that she was pushed down the stairs while they were leading her to him, but that did not make sense in his head. *Her head was on the stairs, so she would have been pushed at the bottom of them, which would not have ended with her lying in a puddle of blood. She would have pushed back, and the assailant would be lying right here instead.*

He flipped her seemingly lifeless body, gently, to avoid adding to what damage was potentially there already. He saw the stream of blood that was mostly dry, but wet enough to sparkle in the light, start at her nose. It looked as if she had slid down a few of the stairs, from the stain she had left behind.

"Miss Faith, are you alright?" he asked with malcontent, while checking her for a pulse. He could see her stomach rise a small amount, which give him reassurance that she was not completely dead. The Man cradled her in his arms, while his legs sat in her blood, the shin portion of his pant legs mopping up what undried blood there was. He shook her, in an attempt to wake her, even though he had his doubts that it would work. As far as he knew she was in a comatose state, and there was nothing he could do about it except for getting out of the building and finding the elves, so they could heal her.

Faith's head bounced as The Man shook her, and while it did her eyes opened. The Man could see the little slivers of sapphires that he had been endeared to since they first met, peeking through. "What?" she asked drowsily, in an almost incoherent fashion, infused with slurring.

The Man wrapped his arms completely around her, embracing the life that she had stubbornly held on to. "I am so glad you are alive, Miss Faith."

Faith weakly grabbed The Man's arms to show that she was glad to see him too, before falling back asleep. The Man wondered if she had even processed anything, through the blue crescent moons that were waning into dreamland. "Do not worry Miss Faith, I am going to get you out of here, and keep my promise to you."

The Man lifted Faith's unconscious body over his shoulder and proceeded to work his way out of the labyrinth, by traveling up the stairs that were forever stained with Faith's nose blood.

Chapter 10

Inadequate Knowledge

The Man did not realize how hard it was to carry a limp body, especially up a flight of stairs. When he reached the top of them, he had to set Faith down and take a small break, something he would regret doing only after attempting to lift her afterwards.

The first time he picked her up seemed as if it were easier, which made sense in his head. *The adrenaline I felt when I saw her on the floor must have helped significantly, but I guess enough time has gone by to make it not as apparent in my bloodstream.* He knew it was him and his lack of strength, not Faith and her weight. She was a tiny person to begin with, and he was not going to disrespect her and fall into the judgmental male stereotype. He hated that he fell into it when they first got to Quii; it was her body, and he had no right to dictate how she should live in it.

He perched her body along the wall and used the hard surface of it to help him lift her. Any outsider would have taken his actions in the wrong way, and hopefully would have come to Faith's assistance. Fortunately and unfortunately, depending on whom you asked, no one came around and found them in the precarious position.

When he finally managed to lift her onto his shoulder once more, he trudged down the hallway. After a while he felt exhausted again, and he had to remind himself that he needed to power through it; otherwise he might not be able to get her lifted once more.

He thought he had climbed at least thirteen staircases and wandered through infinitely more hallways before he finally thought he heard voices; however, since every hallway looked and sounded the same, he could not tell for sure. Before he heard the voices, all he could hear was the blood rushing through his ear canals, and the thumping of his over-exerted heart. He could not tell if his mind was playing tricks on him. He could have been slowly whittling away at his sanity the entire time, like he was some sort of woodcarver cutting chunks of kindling away from his next art piece. *Repetition chews away at sanity,* he thought, trying to keep his mind busy.

His shoulder was becoming slippery with sweat, from Faith's body bearing down on it, and he feared she was going to slip down, out of his embrace. He threw her up and realigned her on the bridge of his shoulder, to verify that she was not going to slide down into an awkward position. His arm crossed perpendicularly behind her knees, pinning the hem of her dress down so it would not feel the need to flutter as they travelled—the last thing he needed was Faith to come to and accuse him of being a perv. He had seen her deal with actual perverts, and the outcome was always a hospital bed.

They rounded one final corner before The Man could smell the lingering scent of fresh-ish air. It was stale, but at least it did not smell like dust and cement, like the lower levels had. He could not figure out why, but there was a particular pungent smell stalking them—he thought it might be whatever was watching him, but the elves were smart, and if they had the ability to heal severe injuries like paralysis or exploded bones, they would not send a spy on foot but would be watching from a camera room, somewhere offsite. They would have millions of angles on him, not just a single subjective onlooker, prowling the hallways for the stranger. *I wonder if Miss Faith got herself into some trouble? Found herself in a skunk tank, perhaps? No way her blood reeks this bad.*

"FAITH?" a random voice shouted, muffled by several walls. It almost sounded like someone was whispering into the corner of a room. If The Man had not taken a moment to catch his breath, he might not have heard it. It was incredibly convenient for him.

"WHERE ARE YOU?" a second voice came, almost without hesitation.

Those voices sound sort of familiar, but I have no clue who they belong to. The Man wondered if he should answer back. *Technically they are not looking for me, so if I answer back, what will happen? Will they have a better chance of recognizing my voice?* He took a second and then had a realization. *What if they are hunting Faith? Did she do something to provoke them? That would make sense on why her nose was bleeding and on why her hip has a nasty-looking cut on it.*

The Man thought about it a little more. *Wait a minute. If these voices in particular are looking for her, then they were not the ones who hurt her; they would know exactly where they left her injured. They would have scooped her up right then, and they would have taken her to a white room like they did with me. I am sure of it.*

"FAITH? WE KNOW YOU'RE AROUND HERE SOME-WHERE!" the second voice said.

They were closer, or at least louder to The Man. He felt like he was running out of time to make a decision, relying on his old faithful; his gut reaction. His mouth grew tired of him trying to make a safe decision and blurted out, "OVER."

~~~

"HERE."

"Marn, did you hear that? Someone shouted back, and I don't think it was Faith," Joena said, semi-concerned in a whispery tone. She was aware that they shouldn't be shouting in the Academy, especially after dark. People were trying to study and throw themselves into their research, and if there was too much ruckus, they tended to become upset.

"That's alright, we have permission from Cline to search the school's hallways," Marn squeaked with a fake half smile. She was fairly confident that they were not going to anger anyone. The walls that separated the hallways from the rooms were pretty thick and if Cline needed to, it would dampen the decibels they were creating; with its active noise cancelling, no one should be able to tell they were running around in the hallways, shouting to their hearts' content.

"If you remember correctly, it gave us permission for the first two floors. Everything below that is restricted, like we were students or something." Joena scoffed at the idea of being treated like she went to the school. She had gone for a few years but realized she learned more outside of her classes than in them. She also hated the guidelines she had to follow while she was a student; a constant barrage of useless information and rules that made the students there seem closer to robots than actual people. "It also only gave us about one hundred and sixty rhonts of clearance. Our time is almost up, Marn. I think we need to quiet down, just in case."

"We can always ask for more time. Cline is pretty easygoing if we ask nicely." Marn paused a second to look around a corner, as if she were deciding which path she should take; the left or the right branch. "FAITH, CAN YOU HEAR US?"

Joena shouted a few seconds after wondering how Marn could be so loud, without vibrating the insides of her nose, causing a sneeze or two to happen. "FAITH, WHERE ARE YOU?"

It was obvious to Marn that her associate was becoming upset and annoyed about their situation. Joena was right; it wouldn't be long before the AI system would come and find them and tell them that their time was up. The thing with Cline, however, was that sure, you could ask nicely for anything, but the moment you did it would always ask for something in return. And unfortunately, it would always ask for the same thing; new information, something it didn't know. It was awfully difficult to provide this information, given the computer system was constantly learning new stuff and stored roughly ninety-eight percent of all the information the community gathered and processed. The likelihood of it allowing them to continue searching was fairly slim, unless they were able to pull some new facts that it didn't know about from their collective brains.

"HELLO! WE ARE OVER HERE!"

"Did that sound like Faith's friend to you, Joena? What's his name?"

"I think Faith called him Jackass," Joena said as her ears perked up and twitched so she could listen to the distant-sounding voice.

"HELLO, CAN YOU HEAR ME? WE ARE OVER HERE."

"That does sound like him. What's he doing in these halls?" Though she considered herself to be analytical, Joena couldn't think of an answer to her own question. "Didn't they take him to the hospital? That would make sense, or they would have taken him to one of the several thousand labs around the city, specifically made for the research of paralysis and regeneration."

"WHERE ARE YOU? WE CAN HEAR YOU, JUST KEEP MAKING NOISES SO WE CAN LOCATE YOU," Marn shouted, nearly in Joena's ear, without realizing it

"THE LAST DOOR WE SAW WAS LABELED TWO-FOUR-NINE-EIGHT."

"That actually helps a lot," Marn said, as her head spun around, looking for the nearest door. She was an alumnus to the Academy, had attended it for nearly thirty years, but there was no way she was going to be able to get to her rivals in the shouting match without looking at a door to figure out which direction they needed to go. There were five thousand doors on the first floor and at least twenty thousand on every floor after that. "Joena, what number is on that door over there, in the opposite direction?"

"Three-zero-zero-two," the other lady responded after locating the closest door to her, adjacent to Marn's.

"Mine is three-zero-zero-three; we need to travel in your direction." The two women backtracked to the intersection they were just at and repeated the process of looking at the door numbers.

Marn had enough knowledge of the place to know that when they were on the three thousand hallway, they needed to enter the main hallway, which was easy enough—they were basically there. They had to travel down the main hallway for a few rhonts and then hitch a left just to get to the two thousand hallway.

When on the two thousand hallway, they needed to count the offset passageways, until they got to four, which would be on their right-hand side, and it would branch into the last of the convoluted system of hallways. *If you were not well acquainted with the system, you'd get lost,* Marn thought, trying to remember the ins and outs of the system.

"STAY PUT, WE ARE ON OUR WAY," Marn shouted just in time for Cline to make its reappearance.

"Your time is now up. Please return to the lobby and wait for the authorities to find your friend."

"You stupid machine, we told you when you restarted that she was here; that's why you agreed for us to search the first two floors," Joena said in frustration. She refused to be nice to the AI system, even though it had done nothing to warrant that reaction. "You ran a quick prediction algorithm and said if she was in the building, there was no way she would find one staircase going down, let alone two. And every floor after that is off limits to the public, so no need to search those floors.'"

"We just talked to them, Cline, they are in front of door two-four-nine-eight. Can you please allow us to grab them, so we can get them into a lab for research?" Marn didn't need to lay on the charm, but she did; her life revolved around her ability to make technology like her. She strongly believed that technology could sense intimidation and anger, and if it picked up too much of that sense, it would misbehave, showing every possible glitch it could until the user threw it out a window or in front of a sledgehammer.

There was a moment of silence from Cline the AI before it responded with, "There is no entity in front of door two-four-nine-eight, please return to the lobby and await the authorities to locate your friend."

"If you please will just allow us to go check ourselves, that would be great," Joena said, biting her lip through frustration. She was at the end of her rope when it came to the computer; she felt it was antagonizing them, just because it could.

"Sure thing," it answered back, changing its cadence so that it sounded nicer and more positive. It had learned years before that if it were asked something, it should try to match the inflection the person asking was throwing out; people were more willing to accept the answer it was about to give and less likely to get angry.

"Oh, thank goodness. I thought—"

The computer vocalization cut her off, before she could fully complete her statement.

"I will gladly grant you more time for your search, if you provide me with one thing. Otherwise, you will have to end your search right now, return to the lobby, and wait for the authorities to find your friend."

"Cline, I am going to assume you want the usual?" Marn asked, fearing they might not have what the AI was looking for.

"That is correct. I would like to learn a new bit of information. Something I have never been taught before, preferably something the researchers do not even know about, but if you cannot come up with that, I would be okay with new information in general."

Without a second of thought, Joena responded with, "What don't you know about?"

"There are plenty of things in this universe that I do not know about; however, I do not know the extent of my knowledge, with relation to what I do not know."

"Thanks, that is no help," Joena said, increasing her frustration. She was not aware that the system would require payment to further their search. She asked nicely, and according to Marn, the computer was pretty easygoing. *That was a lie,* she thought as she reached into the darkest part of her mind, searching for something she thought the computer might not know. "Are you aware of how corrupt our government is? All the lies they tell us but then cover up with reminders of how transparent they are?" She paused to read the room. She could tell Marn was uncomfortable, but without a face it was too hard to tell what the computer was thinking.

"Please continue. I would like to analyze your statements and check them for accuracy."

"Let me tell you this, Computer, I think the government is trying to cover something up. Something none of us are supposed to know about. Something that just doesn't make any sense if you think about it. Can you tell me how a civilization can grow to the extent that ours has, however, when we procreate, we die in the process? Something doesn't add up here, right? Sure you can have multiple births at once, in the case of my grandparents, one boy and one girl. But the most likely thing to happen is a single child, like myself. How do we have so many people in the city? I think the government is covering some important details about our population. And another thing, I don't think the queen has anything to do with it either. There is no way she does. I can't fathom any possibilities where she would be entangled in a conspiracy like that." Joena ranted, like she had practiced for hours, thinking about every counter argument for every argument to grace her with its presence.

"Interesting, and you think these are facts? They sound subjective to me," Cline retorted. It didn't know if she was making something up just to fulfill the request or if she genuinely believed what she was saying. It scanned her body temperature to analyze if it had raised, and if it had, the computer voice would be able to tell immediately she was lying.

"ARE YOU GUYS STILL COMING? IT HAS BEEN A FEW rhonts AND I HAVE NOT HEARD ANYTHING FROM YOU GUYS. IF YOU LET ME KNOW WHERE YOU ARE, WE CAN MEET IN THE MIDDLE." The voice was definitely louder than the last interaction with it. It sounded as if it was only a few hallways away instead of several layers of concrete away. It was starting to sound defeated and lost like it had been left alone again, unexpectedly.

"WE ARE KIND OF BUSY RIGHT NOW. WE'LL BE THERE IN A MOMENT," Joena shouted into her hands, to amplify the sound, before looking up at the ceiling for an indication of where the robot voice was broadcasting from. "There's your proof, just find out where that voice came from and voilà, you'll find our ward's friend and presumably our ward too. Now let us go grab them, and we can resume what we came here for in the first place." She wasn't going to let Marn or the AI know that she was sort of relieved that the familiar voice spoke up once again; she was fairly positive that the AI wasn't going to accept her information as fact because the computer's system was designed by the government, and they probably put in a fail-safe to prevent information like what she provided to become entangled with its binary. It would only be fitting and would apply to her theory just perfectly.

"There were no voices detected, other than yours and Marniple's." The AI's monotonous response was unexpected. Joena was positive that the computer system heard the third voice speak, down the hall. "I have decided the information you have provided is subjective. Please provide new facts to be allowed to further your exploration; otherwise you will have to return to the lobby and—"

"We get it," Joena interrupted the repetitiveness. She was becoming irritated with it, and she wanted to move the conversation forward. "Otherwise we'll have to return to the lobby and wait for the authorities to find our friend. What makes you think the authorities are going to be able to find our ward, if you won't let us investigate a few more hallways, even though we know where she is?"

"I am sorry, but I cannot allow you more time to search the Academy, unless you give me information I do not know."

"Fine!" Joena sulked for a moment and thought about what in the vastness of the computer's knowledge it didn't know. She felt she was playing a stupid game of hide-and-seek, only the hider was the information that could change where it was hiding just by glancing at the seeker, and she was playing the role of the seeker, but she was blind, deaf, or wasn't allowed to smell anything; the worst game of hide-and-seek, one where no one wins, except for those who never played. "What do you know about me?"

"Let us see, Joena Rightmer, dropped out of the Academy two years into her studies, self-proclaimed zoologist of Quii and niece of Siel Beurm, Second in Command to the queen. You are citizen number two-million-three-hundred-fifty-three-thousand-four-hundred-ninety-four, still relatively young at seventy years old. There is no other pertinent information to your inquiry; please provide me with new information to increase your time."

It's right, everything it just said to me is a hundred percent true, so trying to trip it up and falsifying my information would cause us to fail in our mission. Why isn't Marn helping? She would have been helpful for us to figure out what it knows and doesn't know. It finally occurred to the agitated woman that Mouse Queen wasn't helping because she had gone missing. "Marn?" she asked, in disbelief, when she realized that her partner had bailed on her. The amount of confusion in her voice was comparable to that of a chef cutting into a fresh watermelon, expecting the bright red color but instead being met with a globe with chainsaw hands and duck feet. "Where did you go?"

~~~

I hope Joena isn't too upset for me leaving her to fend off Cline. It's the only way we can get Faith and deal with Cline's knowledge-hungry personality, Marn thought as she ran down the remaining hallways toward Faith and her friend a few rhonts previous to her partner discovering she was by herself. Joena wasn't aware that she had said the one word that locks the AI system into its place against its will, and as long as she continued to speak to the system, it would stay conversing with her doing background analysis for any threat to the network. Corrupt, she was so glad Joena had said that word; otherwise she'd be brainstorming with her right now to figure out something the system didn't know.

I'll release her the moment I get back and apologize to Cline for the random threat sweep, but for right now I need to hurry to Faith's friend. Marn wasn't the most active of people—she didn't really have a reason to be—so running down the long stretches of hallway was incredibly exhausting to her. When her sprint slowed to a jog and then to a brisk walk a few millirhonts after she fled where Joena and Cline were conversing, her lungs felt as if they were going to explode. She couldn't inhale enough oxygen to save her life, but she knew the moment she found

Faith and her friend, the world would feel lighter and hopefully that would make her breathe easier.

"ARE YOU GUYS STILL COMING? IT HAS BEEN A FEW rhonts AND I HAVE NOT HEARD ANYTHING FROM YOU GUYS. IF YOU LET ME KNOW WHERE YOU ARE, WE CAN MEET IN THE MIDDLE," Faith's friend had shouted. He was super close to her, maybe a hallway intersection away. He sounded sad to Marn, like he was going to be lost forever, and the slightest glimmer of hope that they had provided by speaking to him had faded away. His sadness made her sad too. She hated seeing people in pain—that was the whole reason she asked Hope if they could help him in the first place. That was also the reason she wanted Faith to be reconnected with him. When they were separated, Faith looked as if she were going to cry, even if it was temporary.

"WE ARE KIND OF BUSY RIGHT NOW. WE'LL BE THERE IN A MOMENT," Joena followed up with significantly farther away than Faith's friend. It was obvious that Joena hadn't realized Marn had disappeared yet, which in her head was a good thing, as the moment her cohort realized she was gone would be the moment she would try to end her conversation with Cline.

"Well, hello, that was fast," a man's surprised voice said as she rounded a corner.

Marn's eyes met his. Excited to see him, she ran to him and hugged him. "I know I don't know you, but I'm just so happy to see you," she said as she embraced him. "We have been looking for Faith for a while. Any clue where she might be?"

The Man stepped to the side and revealed Faith's unconscious body slumped against the wall. "I told myself I was not going to put her down again, but my body needed a rest after climbing several staircases with her over my shoulder. And when I heard you guys shouting, it was you guys shouting, right? I set her down, because help was on the way."

"What happened to her, and what is that smell?" Marn asked as she caught a heavy whiff of whatever pungent stench was following The Man and Faith. She covered her nose and mouth so she wouldn't gag and vomit.

Noticing Marn trying to block out the smell, The Man said, "You get used to it after a while, but before you do, you will have a pretty bad headache and want to puke a few times. My stomach was churning the entire time I was climbing the stairs. As for Miss Faith here, I found her collapsed at the bottom of a stairwell, in a puddle of her own blood. I think she passed out after a fight, and there is a part of me that thought you guys were the ones who did this to her."

Marn threw up her hands as if they were shields, while displaying a face of fear and stress, to show she had no part in injuring her new friend. "She ran away from Joena and me. Before we entered the Academy, she seemed kind of upset when she burst through the doors. And when we talked to Cline, the AI voice that runs the Academy, he said he hadn't seen her. But the weird thing is, he sees everyone who enters the building. The moment the door swings open, he's there welcoming them. Joena and I finally convinced Cline to let us search for her, but we were almost out of time when you answered us." The smell lingered in her nostrils, and she could taste the sourness in the air as she spoke.

"Hmm, interesting. Where is the queen and the rest of your party?" The Man was convinced that Marn had nothing to do with Faith's injuries, but he was not quite as convinced for the rest of her party members.

"When we entered the city, Hope told Joena and myself to watch over Faith, to keep her out of trouble. Everyone else probably went home to their significant others, and the queen said she needed to retire for the night, which is normal. According to the daily reports, she always ends her days at the same time, every day, and it was getting close to that time."

"So the only people who know Faith ran away from you guys is yourself and Joena? Where is Miss Joena, right now?"

"I left Joena to deal with Cline," Marn said with contempt. She felt bad leaving her in the dark of her plan, but if she had said anything out loud while Cline was listening, he would have tried to prevent her from escaping. His focus was directed at Joena, and since she had been quiet since Joena had spoken the lock-up phrase, he wasn't going to be able to track her as easily.

"What does 'dealing with Cline' entail?" The Man was calm; he figured that as long as Cline or Joena were not the ones who harmed Miss Faith, he would do his best to support whoever needed supporting. "Does she need help?"

"In order for us to get more time to search for Faith, we needed to buy it from Cline. Cline only wants one thing, and no one is able to give it to him, so he gets a little mean after a while. He does everything in his power, which is essentially everything short of massacre, to get you to do the one thing he wants you to do. We need to provide information that he does not already know, and my guess is, Joena doesn't have a clue on how to provide this. Fortunately, when I slipped away, she had just locked him up temporarily, by uttering 'corrupt.' I would assume we have a few rhonts to get back and prevent him from becoming dangerous."

"Dangerous, how?" The Man asked rhetorically, not expecting the elf to answer his question and preferring she did not, especially if it made things harder.

"If on the sixth attempt, you don't provide what Cline wants, he has grounds to eject you from the building; if he is locked up, however, the punishment is far more severe and could end in a hospital bed or death, due to exponential compounding." Marn's eyes widened so that The Man could see every square inch of her eyeballs, and her speech slowed to a halt. She completely forgot that her partner would not have known any of this information. They only taught it in year six at the Academy and Marn could only remember Joena attending for two years. "We need to go right now!" she said in a panicky tone. She didn't want Joena to die because of her attempt to be a hero to the Man and Faith.

"Help me with Miss Faith, and we will go immediately after we get her over my shoulder."

~~~

How long ago did that Mouse Queen take off on me? She

was there after I tried giving the new facts to the robot. I know I saw her then, because I distinctly remember her face; she looked displeased and uncomfortable. Did she hightail it out of here after that? That makes me so upset! Joena thought, while racing through other possibilities of unlearned knowledge at the same time.

"Please provide me with information I do not already know; otherwise," the robot voice repeated, this time in a frustrated tone, like it was becoming angry.

I don't think that stupid computer has noticed that Marn disappeared. Could I use that to my advantage? Probably not. What doesn't this computer system know? Joena wanted to hit her head against the wall out of frustration—she figured it might help her come up with an idea or a solution to her problem. *Oh, wait a minute. Didn't our ward's friend say something about different universes?*

"You know what, computer, I do have some information that you don't know," she announced with half confidence. She was certain that the computer didn't know what she was about to say, but there was no way it was going to accept it as fact, and she had nothing to help persuade it; no visual aids, no research, nothing. She wasn't even an authority on the subject, but she felt it was her best chance at the moment. "There are multiple universes, and ours is called the..." She was drawing a blank. She thought she knew the name of her universe, but she checked her memory and the folds in her brain that held them, but there was nothing—she didn't have that information. "Well, I don't know what ours is called," she said, in a more gruff voice than usual. *There's no way now the robot voice isn't going to accept this as fact.* "But our ward's is called the Garf Universe, and in that universe, there is a planet called Earth. That is where she comes from. I bet you didn't know she wasn't from Quii," Joena finally stumbled out, to get it over with.

"What do you have to back up your claim? How can I be certain that what you just told me is the truth?" Cline asked. His voice was firm, like a parent scolding their child for lying about eating the last dessert.

"If you just allow me to go grab Faith, just real quick, I'll be able to prove it to you."

"No need, we are here," the voice of the other competitor in the shouting match said, this time in his normal speaking voice. Joena turned and saw that he was carrying Faith. She was interested to know why, but the current situation was prioritizing her attention. "How can I help?" The Man asked. His eyes looked exhausted, sunken in, and had dark rings underneath them, like he hadn't slept in ages. His presence felt different from the last time Joena had seen him. He seemed more lively, but she figured that was mainly because he was standing upright, instead of leaning on something.

"The robot wants proof," Joena responded, assuming The Man knew what she was talking about.

"Proof of what?" Marn asked, taking the words right out of The Man's mouth.

"Of other universes. We need to prove that they exist, before it will take the information."

The Man thought about it for a second. "I know they exist, and Faith now knows they exist, but I do not know how to prove it without showing you guys. However, Cline, was it? You can see that Miss Faith and myself are not from Planet Quii, correct?"

"If you are referring to your abnormal anatomy of your ears, that proves nothing. Mutations happen all the time in genetics," Cline said before broadcasting a loud, unexpected beeping sound over everyone's heads, indicating that it started its reboot, causing everyone but Marn to jump out of their skins.

"Cline is no longer locked; his background sweep is finished," Marn said with a frightened tone to match her worried face.

"What is that supposed to mean, Marn?" Joena asked, noting the fear Marn was conveying.

"That means we find out if you led him astray too many times. How many 'facts' did you present to him, Joena?" Marn asked sullenly, accusing Joena of much more than her usual over-zealousness of conspiracy formulating.

Joena hadn't picked up on the subtleness of Marn's accusations, even though they were out of character for the Elf Who

Squeaks. "Only two, one of which you guys were present for and the other one I think you, Marn, were at least present for. I couldn't come up with anything, other than the whole different universe thing and how corrupt our government is. The stupid computer didn't like either of them, obviously."

"Oh, good," The Man said, as he lowered Faith to the floor. He figured now that he had help, he could set her down however many times he needed and there would be no problems. He would be able to lift her up once again. "So, Cline should not be upset. That is way under the six attempts it allows."

"Not necessarily. He takes into account how many questions you ask him too, and those are failed attempts in his mind. Joena, do you know how many questions you asked him, while he was locked up?"

"What? No." Joena stressed, her emphasis implying her frustration. She felt like the other two were keeping secrets from her; playing a game of monkey in the middle, where she was the shortest kid in the school and the two tallest kids volunteered to be the one who threw the ball. "I didn't even know it was locked up. What does that mean?"

"I'll explain that later, but right now we have bigger fish to fry. We need to get out of here, before he wakes up from his reboot."

"Is the stupid computer going to hurt us?" Joena asked, upset about not getting an answer to her question.

"This stupid computer," Cline's voice reverbed through the hallways. It was louder and more ominous, like it had been possessed by a computer demon, haunting the hallways of the Academy. It sounded angry, not fueled by a fake temper either, a legitimate rage that would shadow anyone of Faith's outbursts and make them appear as tantrums. "Is going to hurt you. You were unable to give me what I want over your six allotted attempts."

"Cline, we have Faith now, we don't need any more time," Marn said, grasping at Joena's shoulder and a single belt loop on The Man's torn trousers. She was trying to persuade them to step backwards, to show she wanted to run to the lobby and escape Cline and his eventual sadistic tendencies. She knew Cline wasn't going to allow them to get away easily; it went against his programming.

The AI system had already determined that its guests had overstepped their boundaries and had overstayed their welcome. There was no chance that it was going to allow them to leave without punishment, especially when it could take the opportunity to really give them what they deserved for not expanding its already vast knowledge of the world. "You should know that lying to a ubiquitous and all-knowing presence is wrong, Marniple. From my count there are still only two of you. Yourself and Joena. Now prepare to be punished, you ignorant liars."

The sound of whirring turbines began to penetrate the walls and floor when the spindliest of the group cried out in more squeaks than needed, "Run, Cline is going to kill us with electricity!" She took off running, as fast as her long legs would let her, dragging the two she had grabbed a few seconds prior behind her. She made it halfway to the intersection of hallways before realizing she forgot to grab the one person who couldn't run and was unconscious, sitting in the middle of Cline's electrocution path. Faith. "Faith!" she shouted as she whipped around to witness the walls rise up, revealing two tightly wound copper coils that were the size of barrels and were about to be shock cannons.

Marn pushed through the two she was dragging behind her and sprinted toward the spot that held Faith, before a large, firm hand grabbed her shoulder and held her from progressing forward. "I have a feeling she is going to be alright," The Man said calmly, pulling Marn to a position behind himself and Joena.

"No, you don't understand! Cline is about to send one hundred thousand volts and four hundred amps of electricity into that part of the hallway! She isn't going to survive that! She is going to die!" The panic was front and center in Marn's voice, her eyes reflecting the fear she was feeling, and her forehead was covered in sweat. She knew no one could survive high voltage and high amperage electricity, but she wasn't convinced The Man knew this. There was no way he did, not when he was suggesting Faith would be safe.

"Right now we need to get to a safe spot, so that evil AI system cannot zap us. We will return and grab Faith when the coast is clear, you know, when Cline has calmed down a little bit," The Man said in a calming, reassuring tone, to appease Marn's stress levels. "Now how long do we have to wait before we go and grab her, and where is the closest safe place?"

Marn's stomach was squeezing and wrapping around itself, like it was a snake choking its food, with a vigorous constriction. The tightness it was creating made her want to puke. She was not used to this kind of stress, and she was unsure why The Man was so calm, given their situation. He was about to lose a friend; one that would prefer to get herself into trouble to help him than would rather let him deal with his pain by himself.

She explained the plan as she led the way to a zone where the robot couldn't get to them. "The intersections are safe spots from Cline's blasts. He is only going to shock once, anymore, and he will dip into the city's massive reserves, which is incredibly frowned upon. They need it to run the city in case of a city-wide blackout. After he unloads his electric blast on us, he will check to see if we are dead, and if we aren't, he'll let us return to the lobby and nothing more."

"That is nonsense," Joena said after she thought Marn was done explaining her plan. "Wouldn't it try to kill us again? I don't understand why it would stop after one try."

"He is programmed to move on after zapping the life out of those who anger him, because no one can survive that much electricity running through their veins. It is impossible. And when people run, they keep running, they don't stop at an intersection like we're about to. You see, the electrocution panels along the other parts of the walls are going to open up and create an inescapable bridge between the two hallway walls. Intersections can't create that bridge of electricity because the cannons just don't fit in the corners of them."

The group of people gathered in the center of the intersection turned and watched as the bridges of electricity sparked off, one at a time, with a small delay in between each other for the panels on the walls to rise up, just as the initial ones did. The bridges of electricity were bright enough to sting the eyes of anyone who happened to be watching them, as if they were the tip of an arc welder, fusing plates of metal together. They crashed together, leaving a thunderous sizzle resonating through the halls and the smell of melting metal invading the nostrils of anyone who dared enter the facilities.

After the bridges of electricity had stopped, the hallways seemed darker, as they should, given that the retinas of every person sitting in the intersection had just experienced the brightest event in the course of history. Fortunately for them, the moment they saw the first bridge arc across the hallway, they covered their eyes to defend them from any prolonged damage and waited patiently for the sizzling to end, before uncovering the important organs.

CHAPTER 11

REGRET HANDFUL

Ow, Faith thought with her eyes closed, lying on the floor. She lifted her hand and raised it toward her forehead, to rub the pain she felt away. *Why do I have such a bad headache? I haven't had one this bad in ages, not since I turned twenty-one at least.* She opened her eyes to reveal a reminder that she was no longer at home and no longer on planet Earth. She saw a cream white ceiling plastered with large rectangular speckled tiles and to her, the lingering smell of burning oxygen atoms lingered in the air, mixed with the crustiness of dried blood.

She lay on the floor, with her hand pressed firmly to her forehead. Her bangs were being pushed up and unintentionally disheveled. If she was aware of her surroundings, she wouldn't have lain there for so long, but before the world took hold of her, Faith was perfectly content lying on the floor, looking up at the ceiling. She always enjoyed staring off into the void the ceiling created; it allowed her to think about things she normally didn't think about, like how the shower draws the same unsupervised gallivanting thought process.

She let out a sigh as her after-nap confusion started to pull away, clearing the fog, as she remembered that she had collapsed on a staircase. Her head pivoted on the ground, as she tried to figure out how she managed to move away from the stairs, but the direction she was facing she couldn't see the group of people standing a good distance away, in the intersection of hallways. She wasn't awake enough to lift her head, so she took what she saw for granted and assumed she unconsciously travelled the passageways and when her body felt rested enough she woke up.

Every muscle in her body ached and was stiff, convincing her to stay resting on the floor, but she knew she needed to find her way out of the labyrinth of hallways; the only thought that motivated her to finally stand up. She climbed to her feet, struggling to maintain her balance, but when she finally stood on her own feet, she spread her arms out and stretched, like she had never stretched before; a feeling that seemed to relax her.

"Faith! You're alive!" Faith heard from behind her, nearly startling her from the surprise of hearing another human voice.

She turned to see who it was, who was so happy to see her stand up when she heard a second recognizable voice ask, "How? How did you survive that? That's impossible!" It was Joena, one of the people she didn't want to see. Just listening to the harshness of Joena's voice and the cold pessimistic tone that lingered about for an eternity made Faith want to go back to sleep. She scoffed at Joena's questions and refused to pay her any more attention.

"Glad to see you are finally awake, Miss Faith," The Man said, with his usual smile that always conveyed his emotions inadequately.

Faith stretched one last time, fully rejuvenating her strength and awareness and then briskly walked to the group before realizing that they weren't attempting to move towards her in the slightest, and they kept saying stuff like "survive" and "alive." What did they mean? "I don't understand what you guys mean? Why are you over here? And Jackass, where did you come from? I was looking for you, and I found something I never want to speak of—it might have traumatized me, but that is par for the course for my life," she said, referring to her anxiety and the stress she'd felt from it her entire life. "And for you squeakers, how did you guys find me? I thought I was lost for good."

Marn pointed at herself, confused by the new nickname. "Your friend found you and brought you up here," Marn said, her tone indicating she wanted to hug Faith, but Faith wasn't much of a hugger, especially when it came to strangers, who had been parading her around the city and kept telling everyone she was the new research subject for the Academy.

"Hello? Is no one else curious on how she survived that much electricity? She shouldn't be alive right now, but here she is walking and talking to us like it's some sort of family reunion," Joena said loudly, shaking her head as she spoke every word, even though no one was listening to her. The Man was over-whelmed with his friend waking up, and Marn was just happy she didn't accidentally kill someone.

"Please return to the lobby so you can wait for the proper authorities to find your guest," Cline said in the mix of voices, announcing his departure. His voice was back to its monoto-nous levels of boring, and it appeared that his sadistic side had subsided as well.

Cline's sudden announcement startled Faith. She had only heard it before taking off from her babysitters, so its random appearance threw her off. "What the hell?" she asked herself, mumbling incoherently, trying to process everything that was happening to her, or at least what everyone was trying to tell her all at once.

"Everyone, one at a time," The Man said, louder than the rest of the group. It was not a yell, but it was as close to one as he would ever get before continuing his statement in a lower deci-bel. "Before you have a panic attack, Miss Faith, we will gladly explain what you do not know. Just, please, for your own san-ity, calm down. We know you are probably confused. Ask your questions and we will answer them."

"What about my questions?" Joena interjected, furious that she was being ignored.

"Quit being a bitch to people, and maybe people will pay more attention to you," Faith snapped, ironically in the bitchiest tone in her arsenal. Her dislike for Joena was growing out of proportion and there was no logical reason why either. Faith felt compelled to react to what her gut was telling her; Joena just seemed off, and she had no explanation why.

"We will answer your questions too, right, Faith?" The Man said, scolding her for her random outburst. His smile stayed fixed where it was, while his eyes did all the work.

"I guess." Faith pouted.

"Before we start answering questions, can we get out of her before Cline comes back and finds us in the same spot he left us? I'm pretty sure we don't have noise dampeners anymore, so we need to keep our voices down," Marn said. She was worried about the AI returning with a vengeance after not listening to him and surviving his assault of electricity.

The group of humans and elves proceeded down the hallways and found themselves in the entryway of the Academy before anyone started asking questions. The journey was quiet and awkward, but the peace allowed them all to collect their thoughts.

"First question," Faith said when she thought it was okay to speak. She was unsure why everyone else wasn't speaking, but she figured she probably shouldn't either. "What the fuck is that smell following us? I smelt it after we left those initial hallways, and it seems to have just followed us since."

"We thought it was you," Marn said in as nice of a tone as she could to make sure Faith didn't become self-conscious about her potential stench. "We didn't smell it until we regrouped with you, so we naturally assumed it was you, or your blood-soaked garb."

It was inevitable: Faith was offended by the answer, but she understood the reasoning behind Marn's response. Faith also thought the amount of bile she had evacuated from her body might have something to do with the smell; she wondered if micro-sized particles were still in her hair or in the pores on her skin. "That makes sense, I guess," she said to cover up the fact that she was offended. "Next question, why do you guys keep using terms like 'alive' and 'survived'?"

"The stupid robot shot you with enough electricity to kill a Roxapex. You shouldn't be alive," Joena said, still frustrated with Faith while Faith returned those feelings silently, until she spoke.

"Okay, well, I don't know what that is, so you're going to have to elaborate."

"Miss Faith, think the Tyrannosaurus Rex from your world, only larger and more dangerous," The Man said, sliding into the conversation before the two women started a spat once again. "To answer your question, Miss Joena, Faith is not like a normal human or elf, and just as Miss Hope was an anomaly, Miss Faith is one too."

Faith's eyes pleaded with The Man's not to tell them her secret. The elves already wanted her for research because of a stupid reason, and if he was going to tell them the truth, it was almost guaranteed they weren't going to allow her out of their sight.

The Man, who was never great at reading facial expressions, continued, "Faith is an electrokinesis; in layman's terms, she controls electricity, and as a side effect, it does not hurt her, no matter how much power is behind it. Although, I think that was the most electricity she has ever absorbed into her body at any given time. There was a side of me who was concerned that her instincts to ground herself would not kick in while she was unconscious, but I am so glad they did."

"You weren't fucking sure I was going to live? What the hell? I thought you were on a mission to save my life from that curse and you didn't know if I was going to survive a little shock?"

"Yes, I am sorry, Miss Faith, please forgive me. You have to understand, about ninety percent of me was sure you were going to survive, but the other ten percent had me doubting your unconsciousness. You have to remember, I have not had a lot of time to research your unique ability, just the time I have spent with you."

"So you're telling us that Faith can survive a lightning bolt, and she wouldn't even bat an eye at it? That sounds fake, like you're egging us on," Joena said, whose brain was fusing together conspiracy theories of great proportion. Of course she wouldn't believe something as outlandish as someone who controls electricity; there were too many things in her world that made much more sense than a girl who happened to be a lightning rod. "I think the AI was just screwing with us, it wasn't going to hurt us at all, and I bet our ward got no more than a little zap, like it just slightly bit her or something. Nothing more than a few volts."

"No, Cline doesn't go easy, when he has his mind set, he is out for blood, until he sets off his stored electricity through his zap cannons. We learned that in school." Marn denied Joena's theory, because it made no sense to her. Why would Faith and her friend be lying about something like this? Why would they be lying to them in general? "Faith, is it true you control electricity?"

She wanted nothing more than to say no, but to make The Man out to be a liar would mean betraying him. And if she betrayed him, would he still be dead set on helping her survive when the time came? *Probably shouldn't tempt the forces at play,* she thought. "Yes," Faith said, disgruntled. She didn't want to look anybody directly in the eyes, as if she were ashamed that she had her ability; however, her lack of eye contact came more from her devout stubbornness to be honest with the elves than anything else. "And I can't fucking talk to metal either; your tablet thing made that up."

"Prove it!" Joena demanded. She wanted proof that Faith could in fact manipulate electricity to her whim. "I want to see this ability of yours in action. Prove it, right now."

As the group stood in the lobby, a light flickered more than average in their peripheral vision; on the right side of The Man and Faith, and on the left side of Joena and Marn. It was flickering enough to catch the attention of Marn, but Joena and Faith were in the middle of a staring contest; neither of them cared that it was flickering, only because one of them was causing it and the other one was furiously trying her best to one-up and outthink the people she was expected to watch.

"That light is flickering to pattern," Marn said, unwilling to step between the two women to stop their little immature playground tiff. The hatred between the two could be felt throughout the room, and if an outsider had seen what was going on, their first reaction would be to turn around and avoid the daggers each of the women were throwing at each other. Both of them were in each other's faces, but fortunately if fists started to fly, The Man was prepared to step in the middle and break up the brawl.

"That is Miss Faith's heartbeat, Miss Marn. She is probably unaware that she is doing that, especially when her attention is being drawn to Miss Joena."

"I am fucking aware that I am doing it! This bitch wanted proof, there's your fucking proof!"

Joena glanced to her left, enough to see the lights flicker a few times. They were beating in time to a heartbeat, but she figured technically anything could pulse to a heartbeat before she scoffed at the beginning of her statement, "That proves nothing! A ballast could be going out, and it just so happens that it started conveniently when we started talking about your made-up powers. When you lie, you need to make it believable and not so farfetched that people in your company have a hard time suspending their disbelief."

Joena's accusation that Faith was lying was the last straw for the irritable woman. Faith couldn't handle the attitude Joena persistently held and before she knew it, her static-covered hand was flying towards the elf's pastel cheek; she was going to slap some sense into Joena and if the elf received a zap, so be it—she deserved it.

Unfortunately, before her open palm made a connection with the elf's cheek, just millimeters away, The Man caught Faith's wrist to prevent her from injuring the innocent elf. "We do not need to be getting ourselves in trouble with the locals, Miss Faith. Also, I can see in your eyes that this slap was filled with intent to kill, and I cannot allow that," The Man said as he returned his partner's arm to its resting position.

Faith's eyebrows scrunched together, to show she was angry. "I wasn't going to kill her. I just seriously wanted to hurt her, maybe leave a little reminder to stop being so pessimistic."

Marn was terrified by what she just witnessed. Her knees shook and her mouth gaped. She had never witnessed a physical fight before, but that wasn't what terrified her. She could see the blue static around Faith's hand as well as feel the power drain out of the lights and any other electrical device in the building. Her imagination drew Cline in the corner somewhere, wheezing as if he had been the one who just got hit, straight to the gut, with no remorse.

Joena stood still; in shock and awe, she, too, felt the power drain from where it should have been, but she didn't see the glove Faith had fabricated around her hand, made solely out of static and electricity. Power outages were one thing, but this was something else. She could literally feel all the electricity drain from everything all at once and linger in the air momentarily, before it pushed passed her, rioting to get to Faith. She was sure that if Faith's hand had hit her, she would have been dead. There was no way around that kind of power and there was no way she would be able to recover from such a blast to the face. "T-Thank you," she stuttered to The Man, looking at his out-of-place smile. It was sort of comforting to her, leaving a warm pit in her stomach instead of the frigid feeling she had felt when she thought she was going to die.

"Miss Faith, you will stand next to me, as we search for the queen, and you will be the farthest away from Miss Joena, to prevent anymore altercations between you two," The Man said in a fatherly tone that implied he was done with their little squabbles but at the same time proud of both of them.

Marn wasn't great with plan changes, especially when they went against her queen's wishes, and that was exactly what The Man had just proposed. "But Cline has a room for Faith, we have to get her checked in, even though he can't see her for some reason," she said, trying to convince the group that they still needed to do what the queen asked of them.

"Yeah, why can't your advanced technology see me?" Faith asked, as she remembered watching the interaction between the two elves and the AI system when she first entered the building.

"I don't know," Marn squeaked, surprised to find out that Faith was aware of her invisibility. "I would have to guess it was because of your power, like you're somehow cloaking yourself in a layer of electricity and Cline can't track you while you're doing it. That would be my guess, but that doesn't fully make sense, does it?"

"Why not? Sounds like the best guess I have heard. Makes

sense to me," The Man said, half paying attention to the conversation, unaware that the elves' advanced technology could not track his friend. He was more focused on executing his plan to find the queen to ask her some questions, instead of the actual conversation.

"I would assume she wasn't making the layer of electricity when she was unconscious, but Cline still couldn't see her, but I guess she was able to protect herself, so I don't know."

"Interesting, you have a point there," he said, in hopes to draw out more words from her. He was trying to distract her as they walked towards the exit. If she was distracted enough, he might be able to get them outside and walking towards the tallest building, where the voice in his white prison room had told him he would find the queen's chambers.

"Cline, I have a question for you," Marn asked, wishing for an immediate response.

"Stop trying to summon the murderous robot. We don't want to deal with him anymore," Joena said, nearly putting a hand over Marn's mouth before being met with the voice she didn't want to hear.

"Marniple Clourn, presumed dead, how can I help you?" Cline said throughout the entryway of the Academy.

"I was wondering if you had any updates on Faith's location?"

"I have no record of someone by that name, nor do I have location history for said person either," Cline said, acting as if it hadn't tried to kill the group a few millirhonts previously.

"Of course you do; you were going to have a room ready for her when we got here."

"I apologize, Marniple, I have no record of this. Would you like me to get a room ready for when the person you speak of enters the city?"

"No, never mind, Cline, thank you," Marn said politely, even though she was upset about the situation. She was curious about how Cline was able to wipe his memory banks and completely forget the last few interactions he had with the group but also think she was dead—it made no sense to her. "Let's go, guys, I guess we no longer need to be here since Cline doesn't seem to have records of us arriving."

"Great, let us go. I have a few questions for Miss Hope, and we still need to find the technology Miss Faith and I initially came here for," The Man said, stepping outside, taking in the varying shades of gray. "I seem to remember the white room voice telling me Miss Hope will be in her chambers in the tallest building." He looked around, trying to see any specific landmarks and buildings. He wanted to remember what this area looked like, just in case he might need to return to the academy at some point in his future.

"The queen doesn't live in the Orbital Elevator," Joena remarked. Her tone and posture shouted the same thing: conceit. "She lives in the Aurora Castle, so we should go there, not the Orbital Elevator."

The Man was glad to see that Joena was trying to be helpful and complacently said, "Okay, we will go to the Aurora Castle, if that is where you think we will find Miss Hope. Lead the way, will you?"

CHAPTER 12

AURORA CASTLE

The group walked down the streets of Quii's largest city. It was dark, and there weren't many people out enjoying the nightlife. Lights were hung every few yards, so the few people who were out and about could effectively see where they were going. When the group of elves and humans occasionally saw someone, the elves who walked by would quickly look away in disgust, as if they smelt something rank, like the group had just stepped out of a swampy, feces-filled landfill.

"You know, when we left the Academy and entered fresh air, I thought that smell that has been stalking us would disappear, but it seems to have only gotten worse," Joena said, no longer convinced the smell was coming from Faith, even though every logical reasoning would tell her it was. "Something that smells that bad, and gets that reaction every time can't be coming from one of us, but still, where is it coming from?"

"Your—" Faith was able to say before being promptly met with The Man's hand in her face, attempting to muffle the words that he assumed were about to spill out of her mouth, as if it were an automatic reflex. He was tired of the fights between the two women, and he was willing to risk getting shocked by Faith to prevent anymore.

"I am sure the smell will reveal itself sooner or later, but how far are we from Aurora Castle?" The Man asked. He was calm and did not care about the smell anymore; he had gotten used to it, long before leaving the Academy.

"Is that it?" Faith said, pointing at a giant gate that was the little sibling of the one protecting the city. Behind the wall, four spires stuck out over the top, like they were peeking over, watching, observing who might be knocking at the queen's door.

"It is, how'd you know, Faith?" Marn said, amazed, unaware that on Faith's world all castles were built roughly the same, or at least had the same types of architecture.

Faith thought she was being sarcastic and decided to continue the sarcasm. "Just a hunch," she said, hoping Marn would continue.

This is probably the only castle she has ever seen, now that I think about it, Faith thought after Marn failed to give a response. *I mean, technically this is the only one I've seen too, but I have seen a ton of fucking photos from Germany, and there seems to be a castle hiding in the background of every one of them.*

They approached the gate with caution, assuming there were guards watching the exterior of the building. "I assume it is being protected by the same technology the school had?" Faith asked, wondering if she could just enter casually like she planned to.

"This building doesn't have much for security; however, if you think you can fry the electrical system, like you did at the Academy, you're mistaken," Joena said, hoping Faith wouldn't take anything she said too harshly like she had been. "The Aurora Castle has a backup generator to prevent system wide outages and is protected by the simplest of retinal scanners that will only open the gate for the queen, the second in command, or the highest ranked guard on duty."

Faith put her hand up, gesturing for Joena to stop talking. "Okay," she said, as if she had heard nothing the elf was telling her, ignoring every sound that came out of her mouth. "Well, I'm just gonna walk in then and there is nothing they can do about it. Besides, they probably don't even know I'm here, but I'm confident they know you guys are, so I'll handle this in my own way." She walked to the gate, as if there was nothing in her way; confidence emanated off her, as if it, too, was part of the Veil of Hope that surrounded her. Nothing was going to get in her way, she told herself, not even the "fancy" technology that protected the castle.

As to be expected, the gate didn't budge when she approached it. She was not surprised by this and in reaction placed her hand gently on the surface of the thick metal. Under her fingertips it felt cold, like it hadn't been touched in a while, a feeling she almost felt familiar with. *I could zap it,* she thought as she closed her eyes and continued to caress its slowly warming surface. *On the other hand, I could do it the fun way. That would be more entertaining at least.*

Faith removed her hand from the wall, opened her eyes, and looked up to see if there was anything preventing her from enjoying this experience. *Fun way it is then.* "Here, hold these," she said as she took off her heels and threw them at The Man, who was standing with the elves, patiently waiting for Faith to do her thing. He compulsively picked up her shoes as if it was second nature to him.

"What is she doing? Uh, what was your name again, Faith's friend?" Marn asked The Man as she watched Faith begin to walk up the side of the metal barrier. She'd never seen someone before walk up a perfectly vertical incline, but Faith was doing it with ease and precision, like she had done it a lot in the past.

The Man ignored Marn's second part to her question but gladly answered the first part. "She is letting electrical impulses flow into the heels of her feet, so she can walk up that wall. Basically, the impulses are sticking her to the wall through magnetism; she has made her feet attracted to the surface of that wall, which in turn allows her to walk up and down it, without any interference. I think she took off her shoes because a larger surface area makes it easier to scale the wall, in this instance. That being said, I do not understand why she chose to use this method instead of just zapping the retinal scanner over there." The Man pointed at what looked like one of the elves' Terunes strapped to a museum podium.

Marn was fascinated by The Man's explanation—she thought it was amazing that Faith could be so versatile. "Wow, I bet that skill conveniently comes in handy," she said as Faith reached the top of the wall and disappeared from their sight, to walk down the other side.

"It has gotten her out of some sticky situations."

Joena scoffed when The Man finished his statement. It was out of protest to the pun he had wittingly made and the disbelief that such a thing as magnetic beings could exist. "It's probably more likely that she applied some sort of adhesive to her feet after taking off her shoes. There is no way she would be able to do that, I guarantee it."

"She is doing it right now," The Man said, in the voice he always used to persuade people into thinking the way he did. "She did not have anything in her hands when she threw these things at us. You watched her, you saw she did not play around with her feet for too long."

Joena sat for a moment as she thought of a rebuttal to The Man's argument; she refused to grasp the idea that there was an animal, in this case a human, she couldn't comprehend. There had to be another explanation to how Faith was Faith, but unfortunately to her, there wasn't.

~~~

When Faith reached the top of the wall, she looked both to her left and to her right, like she was about to cross a semi-busy street. To her surprise, there was no one in sight. It was off-putting to her to see a royal residence have no security on duty, but then again, from her understanding the elven government could efficiently predict crimes and effectively prevent them before they happened.

She walked down the wall and once again looked around to see if there was an armed guard, somewhere lurking behind a corner; nothing. *I could rob this place blind, if I wanted to. They are lucky I'm not a fucking miscreant.*

The concrete ground beneath Faith's feet felt smooth, and she felt as if she was walking across ceramic tiles, laid in a freshly cleaned kitchen. There was a small expectation to smell the chemical approximation of Pine-Sol and bleach, but she was glad to be met with an almost artificial petrichor smell, which she attributed to the grass patches on either side of the concrete walkway she was standing on.

She strolled down the pathway, casually, like she belonged there, and she regretted kicking her heels off when she found her way into a gravel covered area on the pathway. She thought she could easily walk through the gravel pit, with little to no pain, but she was wrong and realized her mistake almost immediately. *Why the fuck do they have this,* she thought, stepping onto the grass to walk around it.

The farther into the walls of the castle she progressed, the more she understood why it was called the Aurora Castle; the walls were covered, from ceiling to floor, with neon paintings of rainbows and vibrant portraits of attractive young people, whom Faith thought might be Hope's ancestors. She could smell a hint of cinnamon and baking yeast, which subconsciously made her smile, given the pleasantness of it and the absence of the pungent smell that was following her and her group since they left that hallway in the Academy.

The sound of clanging pots and pans told her where the smell was coming from, but she refused to walk in the direction her senses were telling her to go, out of fear of being discovered by the wait staff. She instead decided to climb a grand staircase that split and wove together multiple times, forming a double helix like a strand of DNA.

I don't think I buy that theory Marn was trying to come up with. I know my static is off right now, and I know I'm not generating a cloak that makes me invisible to their cameras—that's just stupid, Faith thought as she climbed the flight of stairs that seemed to never end. *It has to be something else. Maybe they can't predict where I am going to go. I mean, I do have pure free will, but then again so does the jackass. Can they predict where he goes? Can they see him? I don't have enough fucking information to know exactly, but my guess is they can't see him either.*

She reached the top landing and was awestruck. The top floor opened into a large expanse of carefully crafted decor and expensive-looking lights. Faith thought she had found a ballroom, but then she saw the gilded throne, sitting towards the back of the room, centered between two pillars, that served no purpose other than for decoration. "This is excessively vain," she whispered to herself, quiet enough so that no one nearby could hear her.

She looked for any branching hallways or staircases, but unfortunately all she found was a locked door behind the throne and a set of armor standing in front of a poor excuse for an exit, leading to a balcony outside that overlooked the city.

She gazed out over the building covered terrain and noticed a red beacon shooting out from a hill on the horizon. Without a second thought to it, she whispered to herself, slightly louder than she had previously, "I wonder how often this thing actually gets used; it actually looks like they don't dust it at all, or even clean it. That's fucking weird, but more power to the guy in charge of the cleaning duties and getting away with being lazy, I guess."

She returned to the upper floor of the castle and continued her search for Hope; however, the more she searched the grand residency, the more she became concerned. Sure she heard the clanging of pots and pans, which she assumed were the queen's wait staff preparing food for their liege. But other than that, she hadn't run into another person's footsteps or even walked in on someone accidentally while they were talking behind closed doors. There was exactly no one to scold her for trespassing.

I didn't think castles were so quiet, she thought as she found a passageway leading to a downward spiraling staircase. The passage was tucked hidden away, behind a large conspicuous panel, which Faith would not have found by herself if she weren't paying attention. As she walked past it, it wobbled just enough to be apparent that there was something behind it. She peeled the panel back, revealing the poorly lit passageway and followed it out of curiosity; she figured she had no better leads anyway.

The staircase led to a dungeon-like hall; the shortest hallway Faith had seen while on Quii, there were only three metal doors, all of which had a small window about eye level for any traditionally sized elf. Faith, on the other hand, had to stand on the tips of her toes to peer into them.

Don't be any weird sex stuff, don't be any weird sex stuff, don't be any weird sex stuff, she chanted in her head, mentally preparing herself for what could by lying on the other side of the doors. Her toes gave her enough height to just barely look into the first room, straight ahead, at the parallel wall. There was nothing interesting to look at, from what she could see from her limited view, so she moved to the next door.

Faith felt something had to have been in this room; there was something about it that made her think it was off. It was separated from the other two, sitting lonely on its own wall, like it was in a time out. The door sat exactly in the middle of the wall and there was a bright red light above it, holding on to its secret of what it meant.

Faith peered into the window after another moment of mental preparation. She hated the threatening feeling she was getting from the hallway as a whole; it was stressful, and she didn't understand why.

The muscles in her fingertips screamed as she used them to gain extra height to view the contents of the window, but she didn't care. She saw something that would forever change her opinion on the elves and how they were perceived in her head.

"What the fuck? Hope?" she shouted carelessly.

~~~

"She has been in there for quite a while," The Man said, pacing back and forth across the street from the castle. "We should have gone with her. Who knows what trouble she got herself into?"

Marn and Joena sat on the sidewalk as they watched The Man stress, uncharacteristically for him. "I'm sure she's fine. She probably found Hope and is having a nice long conversation with her right now," Marn said, attempting her best to quench The Man's panic. She didn't know him too well, so she didn't know the best way to ease his worries, and instead gave it a shot in the dark.

"That is the thing about Miss Faith, you never know how she is doing with something, until all chaos breaks loose. She is too unpredictable, and that is not a complaint either. Her ability to draw mayhem out of the darkest parts of the universe is unparalleled, and I do not know if that has anything to do with the 'Veil of Hope' or not. But with that being, every single time she goes off on her own, she gets herself in some sort of trouble no matter."

The Man stopped speaking and crooked his head to the side; it was almost instantaneously, sudden and off-putting, alerting the two women that something was off or concerning him more than Faith's time delay in the castle. "What's wrong?" Joena asked, to break the sudden silence. She didn't really care to have an answer to her question, but she would rather not sit in the silence in the middle of the night, centered in the nearly dead city, either.

"You ladies did not hear that, did you?"

"Heard what?" Marn asked. She was about to go into panic mode if The Man kept being so secretive.

"Nothing, it must have been nothing."

A breeze swung throughout the city, stirring up the staleness the urban landscape had been sitting on since the arrival of the humans. The smells of the city life mixed into the air, combining aroma concoctions never before experienced. However, the smell that stood out was the one that had been following the group since their reunion.

Marn gagged as she tasted the rankness in the air. "Guys, I don't think that smell was coming from Faith," she said, covering up her nose and mouth, leaving her muffled vocalization to be carried away with the wind.

"That was obvious a while ago," Joena said as she, too, covered her nose and mouth. "At least to me. I knew when we were walking here; how didn't you realize it?"

"I don't know, I just figured it was Faith."

"And when she went into the castle, what did you think?"

"I don't know, like it rubbed off on us or something? But that smell just got so much worse, and I don't see Faith anywhere."

"Miss Marn, Miss Joena, I need you to be quiet. I heard that sound again," The Man said, interrupting the unnecessary argument the two elves were having.

"What sound? I still didn't hear anything," Joena said; it came out harsher than she meant, but no one noticed, due to the sudden roar they heard down the street.

"RARREWEK!"

"I heard it that time," Marn said, terrified by what could make that sound. "Joena, when we entered the city, did we forget to close the gate?"

"No, it shut automatically like it always does, even with Faith and her supposed electrical manipulation. I watched it."

"Then what was that sound?"

"RAAARREWEEKK!" The roaring noise was louder and closer, and the group of human and elves finally could see where it was coming from. It surprised them all that they couldn't see it before. A few buildings down the road, the creature was slowly trudging, almost limping in their direction. It looked as if it had been beaten to death or at least electrocuted to the edge of its existence. There were char marks where its dripping skin had solidified, near its stomach.

As the monster got closer, in the slowest way possible, The Man started to have an epiphany. *Why would the white room voice tell me Miss Hope was in the tallest building, and then Miss Joena would tell me that she is actually at this castle? Something is not right.* "Miss Joena? I have a question for you." The Man looked to where the two elves were sitting; however, only Marn was sitting there now. She was still covering her nose and mouth and trying not to look in the direction the creature was coming from. She was pretending it didn't exist, because if she came to terms with it, she would feel as if she was in a horror film, a genre that most elves hated on Quii. "Miss Joena?"

"Sheh disahppeared when sheh sawh tha thing ohver there," Marn said, attempting to cover her mouth and nose, while making her muffled squeaks audible.

I think we were set up, The Man thought, distrusting the situation. "Miss Marn, I think all chaos is about to break loose, and I think Miss Faith needs our help, immediately."

Inconveniently the moment The Man finished his statement, the monster who had been moving slower than a snail leaped into action. It moved with speed and precision as if it had just written off all of its injuries. It charged towards The Man and Marn and it was not going to slow down even if it hit a wall.

Sludge rolled off its back, creating small piles of viscous goo on the ground. The several eyes that covered the upper half of its face were all trained on the two people standing on the side of the road, next to the royal residency, like it was a dog returning with a ball in a game of fetch.

"I do not know what this is," The Man said in a worried tone. He did not know how to stop it or how to get rid of it, but at the last second, the monster turned and launched itself over the metal wall that protected the Aurora Castle. It found a couple imaginary footholds, and with ease climbed up and over on its first attempt. "And of course it is going towards Miss Faith; it never fails."

Marn looked at The Man, with eyes full of dread and confusion. "So you weren't exaggerating about Faith? She's always under duress when she goes off alone?"

"Ever since she killed the Goobert, when she was a teenager. I suppose it does not matter which universe she is in, all of them want her dead, and it is because of that curse she carries with her," The Man explained to the confused-looking elf. She looked like she did not know exactly what was going on or how to comprehend the situation, but he did his best to explain it. "I imagine the universe is an animal, and Miss Faith is that itch that the animal just cannot get away from. And eventually that itch gets so bad that the animal will do anything to get rid of it, even jump off a cliff if it felt like that would solve the problem. The universe wants Faith dead, and if Faith remains alive, the universe has no problem throwing itself into death. Anything to fix the problem."

"Is that thing going to kill Faith?"

"I do have a feeling that it is going to try; however, I think Miss Faith will overcome that thing, like she has with everything in her life. She has free will and will act accordingly. That being said,

I think we need to get in there and help her if anything does go awry; she has a way of shutting down if situations get too stressful."

~~~

Meanwhile, across the multitude of universes, on Planet Earth, a significant event was unfolding; the Voidtriss, which The Man and Faith carelessly left sitting in the field outside of that city, had started to decay.

It had only been a few minutes since the two had disappeared from the face of the planet, but it seemed that their time was about to run out; saving the day might not be possible when they got back. A feeling, impossible to convey to a normal human who had not witnessed the series of events that led to this unfortunate unravel.

Not a single human could distinguish a normal day from the one they were currently living. Not a single human could see the Voidtriss, lying dead in that field. And not a single human could tell they were living their last day.

To them, there was no monster and there was no newly formed ravine; they did not have the receptors to properly see into the plane of existence where everything took place. To them, when the time came, death would swiftly take them by the hand and rip their souls out of their body as if they were only stuck down by cheap Velcro. And to them, they would know no difference between life and afterlife, only what was past and is future.

CHAPTER 13

DEAD TYRANNY

Marn uncovered her face, temporarily, to see if the smell had diffused, and to her surprise, it had. She smelt the freshest air she had in a while, like daisies frolicking in the wind on the side of a mountain. Her first reaction was to sniff harder, thinking she was missing something, and as she did it occurred to her that there was a tree on the far side of the castle that would be tall enough to climb, if it were willing to give its assistance.

She was worried that the tree would deny her request, given it was often forgotten about, and only remembered by the few elven children that played by the edge of the pond behind the castle. "I think I know of a way to get into the castle," she announced to The Man when she was done enjoying the scent of summer flowers. She understood by the way The Man was acting that his top priority was protecting his friend.

"Good, we are going to need it, unless you can knock down a wall? What about Miss Joena, what do we do? Do we go find her or do you think she will be alright by herself?"

"I think we go in and help Faith; she is probably in more danger than Joena will ever be, also Joena probably just went home. I can't see her going anywhere else."

"I am glad, that eases my mind slightly. So how do you propose that we get over that wall?"

"Follow me, and I'll show you." Marn started to run towards the castle before even finishing her statement. She didn't have a fading voice like people typically did when they turned and walked away from someone mid-conversation, but instead her high-pitched squeaks allowed her to still be audible to The Man.

The Man followed Marn, without hesitation, to a small pond located behind the castle. There were plants all around it and the water was a dark cyan color. The Man could tell it was man-made, from the preciseness of the shape and the slow sloping that gently curled itself into a bowl. He noticed a beacon shooting into the sky from the horizon, glowing red and standing out precariously. He found it weird that they could not see it shooting into the sky while standing in front of the castle. "What is that?" he asked Marn, hoping she would give him a satisfactory answer.

"What is what?" Marn asked in return. She couldn't see what The Man was talking about, even though it stuck out like a sore thumb to The Man, which he thought was incredibly peculiar.

"That glowing red light shooting into the air? You do not see that?"

"No, sorry, I've never seen something like that before. Anyway, if we climb this tree right here, we should be able to get over the wall and right into the castle after that." She directed her eyes to a tree that was as lanky as she was. It looked as if it had been there for thousands of years, twisting around the side of the wall.

The Man was hesitant to forget about the beacon in the distance—it was calling to him, beckoning him towards it, like it was a siren's song telling him he needed to get closer to it. But there was also something in Marn's face that said they needed to continue with their mission to save Faith, to protect her from that monster that followed her into the castle. "Is it safe to climb on?" he asked after deciding to disregard the beacon, even if it hurt the pits of his soul to do so.

"It should be. It looked like this when I was a kid too; I think it has looked like this for generations. If you want, I can go first, to prove that it is stable?"

"If you feel comfortable doing that, Miss Marn, that would be alright. If you feel you are about to fall, let me know and I will do my best to catch you."

Marn placed her hand on the trunk of the tree, whispered something, and paused. She was waiting for permission from the tree and when she received it, she immediately started to climb the ancient-looking tree without a second thought in her head about it. She felt as if she were a young elf again, doing daring stunts while having the time of her life in the wilderness.

When she reached the top of the tree, she climbed over the wall and, just as Faith had, disappeared as if she hadn't been there to begin with. When The Man saw the elf's last leg disappear, he, too, started to climb the tree. To him, it felt like the trunk was going to snap at any second, and the slightest amount of wind would pressure it into its final resting place. Every step he took creaked with panic and fear; the last thing he needed was to wind up with more broken limbs, especially since the elves were nice enough to fix him up once before. He doubted their hospitality would continue when they found out he was trying to break into the queen's residency.

At the top, he made one last side glance at the glowing red light being emitted across the city and noted it looked closer than it had while they were standing on the ground. *Some other day we will explore that,* he thought, hiding it in his memory bank, so that he would remember to come back to it when time was not so precious.

Inside the royal walls seemed like a completely different world. It did not feel like someone was constantly watching every move they made, and the air seemed softer somehow; easier to breathe. "Where do we go from here?" The Man inquired, assuming Marn had been behind these walls before and knew exactly where the entrance was.

"I don't know. I can tell you where the front door is, but after that, I have no idea where to go. I have only been upstairs in this castle—that's where we met this afternoon, when we were getting ready to go on the adventure to find you guys outside the city walls. I am almost positive she wouldn't be up there, because it is just a giant room."

"That is alright, take me to the front, and we will find her after that. We follow the scent of that creature, because it seemed it knew where it was going. Or at least I would like to think it did." The Man planned to locate Faith, not by the scent of the monster but by his telepathic trick he used to communicate with her while she was recovering her memory during the Voidtriss fight. He did not want to explain this to Marn, however, because he felt it would bring up too many questions that they did not have time for. For all he knew, his friend was lying dead in a hallway somewhere, after being brutally attacked by whatever that monster was.

"Oh, that makes sense, we follow the daisy smell, and we'll find that thing. I don't why I didn't think of that." Marn put on an ignorant smile that said *I'm sometimes a ditz* and began to sprint towards the front of the building. She was light on her toes, and the way she ran was the epitome of grace and wholesomeness. Her run reminded The Man of a well choreographed ballerina.

~~~

Faith had never seen something so out of the ordinary before. In front of her was a queen in what looked like a cryogenic pod filled with transparent silicone. It was connected to many air tubes that snaked themselves into the ceiling of the room; each spiraling off into different parts of the castle. Hope was congealed into the pod, up to her neck, her arms crossed in front of her so that her hands were on top of her shoulder blades, and she was lying there in the nude. Her eyes were closed, making Faith wonder if she was asleep or just unconscious.

From the little window on the door, Faith could see that the room was quite large, due to being unable to see the corners as she had in the other room. She could tell there was at least one other cryogenic pod, sitting next to the one Hope was in; it was empty. Its front eggshell portion was lifted into the air and attached to the top of the machine, like it was a new iteration of gull wing doors.

Faith took her chances and tried the door. She was aware that she might not be alone down there, but she felt she needed to get into that room. It didn't budge. She tried once more, but this time applied a minute amount of force with her static. She collected it around the crown of her shoulder and planned to use it as a cushion of sorts to protect her from when she tackled the door a few seconds later. *This is going to fucking hurt and I know it,* she thought as she charged forward with her right arm and shoulder in the lead.

She hit the door with the force of a semi truck hitting a deer in the middle of the night. Before the twang of the beaten metal halted, Faith was thrown across the hall, hit the wall on the other side with her back, and slid to the ground in agony. She thought she might have broken a rib or two when she hit the wall. If she hadn't, she was going to be surprised and wonder how she got so lucky.

After taking a moment to catch her breath, she stood up, dusted herself off, and looked at the door once more. She was trying to think of other options, since it was obvious she wasn't going to gain access to the room with brute force or her electricity. "I could try kicking it," she said to herself, not forgetting that kicks were brute force. She just wanted to kick something because she was becoming frustrated, and the door was just there.

She was deep in thought, trying to figure out the problem in front of her, when she heard a slimy "RAAAAREWWK" from behind her. There hadn't even been a feeling of another presence in the room, but when she heard the sliminess in the noise, chills of familiar adrenaline ran down her back. She turned just in time to see the monster she never wanted to see again lunge at her.

"I thought I fucking killed you!" she screamed with rage and fear as she dodged the attack by leaping as far away as she could. "Did you fucking follow me here? Are you what stank the entire time?"

The fleshy monster of nightmares crashed through the door, like it was a piece of aluminum foil doing its best to hold up against a strong hurricane wind. It was so easy for it to destroy the one thing Faith seemed to be having a problem with, it scared her to know how much strength a humanoid pile of melting flesh could have. But it scared her more to know that the monster probably didn't even realize its full potential.

It let out another terrifyingly ferocious roar as it immediately forgot about the woman it had been hunting and turned its focus on the helpless woman in the tank. One swipe of the monster's arm was enough to smash the glass cover on the pod. Hope's body slumped forward as all the liquid that had been holding her upright drained out onto the floor. Her body was limp, and she was unaware of what was happening. The grotesque thing swiped once more at the tank, this time pulling the body of the queen out, pushing her through the once solid side panel. Her body folded on her right hip, leaving the sound of breaking bones in its wake.

The cracking and popping of the snapping bones was enough for Faith; she couldn't handle the gruesome sounds. By the time she turned around from dodging the initial attack, the monster had already hurt Hope, to the point of no return. "Hope!" she screamed in a high-pitched, blood-curdling tone as she witnessed a small portion of Hope's mangled body hanging from the broken shards of glass lining the pod from behind the monster.

When she screamed, the tone of her voice reminded the monster of its real mission; it wanted to kill the one who hurt it. Killing the unprotected elf was just a bonus. A sweet treat to avenge all the pain they had put it through over the years— it was nondiscriminatory anyway. It couldn't tell the difference between one humanoid figure to the next, and the only way it knew which one Faith was, was because of the slight odor she was exuding. It was the odor of the room, of its room. The room she had so carelessly left the door open to, to allow it to escape from its prison. It turned to face Faith, towering over her, like it was part giant. But before it could swipe in her direction, it felt a stinging breeze in the center of its stomach.

"I didn't care about her that much, we just met anyway, but we could have been friends someday. How dare you do that to someone in front of me, you fucking piece of shit," Faith said, looking into the multiple eyes of the monster; the rage was apparent. There were flames from Hell, lighting the pedestal-placed sapphires in her own eyes, which were unblinking and staring with intense focus. Her hand was full of melted flesh that seemed to be boiling more than usual. "You will not follow me again. This will be the final fucking interaction we have." She squeezed the goo she had pulled out of the monster's stomach and violently hurled it. A ray of plasma followed the goo towards the face of the monster. She hadn't even gathered any static, like she needed to in the past, but a lightning bolt had shot across the room, connecting the monster with her.

Everything outside the room went dark, while everything inside the room was brighter than the surface of a star going supernova. Even Faith, the person who shot the lightning bolt, was surprised. Never in her life had she summoned so much power at once, and she was graciously thankful for not using her power on that twit Joena. If she had, Joena would be dead, blasted from here to her universe.

The bolt of energy quickly retreated and dissipated into the atmosphere. The room felt sticky, implying a certain bloody humidity had filled the area.

When the lights hit an equilibrium, a balance between the interior and exterior rooms, Faith could see the damage she had done. Where the monster's face should have been was a hole that almost engulfed its entire head, leaving about a centimeter of visceral material connecting the remaining outline of the two hemispheres. The portions of the monster's skull that had never seen a lick of daylight had been cauterized, leaving a bumpy scab of blood and fleshy goop on the surface. Behind the monster, if Faith were only an inch to the right, she would have obliterated the rest of Hope's remains, but fortunately Faith's cannon destroyed the wall instead.

"Faith," a wheezing and gravelly voice said as Faith was recovering from the shock of her now undefined power. "Come here."

Faith looked around, swiveling her head to look at every corner of the room. She was confused and uncertain on where the voice was coming from. Her throat plummeted into her stomach out of terror. *Am I hearing demons?* she thought, wondering if the elves had actually captured a real demon and was hosting it in the same area where they kept their queen. "Who said that? Reveal yourself, and if you don't, I'll find you and kill you, just like I did with that prick."

"Come here." The voice released a long wispy exhale, before coughing like it had been smoking the finest Virginia Slims for thirty years. "Please, you need to know something before it's too late. I don't have much longer."

Faith saw the origin point of the voice this time. It was coming from the remaining un-mangled bits of Hope; her upper torso. It looked as if her chest had been crushed, and she shouldn't be breathing, let alone speaking. "You're alive? How?" Faith asked, sprinting to the deathbed. She lifted the queen's head on impulse, hoping she wasn't hurting Hope more.

Hope groaned, fighting her inevitable death, putting it off to make sure she conveyed the information she needed to.

Hope's battle reminded Faith of when she watched her father pass into the light, after years of battling brain cancer. It reminded her of the good times she had with him. But most of all it reminded her of the sadness and emptiness she'd felt when she watched the lights burn out in his eyes. She was only six at the time; she didn't fully understand what had happened to her father until she was older and wiser, but that didn't mean it hurt any less. The same was true now. She might not have known Hope, but she despised when people died in front of her, and to her, it was her fault. She was the one who left the door open, ignorantly. It was obvious she was the one who led the monster there. And she was the one who jumped out of the way. It was her fault, and she couldn't help but to feel overwhelmed with guilt.

"You should save your energy," Faith said, choking back her remorse and putting on a brave face. She had read somewhere at some point in time that the dying don't like to see tears regarding them.

"*WHEEZE*. No, *WHEEZE*. I need to explain a few things to you. *WHEEZE*." Hope inhaled as much air as she could in an attempt to prevent the wheezing. She sounded like a humidifier, releasing vapors into the air. "Nothing is as it seems, here on Quii. Many centuries ago, our race discovered cloning. We perfected it, and we thought it was the end-all solution for something that plagued our people for even longer. *WHEEZE.* As you know, our women die when they give birth. Our significant others, our partners in life, are connected to us, through a very powerful ritual that ties our souls and our hearts together. *WHEEZE.* And when us women die, our partners follow us to the grave, leaving our child orphaned."

"So what? Why is this important? You need to save your breath."

Faith's hair drooped over Hope's forehead, in a way to hide the queen's eyes. Faith didn't want to see the fire go out and was doing her best to stoke the flame.

"It's alright, *wheeze.*" Hope's breathing was getting lighter and it was obvious it was getting harder to keep her thoughts straight. "It becomes very apparent that if we progress into the future, our population shrinks. *Wheeze.* We thought... we thought... we thought that cloning would allow us to continue our lineage, but unfortunately, we were mistaken. *Wheeze.*"

Faith didn't want to ask any question, to make it easier on Hope to explain, but a question stuck out and her mouth operated without permission. "But what about your vast population? Joena said you guys had a lot of people in this city."

"Mostly clones. *Wheeze.* There's not a lot of us left. The clones have no ability to reproduce effectively. The offspring, *wheeze,* the offspring melt within a few rhonts of birth, usually leaving a hand or foot and their consciousness. *Wheeze.* We had to hide those children away, and nobody but myself, Siel, and a few of the ancients know where they are. *Wheeze.* Every real person in this city has no idea that the city consists of clones. We keep them in the dark to protect them. *Wheeze.* We encourage them to be productive and learn something, to distract them from making any meaningful relationships. *Wheeze.* We tell them that we are being a hundred percent transparent with them, so they don't ask any questions. Our culture, our society, it's all built on lies. *Wheeze.*"

From the muscles on Hope's forehead, Faith could tell the dying queen had shut her eyes. As a precautionary measure, Faith shook her, to make sure she was only resting her eyes and not slipping into the void. "Come on, keep talking. You're going to be alright, just keep your mind active. I can tell you something you don't know, to keep you thinking. We'll get you to that doctor of yours that fixed my friend. I'm sure if my friend was here right now, he'd thank you; you guys saved his life."

A faint smile appeared on Hope's face. It was just as bubbly as it had been when Faith first met her a few hours before. Her dimples were just as deep and if you couldn't see the rest of her body, one would assume she was perfectly fine. "That makes me happy that he's alright. Before I go, *wheeze,* your friend was looking for some technology to save your world? Go to the top of the Orbital Elevator; he'll find what he is looking for, and you'll find something of interest too. I just have one...*wheeze*...one request. When you and your friend leave this planet, take the rest of the real people, there's no more than twenty of them. *Wheeze.* You'll...you'll find a record of who is left on the top floor of the Orbital Elevator."

The room flooded with silence as the last of Hope's breath escaped in one final hissing wheeze. Faith could feel the coldness take over Hope's body, leaving whatever heat was left to be engulfed by the void. The fires in Hope's eyes were finally snuffed out.

CHAPTER 14

PARALLEL PLANE

Faith was shaking from her experience. She could hear her heartbeat in her ears and could smell the lingering smell of daisies in the air. She had processed some of what she was told but not all of it; that last part that Hope told her, to be specific. What would she find that would be of interest to her? How would she know which record to look for? And most importantly, how was she supposed to get to the top of the thing that she was told only a select few could access?

She refused to move, embracing the remains of Hope's body as she stood. The questions sprinting through her head kept her frozen. She wasn't even aware that she was still clutching the dead body while the stillness in the air precipitated on her forehead, mixing with the haze of blood from the fried monster and her hair. She was surrounded by death, the monster at her feet and Hope in her arms, but her eyes were glazed over with a pungent despair, keeping her mentally occupied and preventing her from realizing where she was.

It took a couple minutes for her to fully process everything that had happened. When her eyes refocused, there was a question louder than the rest, shouting through the folds in her brain. Her thoughts were an incoherent mess, pushing her ever so slightly to the edge of complete insanity; a panic attack was about to ensue, and there was no derailing it. *WHAT HAPPENS IF SOMEONE SEES ME IN HERE?* *I will surely be called a murderer, probably arrested, if elves even did that, and forever be known as the person who slaughtered the queen. Because let's face it, this scene is super incriminating and if the government was willing to lie about those other things, I am pretty sure they would be itching for a possible scapegoat. Me. I would be the scapegoat. I need to get out of here, I need to get as far away from this crime scene as I can. What do I tell the jackass, though? I couldn't find her? Should we try the place he originally said? Nope, I can't lie to him, he'll know immediately. If I lie to him, I'll have to keep that lie up, I'll have to remember it, and when I am confronted with questions, I'll have to lie more. I can't do that. Oh my god, what do I do?*

The internal panic she was suffering from set in, blocking whatever outside thoughts were trying to penetrate. At first, she didn't hear anything, but when she calmed down enough to slow the rumble in her ears to a mild rolling bass, she heard a familiar voice; The Man's.

"Miss Faith?" the voice said in her head. She had forgotten The Man was able to telepathically communicate with people, even though he had only used it a few hours previously. There was just too much that had happened in that time frame to remember everything. "I do not know if you can hear me, but Marn and I are coming in to find you. A fleshy monster broke through the security of the castle, and I think it is going to find its way to you."

Faith weakly smirked at The Man's statement. He was behind on the times. She had already killed the monster and it was lying at her feet with a giant hole through its chest. *It is nice of him to try to find me, I guess. But that means I have to get out of here even sooner. I wish I could tell him that I'm alright, and he doesn't need to worry, but I also need to tell him the situation without Squeakers finding out.* "Wait a minute? Why didn't Joena follow them into the castle?" she said aloud the moment it occurred to her.

Her thought broke the quiet she had been sitting in, stirring the air and turning Faith's stomach. The taste on her lips when she said those words sent her into a panic, unlike her anxiety-fueled panic attacks she had been prone to but something different. Something more unbalanced. Something more wrenching. "He definitely would have included Joena in his statement, if she were with them. That's just how he was. Did that monster kill her? Would I be that lucky?"

Without realizing it, Faith had found her way out of the hidden corridor, away from the death and destruction. Her imagination had run rampant, trying to figure out the best and most enjoyable death Joena could suffer, leaving her legs to think for themselves, allowing them to lead her out.

"Miss Faith? Where are you?" The Man's voice said once again in her head; she could hear him, but her mind was elsewhere and her emotions were a roller coaster with winds and turns she had never experienced before. She had no way of answering him, nor did she want to. She had taken a back seat to her consciousness and was just allowing the universe to move around her, something she had never done before.

"Look I know you can hear me," he said, implying that he knew something she didn't. "I feel you might be having a rough time, which is fine, you do not need to answer me, but please just send me a sign so that I know you are alright. Otherwise, we will have to continue our search for you. I mean we probably will anyway, but this way I can ease my mind a little. If you want, we could even meet on a parallel plane, and talk. I feel you need it."

A parallel plane? What is he talking about? Her thought sounded as if it had been sucked through a vacuum, while her breath seemed to come in short segments and the world turned to a grayscale all in a matter of a second. It reminded her of when she first talked to The Man; how it seemed no one was around, but she could still feel movement and emotions around her. "What the hell?" she mumbled before seeing a figure in the distance.

The figure moved closer, approaching her like it intended for her to pay it some money. It held a steady hurried pace, swiftly becoming apparent to Faith what was approaching her—it was none other than The Man, himself, or at least something that looked like him. "Miss Faith, come here."

"I would rather not. I don't know who or what you are?" The distrust in her voice would have sent chills down anyone's back, except the one person walking towards her.

"It is me," The Man said in a reassuring tone. His usual smile was there, presenting himself, controlling his range of optimism. "I heard it. Just because I said it is me does not mean it could be me. I see the distrust. But please allow me to explain."

Faith realized it was The Man after he said that; his enunciation of all the words clued her in, but she was willing to hear his explanation to ease her confusion.

"You have been here before, or at least someplace similar, multiple times, even if you were not aware of it. This is a parallel plane. A place where almost all of your fights have taken place. It floats in alignment with your own, or I guess the world you currently reside in. It denies access to most people. But somehow you gave yourself access by willing a key to it, into existence. You remember how when we first learned of each other's existence, you could not find another human, but somehow you and I crossed paths? And you fought the Goobert that started everything in one of these planes. Unfortunately, what happens in here can also sometimes affect the plane you live on. Which is why no one can see the Voidtriss on your world, but the black hole that is probably currently forming as we speak will be felt, and will affect everyone."

Faith looked upset to The Man, but he could not fully place her emotions. Was she angry to learn about the parallel plane? Was her range of melancholy from something else, something he was not even aware of? "What is wrong, Miss Faith? I hope I did not sadden you with this information."

"No," she said, holding back her tears with a gulp, placing a facade in front of her to keep The Man in the dark. She didn't want to explain to him what had happened, but before she could gain complete control over her motor functions, she broke down. She shed tears of anxiety, of confusion, and of heartbreak. "I might have messed up, really bad."

"Do you want to talk about it?" The Man said, getting closer to her, so he could place his arm around her shoulder.

"N-no." She sniffed, returning to her hard, stubborn exterior.

The Man attempted to scold her and said, "That is alright, Miss Faith, if you do not want to tell me and feel better now, I will wait patiently for you to be ready, and when you are, we can have a nice conversation. But remember that sadness you are feeling only gets worse the more you allow it to cultivate in you." He sat down, his arm still wrapped around Faith's shoulders, forcing her to sit down too. "Look, I understand that sometimes it can be difficult to be honest or talk about how you are feeling, but it is very important that you do talk to someone. Light only pokes through darkness if you do not allow the darkness to grow."

There seemed to be a cool breeze surrounding them. Circling about like it was dancing around a campfire. Faith's head was in her arms, which were resting on her bent knees. Her hair was in a tidy mess, being constrained by a few hair clips and tucked behind her ears.

She looked up after a few minutes of silence and said, "Hope is dead. I didn't kill her, but I watched her die. That monster is dead too. I killed it because it killed Hope. Before she passed away, she told me some things that I don't know how to really process. This city was built on lies and corruption, but no one is aware of it. And on top of all this, Hope asked me to do something I don't even know how to do."

"What do you want to unwrap first? The death? The murder? Or the task?"

"Why does everything happen to me?"

"Well, to put it bluntly, Miss Faith, everything happens to you because you are you. The anomaly the universe does not know what to do with. The woman sitting in an abyss of uncertainty, paving her own path. Technically you are doing 'this everything' to yourself, but you have also found a way out of 'this everything' by yourself too."

"No, you've helped me a lot, asshole." She sniffed.

"Think about it; if you would not have willed yourself a key into this parallel plane, or rather the one back on your planet, our paths would have never crossed. You and I conveniently crossed into the same plane of existence, briefly, but long enough to learn about each other. I think you summoned me, without knowing it, because you were looking for someone to help you. And who else would you summon, other than the guy who knows basically everything about everything? Of course. Knowing myself, I came because of who I am. I do not know if you have noticed, but things happen conveniently in my favor."

"What do you need me for? If I am convenient to you, I'm obviously needed for something. What are you fucking planning?" Faith said, glancing at The Man's silhouetted figure, displaying a sudden mountain of distrust towards her only friend.

"I feel you have misinterpreted my words. What I am saying is we need each other; without you, there would be no me to help you. And without me, there would be no you. You and I are slated for something greater than either of us is ready to know about. All I know is everything is going to be alright, no matter how dark or near impossible things seem to get. You and I will always come out swinging, fighting for our last breaths. And in the end, we will manage to do what we do best, win."

Faith sniffed one last time, wiped her eyes with her hand, and attempted to put on a smile, to show The Man she was feeling better, denying the smorgasbord of emotions she had laid out in front of her. "Thanks," she said while her palm was fishing out the last of the tears. "I needed that."

"Of course, Miss Faith, you are welcome."

An elongated silence awkwardly sat between the two figures while the stillness of the parallel plane rustled about. "So how do we tell Squeakers and Bitch that their queen is dead?"

"Miss Marn and Miss Joena? I think we need to let them know with the best courtesy we can, but unfortunately we have no idea where Miss Joena disappeared off to. She ran the moment she saw that monster."

"I would expect nothing less of that fucking chicken. She and that fucktard Siel, I can see both of them running at the sign of any danger." Faith's dislike of the two elves overshadowed any respect she had for them. "So here's the deal. Before Hope died, she told me a few things, like how the majority of this population are just clones, and the clones run this world. Unfortunately, this world is dying and the elves aren't even fucking aware of it. She asked me to take the remaining elves, the non-cloned ones, to my planet, so they could live out their lives in freedom. Away from any corruption or manipulation, like they have experienced their entire lives on Quii."

"How can you tell if they are clones? How is this planet dying? Maybe we can help them," The Man said, for once not knowing all the answers.

"No. We can't help them. They can't reproduce with each other, or they will die, and there is nothing we can do to help them with that. And when the clones reproduce, that monster you saw is what happens. I think. I am still trying to process all of this myself. But Hope told me there was a way to tell which ones are clones and which ones are normal elves. There is apparently a record of the remaining real elves sitting on the top floor of that building you originally wanted to go to; you know the thing they call the Orbi-vator? She also said there might be something of interest, for you and I both. I think the machine you were looking for is up there. Now here's the thing—according to those elves on the way here, they don't let just anybody into that tower. You need special permission."

"Okay, wow, that is a lot of information to take in at once," The Man said, bringing his fingers to a steeple below his chin. "Well, I guess the first thing we need to do is reconnect in the real world, and then I guess we will have Miss Marn lead us to the Orbi-vator, and then from there we just need to figure out how to get to the top of it without being stopped." The Man stood up and started to walk in the direction he originally came from, mumbling to himself as he did. He stopped for a moment to swivel around and say, "Did you happen to cross a random gravel pit in one of the paths on the outer perimeter of the castle?"

"Yeah, it only stood out because it didn't make any fucking sense."

"Great. We are there; meet us, will you?"

"I guess. It might take me a few minutes to find my way out of this place and back to that pit, though."

"That is fine, Miss Faith, I am sure it will not feel like it." The Man walked into the distance and vanished, exiting the parallel plane, leaving it undisturbed like he had not even been there.

~~~

It started with the field, the battle-scarred terrain, outside the city limits. It stretched and warped, bubbled and flexed. The black hole had started to suck planet Earth away.

The hill Faith had been thrown into a half an hour or so previously was pulled into a pinpoint of denseness, only to be ripped apart during its spaghettification. Particles of dirt and stones the hill was built upon wouldn't have a chance to land, but instead would be sucked into the ever-growing mass as well.

It would be at this point that the humans in the city would hear the Earth growl in agony, a sound they themselves would not be able to process, before their untimely doom.

One final thought would be shared across the planet as every person's last breath was snuffed out to feed the growing black hole. *The end is here and there was no warning.*

The last second of Earth was marked with a slight shimmer against the blackest of blacks as the mass of rock stretched into a hole no larger than the small toenail of a baby.

CHAPTER 15

ORBITAL ELEVATOR

"Alright, Miss Marn, Miss Faith is going to be here in a few minutes. We have talked things through, and we know what we need to do," The Man said, breaking the silence they had unintentionally created between them.

"What do you mean? You've been here the entire time. How did you have time to talk to Faith?" Marn said, displaying her innocence to the situation. "You stopped in front of the gravel pit. I thought you were praying with me."

"Praying? No, I was communicating with Miss Faith. We have ways of communicating with each other when we are not next to each other."

"We pray at gravel in honor of our ancestors; it's just something we've done since the beginning of time." Marn looked at The Man with interest and intrigue the moment it occurred to her that he had said what he had said. "Apparently people with Terunes can communicate with others without being next to them, do you mean like that?"

"Similar, but I think you are referring to something different. We are telepathically linked across parallel planes of the universe, and we just had a conversation. When Miss Faith gets here, there is something very crucial we need to tell you. Actually, we need to tell all of you, including Miss Joena and the others."

"Why can't you tell me now?" Marn squeaked, her face revealing worry and surprise like she was expecting a gift from someone.

"I think it is best if you hear it from Miss Faith herself. I would not know where to begin. She should be here in a few rhonts as it is."

"No, I think she is here now," the elf said, glancing behind The Man as she tilted her head towards the filthy woman limping her way to the two standing there.

"Where are my shoes? My feet are killing me," Faith said, approaching at turtle speeds. The blood she had been hazed with had dried to a crusty, flaky mask. The whites of her eyes stood out, as they contrasted the dark brown that had been smeared across her face in a failed attempt at a Jackson Pollock painting. She walked around the gravel pit as she had when she had entered the castle walls, leaving Marn with a glimmer of respect. "Squeakers, I have some bad news for you, and you know what, this is probably the hardest thing I've ever had to tell someone," she said as she stopped in front of the two who had been standing there.

The Man could tell Faith was putting up a wall. She was avoiding eye contact, and though her outer facade was that of a tough person, her interior personality was on the verge of tears like she had been on the parallel plane. "Miss Faith," he said, hoping she would calm down, hoping she would shed no more tears for the events that had happened in her life. "Remember to show some courtesies like we talked about."

"Yeah, yeah," she said, ignoring almost every word The Man had said, like a delinquent avoiding being chastised by any form of authority. "This is hard, and if you want to tell her, be my guest, but I get the feeling you don't want to."

"Tell me what?" Marn looked scared. She watched the two strangers bicker between each other. "You guys are stressing me out."

The two humans looked at each other, trading glances. "Squeakers," Faith said, finally turning to the elf. "I witnessed your queen die, and she told me some things before it happened. I honestly don't think you're mentally capable of learning

183

them, or even understanding them."

The lines portraying fear along Marn's face shifted and darkened her smooth complexion, trading the look of fear for glum, forecasting a storm of sadness. "No, I think you guys are lying to me," she said, lashing out to the unfortunate information Faith had just provided her with. Her whimpers sounded like a kettle boiling water; the whistling sound they make when the water inside gets to the right temperature. "If you watched her die, then why didn't you prevent it?" Marn asked suddenly, her squeaks deeper.

The Man and Faith could tell she was enraged. "That was the quickest leap from one stage of grief to the next I've ever fucking seen," Faith said, concerned about Marn's health.

"Miss Marn, we know it hurts, but Miss Faith tried her best to protect Miss Hope."

"Well, she didn't try hard enough, she should have done better, but now our people are left without a ruler and protector. We are never going to recover from this and all you have to say about it is 'oh, well, she tried her best.'"

"Look, Squeakers, if I had a choice, I would have gladly saved her, but she was dead before I even realized what happened. And if I could have healed her, I would have. But I don't have fancy fucking technology that can heal broken arms and damaged spines like you guys do. Okay. All I have is the power to screw things up, attract universal dangers, and shoot electricity out of my fingers, so don't blame me for this."

The Man placed a hand on both of the women's shoulders to try to calm them both down. "I am sorry to say this, but I get the funny feeling that we are running out of time. I wish we could mourn over her right now for as long as we wanted but I fear the worst is already happening on Miss Faith's planet. We should really think about hustling, so we can get back in time."

"Now's not the time, jackass," Faith snapped angrily at The Man.

"I beg to differ, Miss Faith. I fear it might actually be too late at this point, but I get the feeling that your universe is no longer there. And as a Watcher, it is my job to stop massive anomalies such as the one we left behind on Earth. Do you catch my drift?"

Faith sighed and decided to briefly hug Marn, a motion so out of her comfort zone. The Man stared in amazement, with his mouth gaping, unsure of what she was doing. "Marn, the asshole is right. Can we offer you a slight distraction, so you can keep your mind off of the news we just gave you?"

Marn nodded, her silence cumbersome for the two humans to carry. Her eyes were puffy and red, and her ears drooped, leaving her hair dangling in front of her face. "Miss Marn, could you lead us to the Orbital Elevator? Before Miss Hope died, she told Miss Faith that what we were looking for would be found at the top of it." Again, Marn nodded. "Could you do one other thing for us?"

Marn stared at The Man with her sunken eyes; she felt that was enough response to his question. "Could you tell us your favorite thing about your queen? Remember her as a hero, because in the coming hours, you may learn stuff you may not want to know about." She refused to speak. She would rather just lead the two humans to the Orbi-vator and then disappear for a while, so she could mourn the death of the only queen she had known throughout her life.

She led them to the front of the castle's gate, released the lever that was holding it shut, and walked down the road without hesitation as if it were a normal thing for her to do.

~~~

Traveling to the tallest building in the city was pretty easy; when you looked up, however, Marn refused to consider that an option as she moped her way down every diagonal street and every perpendicular avenue. Her ears remained drooped and level with her frown while she led the humans away from the castle and to the Orbi-vator. It was easy to tell she had reverted to the quiet somber individual that had greeted the strangers a few hours before. She was planning on going her separate way, after she arrived at the building that stood higher than a mountain, literally touching the sky, but her plan changed the moment the group of people arrived at the doors of the elevator.

"Marn, are you coming with us?" Faith said when she noticed the elf was readying herself to run away from them. "This might be your only chance to see what it feels like at the top. You'll definitely have a story to tell your friends. I mean, not that you don't already, but how would it feel to be one of the few elves to actually stand on the top of this building?"

Marn knew Faith was trying to manipulate her into helping them; however, it still worked. The intrigue and curiosity got the best of her, and she wanted to know what it felt like standing at the top of the world. Would endorphins rush through her body and give her a fleeting sensation? Or would she learn something new by brushing against the thin layer of atmosphere that separated space and the place she called home? It was exhilarating to her, and for some unknown reason she felt a little better about the death of her queen. She nodded her head, filling her body with excitement.

"Now the question is, how do we enter the building without being fucking caught?" Faith said, hoping someone else would have an answer. "I know I can enter and not be detected, but I know you two are going to set off every alarm this fucking building has."

Conveniently, the moment Faith stopped speaking, the heavy armored doors slid open, enticing the group to enter. *It is almost too perfect,* Faith thought as she read the faces of the other two people standing with her. *It's the middle of the night, we show up unannounced, and the building that is allegedly impossible to enter if you're a normal civilian opens its fucking doors like a street walker opens their legs. There is no way anything good is going to come out of this.*

"Well, we might as well walk in," The Man said, displaying his typical grin. "I guess they have been expecting us."

"I've never seen the doors open like that before," Marn said quietly with surprise. "Actually, I've never seen the doors open before. And I am pretty sure no one other than those who are allowed in there have. I think they have been waiting for us."

"It's a fucking trap," Faith said, looking at The Man with exasperation. "Squeakers broke her short vow of silence to tell us she has never seen that door open before."

"It may be a trap or it may be good fortune; we will only know if we enter," The Man said as he took the first step toward the open door. His stride was jaunty, which paired well with his grinning face.

"If there is another one of those fucking monsters, I'm going to be a little pissed," Faith said, catching up to The Man's quick stride with Marn not too far behind.

"So, you have finally made it, I see," a familiar smug voice said as the trio entered.

"It's worse than the monster, it's fucking Siel," Faith shouted as she rolled her eyes at the sight of one her least favorite people. "See, I told you it was a trap."

Siel was standing at a counter adjacent to the entrance. He was the first thing everybody noticed when they entered the building. His appearance hadn't changed since the last time they saw him, but his attitude definitely seemed different, less conceited. "I thought you guys were going to be here sooner— all the reports I received told me you left the Aurora Castle twenty rhonts ago."

"Why are you here?" Faith asked almost instantly, disregarding anything that came out of his mouth.

"I am here by order of the queen. She told me to greet you when you finally made it here."

Faith took a step forward, her fists clenched like she was about to attack. "How? I watched your queen die. I held her in my arms. When did she have time to tell you to meet us here?"

"You don't understand yet, do you?" Siel inhaled excessively to ensure all the eyes were on him. His chest puffed out and he stood up straight.

Before he could continue his statement, Faith quickly quipped, "No. Shut up. I don't want to hear any monologuing. I know you're the villain, all the signs were there. Joena is also in on all of it too, right?"

Siel was more confused than a dog trying to figure out a magic trick; he didn't quite understand what Faith was going on about. "Monologuing? Villain? I don't understand. I'm not a villain, I work for the queen, and my niece has nothing to do with my job."

"Miss Faith, I think we should hear him out. I think he can be trusted," The Man said, holding the furious woman back. His firm grip on her shoulder was enough to prevent her from marching into Siel's face.

Siel nodded at The Man graciously, thankful that he was allowed to speak. "Please, if you would, follow me." He left his spot at the counter and slowly walked across the room to a cylindrical protrusion sticking out of the wall. It, along with everything else in the room, was aesthetically pleasing, nothing out of place. There was an aura of cleanliness, like before that moment, no one in the city had stepped foot in that room. The cylinder rotated, revealing an empty chamber, while Siel swung out his arm to usher the people into it. "This will take you to the top of the space elevator. Are you prepared for what you'll find at the top?" he said, sweeping his eyes across the room. "Marniple, I'm glad you're here too; that means we'll have to contact less of you."

Marn's ears perked up when she heard her name. "What do you mean by that?" she asked as she stepped into the cylinder.

"I will explain while we ascend to the top. Or rather, the one who has been expecting you will explain when we get to the top," Siel said with a calm, unwavering tone.

Faith blinked, realized what they were about to enter, and asked in an alarmed tone, "Why are we using an elevator? Where are the stairs? I'll fucking walk."

"Miss Faith, would you calm down? Surely you do not want to climb thousands of stairs to the sky. That would take you longer than we have time for," The Man said, pulling Faith into the cylinder. "Also, it is a space elevator; how else did you think we were going to reach the top?"

"Machines that run on electricity hate me. I didn't fucking realize we had to ride one to the top of the world." Faith's panic was unique, and she had never been so nervous before. She knew she hated elevators, but she never actually had to ride one. There was always a stairs option, and she would always gladly take it.

"You will be fine, Miss Faith. I promise."

Faith was shaking hard, making it difficult for her to stand. She pressed her back against the wall and slid into a squatting position. As she lowered herself, she wrapped her dress around her knees to prevent unwanted constriction. She wanted to be as close to the floor as she could get without lying on it, and the ball she had formed was the best solution her anxiety-riddled mind could come up with.

Siel stepped into the elevator last, the door rotating around the group of people as he did. "You won't believe the view from up there," he said, over the normal compression and grinding sounds the elevator was making. "It's like nothing you've ever seen before."

Chapter 16

Abundant Confusion

Faith was the first one off the elevator after the thirty-rhont ride. She forcefully pushed her way through the other bodies standing there to exit the half full cylinder as soon as it reached its destination; she wasn't going to spend more time on it than necessary. Her fear of the elevator, mixed with everything else that had happened that day, left her anxious, wanting for her inter-dimensional escapades to come to an end. "I'm walking when we go back down," she said, out of breath, the moment she pushed through the wall of humans and elves blocking her path to freedom.

The ride up to the top was quiet. No one uttered a single word in the time it took to ascend to the highest point of Quii. "Welcome to the top of the world," Siel said, allowing the elevator riders to exit past him. His tone had reverted to that of a more enjoyable, less smug tone. He genuinely felt like a completely different Siel compared to the personality they had met earlier in the day. "Your guests are here. They brought a bonus too—you can come out now." His eyes stretched across the room, looking for anything out of place. "Madam?"

The wide open room was essentially empty. It surrounded a group of walled off sections. There were bookshelves lining the interior walls and a small ritzy metal table that housed a single pair of chairs; however, for the most part the attention grabbers were the windows that provided a full three-hundred-sixty-degree view across the cityscape. A sight so breathtaking, even if Michelangelo were given multiple lifetimes, he would have a difficult time bringing out its beauty.

When standing against the glass, the ability to see halfway across the world was an understatement. The building-riddled landscape stretched for what seemed like miles and eventually transitioned harshly into greenery. The curvature of Quii remained visible through light blue outlines of the stratosphere, only to be backlit by the void of space. Faith saw the beauty, and she immediately forgot about the ride to get to it. Her eyes dilated with excitement as she sprinted to the edge of the room to glance down at the scenery. She couldn't hide her awe.

The Man had noticed, while examining the view, the red beacon that had drawn his attention into compulsion had disappeared. There was no sign of it, even though not too long before it was calling out to him, expanding outward like it was looking for something, leaving the planet undisturbed while it searched.

The Man and Faith turned around in synchronization, the distraction the view was providing interrupted by a calm feminine voice. "I'm glad you finally made it here. All the seeds I planted, all the strings I pulled, just to get you here," it said, taking an overwhelming presence in the room. "Siel, go grab a few more chairs for our guests. I think they are going to need them."

"Yes, ma'am," Siel said, leaving the main room they had been standing in. He returned moments later with three small chairs, all matching the two already set at the table.

Faith was undeniably shocked by who was standing across the room from her. She couldn't put into words what she was feeling. Marn noticed the surprised faces from her human counterparts and was the first to speak. "Faith said you were dead." Marn's voice was higher than usual, her shock just as obvious.

Standing in front of them was the queen of Quii herself, Hope.

"Kind of, but not really. I'll explain it. Please have a seat." Hope said calmly with charisma swinging out her arms in a welcoming fashion.

"You can't be real. I held your dead body in my arms," Faith said as the shock wore off, endearing her to the invitation of a seat. She slumped into one of the chairs and kicked off her heels, as if she were sitting at home in front of her television.

"Miss Faith, remember we are in the presence of a queen," The Man said, taking the seat next to her, with Marn behind him, following and duplicating his actions with added hesitation.

"It's truly alright, she deserves a rest from what I've witnessed today," Hope said, sliding into one of the chairs across from her guests. "Siel, go round everyone else up, be back before we leave. I've got some explaining to do, and I am sure they have plenty of questions; hopefully that gives you enough time."

"Yes, ma'am, we'll be back in no time," Siel said, exiting the room and entering the elevator. His face was stern and unchanging as the door to the elevator slid in front of his glazed over look.

"So, let me begin with something I know you all are curious about," Hope said, watching the three faces in front of her carefully. "I am not the Hope you met earlier today. That Hope, the Hope you watched die, was a clone."

She crossed her legs to get more comfortable, an action she rarely did, but this time she felt it was necessary to give off a serious aura. She didn't want the guests in front of her to misinterpret her words as a spiteful joke.

"Centuries ago, our planet started from the grains of the universe. These grains grew into a plethora of organisms that would live side by side for centuries to come. We adapted, we grew into our roles of cohabitation and became one single entity, us, the Rymuth elves. We avoided wars and plagues and encouraged intellectual growth, but the once thriving society that we had created had gotten greedy. We looked up to our gods and pleaded with them to send us an answer to help us thrive even more. In response the Orb of Blood Disdain, an object rumored to have started the universe, was sent from the heavens. We cherished it, we protected it, and to this day we watch over it, waiting for the perfect time to use it." Hope paused her story to watch The Man's face. She could tell he was thinking about something, and she could tell that something was about the Orb of Blood Disdain.

"Over the years we have done several tests and inquiries on the orb; however, our finest scientists have concluded that only a select few people who have been chosen by the universe can operate it, and can restart the universe or force its inhabitants to thrive. Meanwhile, our society began to shrink. We ran tests to figure out what was wrong with us, and the unfortunate thing is, the thing that was supposed to make our people thrive has cursed us. We, the Rymuth elves, the people of Quii, we are cursed with the inability to reproduce and grow our society. We were forced to live on, watching as couples would have their children and then proceed to die within hours of childbirth. It needed to stop. We needed an answer, and so the intellectual beings we were came up with a solution. We worked tirelessly, to crack the case, but as time passed, our desires were slowly eating away at us. Occasionally parents would pop out twins, like Siel and his sister, but for the most part for every new birth there were two deaths to contend with. The solution, clones. We would clone our people and then our population would rise; it was easy. The solution was so clear and obvious. We rebuilt our government and society around this idea, but unbeknownst to us it was an immediate failure. The first generation of clones always worked, without a doubt, but the moment they started to reproduce was the problem. We had created sludge people that could live through a lot, and were almost impossible to kill, but as it turns out the sludge people acted like a hive mind. One would always grow bigger than the rest—it was their leader, it was the one in control of the hive mind."

"Why isn't this common knowledge?" Marn asked in confusion during another one of Hope's silent pauses. Her eyes were watering from the information load she had just received, but she kept her composure as Hope continued to speak.

"We did everything in our power to prevent carnal urges. We continued to encourage you all to focus on your studies, 'learn something no one had learned before,' we would tell you. We hyped up stories of animal attacks outside the gates, to keep you within the city limits, and we installed cameras and microphones everywhere, but unfortunately for most of the population, the urges were strong and unpreventable. We had no control over the clones; they did as they pleased, and eventually the sludge people problem grew out of hand. We trapped the sludge people in a room, way below the surface of Quii. We wanted to forget about them, but we still had the clones to remind us. The clones, they were nearly flawless. They would have been flawless, if it weren't for the whole sludge people debacle. We continued with the clone idea, modified it, and prevented further complications by removing the clone's genitalia. But in the end after centuries of doing this, we were left at square one, and no progress had been made on our dying society. The Hope you met earlier today was me, but it wasn't. It was me from years ago, when I cloned myself. I went into hiding for scientific experiments, and let that version of me run the world, as I had told her to. She was under my command, so everything she did, I was the reason for. I was able to watch from a distance, from up here, and intervene if I needed to. The videos that the cameras and microphones picked up were streamed live to me. I knew what everyone was doing at all times. If a spore so much as thought about blooming, I knew it—there was nothing I didn't know."

Hope relaxed her legs and then crossed them again in reverse order. She had remained motionless and only moved when she would take a breath.

Faith was supporting her head with her arms and knees while her hands were on her cheeks, curled up into fists; she looked bored from this information. "Get on with it," she said in an annoyed tone. "How does this pertain to us? Why are you retelling me what your clone already told me?"

"This is good information, Miss Faith. I know you are bored and would just rather go home at this point, but remember you potentially do not have a home at the moment and Miss Hope, here, is going to help us hopefully with that," The Man said as he stood up to stretch his legs. He was intrigued by all the information Hope had laid out and had his own questions he wanted to ask, but instead he waited for Hope to finish her story.

"Decades ago, I gave up on looking for a gifted individual who could control the Orb, but then something happened. Today a couple strangers appeared out of nowhere, in the middle of the trees. I could see their mesmerizing auras, even from this great distance. They radiated throughout the trees, leaving me to theorize that the people who could control the Orb had finally arrived. Both of the strangers radiated a sense of free will; however, only one of them radiated a slightly different aura. I sent Siel out to alert the other me that the people we were looking for had potentially arrived. As you are aware, those strangers were you.

"The other me was instructed to bring you to the city, heal the broken one, and then bring you to me. I was the one who allowed the broken one to exit the room he was in, even though every report I received on him predicted my untimely death by his actions. He was the easy one to track. The other one, you, Faith, however, were impossible to track. I couldn't track your movements, I couldn't predict your actions, and most of all I couldn't predict your thoughts, and I assume this is the case because of your powers you demonstrated throughout your time being on Quii. I didn't expect you to run away from Joena and Marniple. I didn't expect you to wander into the sludge people's jail, and most of all I didn't expect you to release the leader of those sludge people by forgetting to close the door.

"I told the broken one where to find me, but a fortunate stroke of luck allowed Joena and Marniple to tell you where the other me lived. That was when the broken one had decided to check the Aurora Castle. It was there the sludge people's leader found you, Faith, and it was there my supposed untimely death happened as the predictions had come true. The other me was finally able to set you on the correct path and lead you to the Orbi-vator, the place I've called my home for years now, only to pass away moments before she could tell you the full truth.

"Every camera and sensor I had in the other me's incubation room told me that you were the one to finally kill the sludge people's leader, a task we've been burdened with for decades but couldn't succeed over. As we speak, the other sludge people are dying. Being left without a leader will only allow the strong to survive, but from lack of nourishment and sunlight for decades,

I don't expect them to survive very long.

"So now you are here, and I do believe the other me told you a few things about our predicament. We need your help. Those of us non-clones need your help. Our planet is dying and all I want is for those of us who remain to live out the rest of our days on a planet that has more than artificial beings. And from all the intelligence I have gathered on the strangers that appeared out of nowhere, I have confidence that you people will allow me this one favor. Save my people, take them to your world. Let us live the rest of our lives in peace, away from our dying civilization. I beg of you, please allow this one favor."

There was a stiff lingering silence in the room as the group of people shared glances at each other. The queen's story had been laid out in front of them and the only sound that could be heard was the sound of confused blinking. By this point it was becoming daylight, and the sun shone through the windows, casting rays of orange light across the room. Shadows bounced off of every reflective surface as the people sat in their chairs.

"No," Faith finally said to the disbelief of everyone around her; the solemn tone she spoke through left the room in a deeper silence. "We can't help you."

"Now, Miss Faith, do you really mean that? We could easily help them," The Man said, disappointed in Faith's response.

"No, we can't. As we speak, my planet is either gone, or about to be gone, have you forgotten that? We came here to save it and so far, the only thing we have found is trouble. We haven't found the machine you were looking for, only a race of people who are asking for help because they themselves can't save their planet. How are we supposed to save them if we can't save my planet?" Faith said aggressively.

"How could you say that, Miss Faith? These people need our help, and I for one am willing to save them. Besides, were you not listening to Miss Hope's story? They do indeed have the object I was looking for. Now we may not be able to restart their planet, and it seems they have come to terms with that, but we could definitely restart yours if needed."

What is he talking about? What machine is he looking for?

"Look, I don't want them to die either, but how are we going to save them and my planet all at once? We might be stretching ourselves too thin."

The elevator opened halfway through Faith's statement. Behind the doors was a group of elves, no more than twenty or so, crammed into the cylinder that had delivered the two humans and Marn a while earlier. "I've gathered those who wanted to leave. The others refused to believe my story and have decided to live the rest of their days out on this planet. They are aware they will have to live the rest of their days out without the watchful eye and ever looming presence of their queen, ma'am," Siel said as he and the last of the elves stepped out of the elevator.

"How many said no?" Hope asked, displaying a face that revealed her concern.

"Only two, ma'am. Rirr and Estel, the other two ancients who helped build the new government. They said they would rather live out the rest of their days on the planet they watched grow than start anew. Everyone else has come, including those who went on the journey earlier today."

"You pleaded with them? Begged them to come with us?"

"Yes, ma'am. I did."

"Then they have decided their fate, and there is nothing we can do about it," Hope said, lowering her ears in an attempt to mourn the two she would never see again.

"Wait a minute," Faith said aggressively towards Hope. "We haven't even decided if we are taking you with us. Quit trying to manipulate us."

"Miss Faith, I think you know you have already decided on what is right. I know you are trying to put on a tough facade, for whatever reason, but the time to show your true persona is now. Please, let us help these poor elves, so we all can help each other."

The Man was right, Faith had already decided to help the elves, but for some reason felt like she needed to gain control over the situation, and demanding to stop being manipulated was her way of doing just that. "Fine, let's fucking do it," she said, staring into the eyes of all the scared elves she was about to save. "But if any of you start to annoy the hell out of me, I'm leaving you fucking behind." Half sarcastically she said that but half warning the three elves who had upset her or annoyed her earlier in the adventure.

"There is one thing we do need from you all if we are going to help you," The Man said, looking at the queen for acceptance with his conditions. "We are going to need the Orb of Blood Disdain."

CHAPTER 17

HOME

Hope was willing to accommodate The Man's desires and without speaking a word exited the room, disappearing into one of the other rooms that was hidden away behind a locked metal door. She was gone for long enough to make everyone wonder if she had a change of heart. But when she re-entered the overwhelmingly silent room filled with an abundance of body heat, a small gasp of relief could be heard throughout the crowd of elves. In her hands, she held a small, dark, black sphere no larger than a softball. It glimmered with exceptional beauty, polished to perfection to ward off any fingerprints that may have found their way onto the surface of it. Inside the sphere a swirl of red rotated and squirmed about, as if it had sentience. "It's yours," she said, handing it to The Man gently. "I know my counterpart would hate to see me give it up, but she is dead, and I am my own authority. If you can make it work, and save us and yourselves, then more power to you. We have sat on this thing for millennia and could not figure out its great and mystical power. I graciously give it to you in hopes that it shall serve you well."

"Thank you," The Man said; a semi-automatic response that he had no control over. "Okay, Faith, time to go home now."

"Hey, jackass, I have a question for you," Faith said in response as she watched The Man shove the Orb into one of his jean pockets, carefully to not damage it. "How are we going home?"

"The same way we got here, Miss Faith," he said enthusiastically. "Through my home. This way we can see if there is a landing spot for us." He flashed an excited grin towards Faith and then stood up once again to look around the room. "Now Miss Hope, may I inquire about your Terune? Does it have snapshot capabilities?"

All at once, Hope, Faith, and Marn gave The Man their version of a confused face. A face that twisted into an inaudible *huh*? "Would you not like a photo of your planet for a keepsake? This might be the last time you see it."

Marn squeed at the idea in excitement; of course she wanted a keepsake to remind her of her home. The big universal move was unplanned and it scared her, but if she could have a small photograph of her home, she knew she would feel better about the sudden uprooting. "Please, Hope," she squeaked, perking up her ears and wiggling them to show her excitement.

"That sounds like a wonderful idea," Hope said, running out of the room again, this time to grab her Terune to fill her last moments on Planet Quii with enjoyment. When she came back, the elves had organized themselves from tallest to shortest, from Siel's persuasion. She raised the device, quickly took a shot of the group with the planet of Quii floating in the background, and then one without the group in it. The dimples on her face widely gaped as she smiled at the sight of her world and her constituents together for the last time. Her smile shadowed the sadness she was feeling, but she just had to remind herself that it was for the better, for her people.

The Man approached her and grabbed the Terune out of her hands. "Stand with them," he said, displaying an understanding grin across his own face. She was endeared by his sincerity, walked over to the group in front of her, and stood with her Quiian family. The Man took a picture and then another one for good measure. He handed the Terune back to the queen and said, "Alright, are you all ready to go? Miss Faith, say the words."

"What? No, why can't you this time?" Faith argued. She didn't want to tell The Man that she had already forgotten the Latin phrases he had made her speak and not to mention the dumb motions he made her do too.

"I figured you might say that; that is alright. I would like every-one to hold hands and gather in a circle, please. Those of you next to me, grab on to my shoulders." Faith hurriedly grabbed one of The Man's shoulders before anyone else could while the new migrants did as they were told. None of them muttered a single word or a groan of grief. They latched hands as The Man stood awkwardly on his right leg and stretched out his left arm with his fist in a ball. Hope grabbed on to the unoccupied shoulder, while Siel, Joena, Bramish, Qunor, Kithor, and Rein tied hands together with the rest of the elves, looping around to Marn, who filled Faith's other hand. Looks of worry and concern were shared across the group. "Aperi Portam, Lacus Domum Realm, Amici Accipiat," The Man finally said, blinking the room they had just been in, in the highest building on Planet Quii, away from them like it had not been there all along.

~~~

"What is this place?" Qunor asked, looking around The Man's home. His first reaction was to start walking away from the group, before Joena grabbed him by the back of the neck.

"It doesn't matter, just stay put. I have a feeling this isn't where we're supposed to be anyway," Joena said in a stern motherly tone. She had the same question but figured eventually they all would be informed about the full truth.

"He,y Joena, I have a question for you," Qunor said when the back of his neck was released. "Why didn't you stick with Marn and Faith, like the queen asked you to? I saw you get to the Or-bi-vator a rhont before myself."

"That doesn't matter either. I had other things I needed to do, so I left the job the queen gave me." She shot him a warning glance that implied if he asked another question, she was going to kill him.

"Qunor, was it?" The Man said, breaking away the group him-self, swinging his finger around, like he was directing an orches-tra. "This is my home; it is a linking point between all time and space. This is how we are getting to Miss Faith's world." He poked at the air, swiped his hand in the direction of all the elves, revealing the screen that was there but was not. Like clockwork the elves gasped at the impressive feat The Man had just done. To them, it was magic, but in reality, they could not comprehend the Watcher's science; no one could.

It took The Man no time at all to find Faith's universe, the Garf universe. He found planet Earth even faster, or at least the location of where Earth should have been. "Well, that is not great," he said, staring intently at his magic screen. "Miss Faith, just as I had expected, your planet and its solar system are gone. It looks like we are going to have to restart, from scratch."

"Wait a goddamn fucking minute. I thought from here you could jump to any point in time, rewind this bitch to when planet Earth was there," Faith said, feeling the stress and anxiety that had been built up throughout the day. She insisted he did it without any hesitation in her voice, or forethought in her mind.

"I can rewind it, but not too far. If we go too far, we risk destroying other timelines in parallel universes. I will go just before your fight with the Voidtriss, no farther. We will have to be placed in your city, out of your own path. If we go back, we cannot intersect with ourselves; otherwise, everything we went through today will be pointless. If we cross our own timelines, the universe will just implode on itself, right then and there. Got it?"

"Do what you have to do, just do it. I won't be able to live with myself if I knew Mom and my grandparents were dead because of something I did," she said, smacking The Man on the back. She sounded rushed and panicky as the current situation set into her mind. It had finally occurred to her that she was the reason why everyone on Earth was no longer there. She was the reason Earth wasn't there and that realization made her heart sink and her stomach twist. She wanted to keel over but knew the longer she waited the less likely she would be able to save the few people in the universe that she loved.

The Man poked at the air one last time, to watch the solar system return to where it had been. It was floating there in the dead of space, unprepared for its unforeseen extinction. Pluto appeared first, like it was the awkward guy at a house party who confused arrival time as the start time. The rest of the planets blinked into existence shortly afterward, unrattled by the sudden feast the black hole had just thrown up. "Miss Hope," The Man said, looking away from his magic screen to glance at the once-been queen of Quii. His tone was grave and serious, the smile he usually wore nowhere to be found. "I think you and your people should really stay here while Miss Faith and I try to fix what we broke. It is better if you all stay here so you do not lose two homes in one day. I will not stand for it."

Hope squinted her eyes and tilted her head in response. She almost looked confused. "No. My people can stay if they want to, but I'm going. I want to help you people if I can. I mean, it is the least I can do, for how humble your hospitality has been."

"Look, lady, I screwed up pretty bad on my planet. I don't think you'll be able to see what we're fighting, and I don't need you getting in the way. You don't need to come; this is my problem to fix," Faith said, annoyed by the time waste the elf had provided.

"Oh, that is a great point, Miss Faith!" The Man said enthusiastically. He whipped his head around, as if he were searching for something. His hand reached out and from nowhere a pair of glasses appeared. He spun around again and dropped them into Hope's hands. "You should be able to see the Voidtriss now, Miss Hope."

"Dude, asshole, what the hell? Didn't you just fucking hear me? I didn't want help," Faith said in shock.

"Miss Faith, I think it would be handy to have Miss Hope help us in our fight. Besides, she might be the only person who can tell us how to use the Orb." The Man patted his pocket to verify the object that was going to potentially save them was still there. "Miss Hope, just one favor to ask from you. Please do not look the Voidtriss in the eyes. Your memory will be wiped temporarily, and unfortunately we do not have time to do that again."

Hope nodded in agreement. Her ears drooped slightly as she processed the words The Man was using. "What is a Voidtriss?" she asked, quietly to herself. She'd never heard that term before but was excited to learn what it was.

The Man swiped his hand through the air and in front of them appeared a window. Through the window was a bustling, post workday street. "Are you ladies ready to go then?" he asked. The window moved from the bustling city street to a more horizontal perspective. A perspective that blocked the light and made it impossible to identify where they were going to land.

"What's wrong with your fucking portal?" Faith said, unsure if The Man had realized anything was wrong with it. "It didn't do that last time."

"Do what?" The Man asked curiously.

"When we went to the elves' planet, the portal was stationary. It didn't move whatsoever, but this one, the one you just made, just moved. It was looking straight ahead, maybe on third street, and then it changed to black. I think it moved."

"These portals do not move, Miss Faith, something probably just crossed in front of it or it is reacting to the time dilation. No need to worry about it."

"Are you sure? Because it looks like we are staring at the ceiling of an ambulance now."

"That cannot be," The Man said as he pressed against the surface of the portal with both of his arms. "It is sort of difficult to push through it too. I think I just brushed someone by accident. I hope they do not notice." His shoulders moved in an attempt to widen the portal, to make passing through it easier. "I have never had so many issues moving through one of these things before." The Man's voice stopped with a sudden impact, and he turned to the group with a small amount of fear in his face. "That is weird. Something is purposely touching me. I will finish going through to see what it is and then Miss Hope, Miss Faith, you both follow afterward."

"How do we know it isn't a monster trying to eat you?" Hope asked. She was concerned and fearful now, even though she felt she had to be brave in front of her people.

"Because we are in the middle of my hometown, and the worst thing to ever come out of it is a few hobos who like to relieve themselves near parks, and I guess that stupid fucking Voidtriss and the Goobert, not to mention a few other things too," Faith said proudly, only to realize seconds later that her city was actually pretty dangerous. "You know what, jackass, Hope has a point—how do we know we'll be fine?"

The smile The Man wore was all the response Faith needed. He pushed his body the rest of the way through, leaving the human and elves to soak in the contradicting silence he had left behind.

"Last chance for you to say you don't want to go," Faith smugly said to Hope.

"I'll go, but what if we are to expire? What do my people do?"

"Live out their lives in the safety of a multitude of universal knowledge? I don't fucking know, but I'm sure they will be fine."

Hope was hesitant to jump into the gateway that led to a foreign world. Faith could read it across her face, stepped behind her, and pushed her in forcefully. "I'll see you annoying bunch later, be good in here. I'm going to go save my home now," she said to the remaining elves, who were bunched together, hugging each other in fear, as she stepped through the portal.

CHAPTER 18

PLANETARY DISSONANCE

"Well, that is not great," a masculine voice said in the back of the ambulance Ron was driving.

"Did the patient wake up, Kev?" Ron said, approaching the hospital's emergency room entrance. As he pulled in, with speed and precision, he looked back to meet Kev's pending response. To his surprise there was a man's head now protruding through the patient's stomach to go with the set of arms that he had seen earlier. "What the hell?"

Kev stood with his mouth gaped and his eyes open. He had witnessed the head emerging out of the poor patient laying on the cot in front of him. He had seen some gruesome things in his short career as a paramedic, but witnessing a fully grown human birth himself out of another grown man took the cake.

"Oh, good," the head said, noticing the pair of paramedics staring, horrified in its direction. "Could you gentlemen give me a hand? I would greatly appreciate it if you did. I am on a bit of a time sensitive mission."

Kev shook his head vigorously in dismay. His lips began to tremble, looking for the missing words his brain was attempting to send. "I, uh, uh," he finally stuttered before Ron stood up out of his driver's seat, crossed in front of his stumbling colleague, and started yanking on The Man's arms as if he were a gardener weeding his garden.

"Thank you, I have a couple friends coming through too," The

Man said graciously and respectfully. "So do not be surprised when more arms appear."

Ron provided a half smile, nodded in response, and continued to pull on The Man's torso until only his feet were submerged into the stomach of his patient. "Son," he said in the most fatherly way he could after The Man was completely out, "I don't know how you got in there, or why you would be in there, it defies all logic, but I am glad to help you, just as long as this man right here on the cot is going to be alright."

"I wish I had an answer to that; however, it appears there is something inharmonious happening with my portal and this world. I have never landed in someone before and I wish this man the best recovery all the same, but unfortunately you, me, your friend over here, we all have a much bigger fish to fry right now," The Man said, speaking carefully as to not disrespect the two men who helped him emerge.

"I have many questions about what you just said, young man, but we need to get this poor guy into the hospital." Ron gave a hard shove on Kev's shoulder to wake him from his shock and fright, stepped around to the foot of the cot, opened the back doors, and started to pull the man on the cot out of the ambulance. The wheel dropped and hit the black asphalt before the next set of hands appeared out of the unconscious man's stomach.

"Please, I beg you not to take that gentleman into the hospital. You need to start driving to the south of the city instead. You know where that field of wheat is, outside the city limits. My friends will be here any moment now—you can see the first set of hands coming through now."

"The doctors are highly capable of helping your friends when they appear. I'm going to have to ask you to get out of my ambulance, because you are preventing us from saving this guy," Ron said sternly, raising his voice, forcing it to become more gruff. "Kev, help me, would you?"

"Ron is right, this is an ambulance, not a taxi service. We will need you to exit the ambulance, or we call the cops," Kev said, now fully out of shock.

The Man stood there, in hopes that something convenient would happen to persuade the two paramedics that his mission was more important. Save one life, or save billions, to anybody else the moral dilemma was near impossible to make, but to The Man it was black and white. He would gladly save the billions. He had that power to do so. Of course, he felt awful for accidentally placing an inter-dimensional portal in someone innocent, but he literally needed to save the world, and if he could save the world, he would be able to come back and help the man on the cot.

The second set of hands continued to grow into arms and then dainty shoulders. The scent of daisies came out of nowhere and met the two emergency room nurses, who ran out to greet the paramedics with a pleasant surprise. Both were confused and terrified by what they saw when they ran around the open door to the back of the ambulance.

When the lights started to flicker, The Man knew who was arriving. "She is getting frustrated; we might want to help her out of there," he said, looking at the four humans staring back at him with either disbelief or fear. "My friend has a bit of a temper. I would not keep her in there too long; otherwise, things might get...bad." He released the cot and prayed the EMT he was fighting with would also loosen his grip on the tug-of-war they had going on too.

"Kev, help these nurses pull this guy's friend out of there, would you? I'll keep this thing from rollin' away on ya." Ron pressed his foot against the wheels of the cot and eyed the stranger on the other side.

Kev and the two nurses bent over the body simultaneously and reached for different parts of the arms that were desperate to get out. They made brief contact before feeling a numbing sensation climb through their own limbs. "What is that?" one of the nurses shouted, before releasing the set of arms. "I could feel a shocking feeling through my teeth," she said, weary to reattach herself to the arms.

The EMT and nurse pulled forcefully at the arms, desperately wanting to let go, but found their muscles contracting from the numbing sensation and found it impossible to do so.

"It feels like we are being stung with a thousand needles," the nurse said, whimpering in pain as she did. "I don't understand what is going on, but I want this excruciating pain to stop."

The Man stepped around the cot that was housing all the chaos and started to help pull on the arms too. His neutral grinning face did not change as he felt a little tickle of static burst through the skin on the emerging hands. To him, it seemed the two people trying to help were exaggerating the pain they were feeling; he was not certain about it, but it definitely seemed that way to him.

When the head of a woman in her mid-twenties popped out of the unconscious man's stomach, the numbing feeling ceased almost immediately, synchronized with her realization that the people touching her were trying to help her. The two nurses were baffled as the woman easily slipped the rest of the way out, without much resistance. "Sorry," the woman said shyly to Kev and the nurse, caked in a dried red mess, pulling at her severely torn sundress to prevent any unwanted accidents. The smell of daisies filled the area as she looked around. "Where are we, jackass?"

"We are in the back of an ambulance, Miss Faith. I think the universe is attempting to persuade us to not do what we need to do. I cannot imagine why else my portal ended up in this poor man," The Man said, forgetting about the other people in sight. "Miss Hope is coming through too, right?"

"She was right behind me. I don't know why it is taking her so long to come through."

"She will be here shortly then. Ron, is it?" The Man said, making eye contact with the EMT supporting the cot with his foot. "Here is the deal. We desperately need you or your friend's help to drive us to the south of the city, where that field is. We are sitting in the most literal interpretation of a life-or-death situation. Our friend coming through is not from around here, and she might be able to help this poor guy sitting on the stretcher, if things turn for the worse."

"No I—" Ron started to say before being cut short.

"Oh, for fuck's sake," Faith angrily said, revealing her temper to the nurses and EMT. "We don't have time for this. If you don't give us a lift to that field, right now, you will die, your partner will die, both of those nurses will die, I will die, this jackass will die. If you have any children, they will die, their friends will die, everybody is going to die. Do you want to be known as the people who could have prevented a calamity, or do you want to be known as heroes? This is your defining moment. Take us to that field right now, and help us stop the end of the world."

"I am confused about something," Kev said, sharing glances between the ill-tempered woman and his partner who had moved his foot away from the wheel of the cot. Kev could tell the woman was slowly convincing Ron to help them. "If you feel your situation is so important, why don't you just commit to grand theft auto? Take the ambulance and leave us out of this situation?"

Faith squinted as she turned her head, switching on her scariest smirk. If she wasn't careful her static might have leaked out and caused an evisceration of mass proportion. By then the group of people standing around the man in the cot had noticed the third guest initiating her arrival. The tips of her ears were showing and somehow conveying that she was displeased about her trudge through the inter-dimensional portal. "I don't know how to drive, and neither does he, and I am going to take a stab in the dark and say the third person arriving doesn't know how to either. Any more stupid questions? You might be careful. I don't know how many more I can answer without absolutely frying you. Are you going to help us or what?"

"I'm sorry, but we have priorities, and unfortunately you don't stand very high on the list," Ron said, remaining in a position of power he had sat himself on.

Faith looked upset; it was written across her face. The smirk she was previously wearing had transformed itself into a disgusted frown, discouraging the men and nurses from continuing their conversation. Outside the door of the ambulance, between where the two paramedics stood, a bolt of lightning struck the ground. A peculiar happenstance, given there were zero clouds in the sky.

The blinding light the bolt generated was enough for the nurses to scream in terror, a sound unable to pierce the deafening cracking sound the bolt had made. It was a wonder how anybody in the vicinity, in front of the hospital, didn't lose their hearing. When the light from the lightning bolt had dissipated, the two nurses had disappeared, running away from the chaos the paramedics had brought with them. "Miss Faith!" The Man scolded, implying he felt upset about what had just happened.

"I didn't do that," Faith retorted, to claim her innocence. "It was surely convenient, though, right?"

"Are you guys crazy? You can't control lightning," Kev said, nearly cowering. His fear from the random, rogue bolt of electricity was about to overtake him.

"Sure she can," a new feminine voice said, coming from the man on the cot, more precisely his stomach. "I haven't witnessed it personally, but I trust her. She stopped a threat to my people somehow, and she doesn't strike me as someone who fibs. Who are these people?"

Hope was slowly being birthed by the man on the cot. Her neck was fully visible, allowing her to look around with intrigue and interest. She had many questions but felt it to be more important to compliment her new home. "You have a very nice planet here, Faith; it is sort of small, though, are you sure we could live here?"

"We are in an ambulance, Hope," Faith said, facepalming as she tried to pull on the elf to emerge her faster. "We are trying to convince these men to take us where we need to go."

Hope giggled, attempted to push the glasses that she received from The Man up and said, "Oops, silly me. I can be a ditz sometimes, but I guess it will happen a lot in our new home, until we learn the ways of your people."

Faith ignored Hope and looked at the two paramedics. "You just watched three people emerge from this poor man on the cot, and you're telling me that you refuse to believe that someone can control electricity? Bullshit." *CRACK!*

~~~

"I swear those two lightning bolts weren't me, but it fucking worked, didn't it? I wish I had that much control over my static," Faith said, standing next to The Man and the now fully emerged Hope. The trio watched as Ron carefully drove haphazardly (sounding the siren when Faith asked him to, to get a childish, giddy response from Hope) to the south, where the biggest fight the world and universe had ever known was currently progressing. Kev was slouched in the passenger seat, unconscious from the sudden fear of the second lightning bolt hitting so close to him and unaware that he had been brought along.

The man on the cot had regained some of his color in his face, after Hope had emerged, indicating to The Man that his inter-dimensional portal had closed. Seeing this was the real reason Ron decided to go along with the group of "interesting" characters, Ron was unsure of how he knew, call it a sixth sense of sorts, but he was certain the man on the cot was going to recover from his unnatural circumstance.

The drive to the field was, to put it mildly, unique. Bolts of lightning struck around the ambulance on a precise schedule, every minute or so. All of them coming within centimeters of the vehicle, but none of them really touching it. "Something is supremely wrong. I think the universe is reacting to our forced restart. I have never had to bring a planet back from death before, and I suppose there would be side effects to reviving a planet potentially about to plunge itself back into the abyss," The Man said as he watched out the window.

"That's quite intriguing," Hope said, enthralled with her new surroundings. Her dimples shaped her face as she looked around, distracted, trying to figure out what all the tools hanging on the wall did. She couldn't be bothered to push up the glasses that were now perched on the tip of her nose. "Hey, Siel," she yelled, out of habit compelled to touch everything she could get her hands on, before realizing Siel wasn't there.

"Miss Hope, did you need something?" The Man asked kindly, removing his gaze off the road to serve the retired queen.

She's just a child in a grown woman's body, Faith thought, noticing the lightning was only striking around the ambulance and nowhere in the distance. "Hey, jackass, if the universe is reacting to us, is it trying to lynch you, me, or her? The lightning is following us."

"I assume since we were all sitting there when we reversed the trajectory of this planet's destiny, it wants to get rid of all of us. I am sorry to say our fight just became that much more difficult."

Ron had been so careful driving that the group had forgotten they were in an ambulance; however, a sudden stop throwing them from where they stood was the only reminder they needed. "What the hell was that for!" Faith complained, regaining her balance like a drunk fist-fighting. Her hand had instinctively caught the edge of the cabinets that were attached to the wall, saving her from a concussion.

"I'm sorry, but there seems to be a traffic jam. I can't take you any farther. We're pretty close, fortunately, maybe another ten minutes on foot and you'll be in that field you so desperately want to go to."

"What are you fucking talking about? There wasn't a traffic jam here last time. It's past rush hour, and everybody was minding their own business."

Ron squinted in confusion as Faith spoke.

"This is how it is trying to heal, Miss Faith. I think the universe found another world, quite similar to your own, and it is trying to fill in the gaps. Nothing will be the same from when we left, except for our fight with the Voidtriss. We have added extra grains of sand into the hourglass of time."

"I thought it was your job to fix the universe, so why is this happening?"

"I was the one who broke it. We have entered uncharted territory, and everything that happens from this point on I have no control over."

"I don't want to alarm you guys, but there seems to be a large yellow aura floating in the sky over in the direction we were traveling to. You guys can't see that, can you?" Hope said, finally joining the conversation.

"What? No. What does yellow mean?" Faith asked, nearly forgetting Hope had the ability to see auras.

"The edge of calamity."

Chapter 19

Calamity

"I mean, obviously," Faith said with a load of sass. "We are here to prevent the end of the world, aren't we?"

"Miss Faith, what I think she is saying is the end is now. It is not riding the same timeline you and I left behind. Instead, we have run out of time. If we stop right now, we will never make it to the Voidtriss's corpse; we will not be able to prevent the black hole."

"Then what are we fucking sitting here for? If we need to go now, we need to move!" Faith howled.

"There is no way to go around all the cars, young lady. Not to mention all of this lightning that is surrounding us, it's sort of making it difficult to traverse this road," Ron said, hoping his reasoning was enough to get him out of helping the trio of characters any longer.

"Fuck it," Faith said, placing her fingers to her temple, showing she was focusing on something. "Everybody hold on to something. I've never done this before, so I don't know if it is going to work, but I think it will."

"What are you planning, Miss Faith?"

"I control electricity, right? I don't know if this is some sort of logical fallacy I have come up with, but if I control electricity, then I could potentially pick up this hunk of metal we are traveling in and chuck it. We're going to fucking fly to the Voidtriss."

"That seems incredibly reckless, Faith," Hope noted. "But

now that you have said it, I'm curious. Can you really do it? Can you really throw us towards the calamity?"

"I don't see why not," Faith said, closing her eyes to focus harder. "I don't hear any onlookers complaining and calling me out on thinking I can do something like that."

What onlookers? Every conscious person in the ambulance thought as the vehicle started to shake and lift away from the ground. "I'm going to recommend you all ground yourself; otherwise you might be electrocuted.

"Ground ourselves with what, Miss Faith?"

"I don't know. Hey, driver, you got any rubber gloves, or is everything latex?"

"There is a protective mesh around us that moves electricity around the ambulance, sort of like airplanes. It's unlikely that an ambulance gets struck by lightning but, on the off chance it does, there is a safety measure in place."

"Oh, good, then I don't feel too bad about doing this." Faith threw her left hand down like she was throwing something onto the ground, making sure to follow through with the motion as a bolt of plasma shot itself into the ambulance. Two singed and melted holes, one on the roof and the other in the floor where the rear axle had set, appeared, as fast as the lightning had struck. The force of lightning sent the ambulance spinning through the sky, over the crowd of cars, leaving what wasn't tied down or attached inside the vehicle rotating chaotically, except for Faith herself, who had firmly planted her feet to the floor, like when she climbed the walls to the Aurora Castle.

Screams of panic were heard both inside and out of the flying vehicle as those who sat safely in their passenger cars watched the show. When Faith felt the ambulance start to descend, she shot off another blast, this one hitting and splitting the rear axle, rendering the vehicle useless, but spinning it even more vigorously in the sky, allowing for more hang time.

Miraculously the emergency vehicle had jumped over the crowd of cars that had stretched for miles, taking its passengers straight to the cause of the traffic jam; the Voidtriss.

~~~

"I think I hit my head too hard," Ron said, attempting to dizzily stand up after his ambulance had crash-landed into the field he was trying to drive his eccentric passengers to. He was holding his head, forcing an act of stabilization. "Because I think I see something outside that shattered window."

"Then I hit my head pretty hard too, because I too see it," Hope muttered, shaking her head in disbelief. Her hair smoothly flowed around her disheveled face like a creek; not a hair out of place as she did.

"It is really there. That is the Voidtriss, the consumer of worlds, the walking abyss. Whatever you do, do not look it straight in the eyes. We do not have time for that," The Man said, slightly intrigued about how Ron could see the monster in front of them. "This is what we are here to stop."

The sound of honking was apparent, as the rowdy travelers behind the field were conflicting with each other, growing more and more impatient and inconvenienced. The front cars were stopped because they could see what they should not have been able to see, wanting no more than to shift into reverse and run away; however, the cars in the back could not see what was causing the jam and did not share the same ideas of fleeing. No one was going anywhere as long as the walking abyss stood in the way.

"W-what happens if we look it in its eyes?" Ron asked, stuttering in fear as he did.

"Nothing too terrible, only a temporary memory wipe, but at this point, we do not have time to deal with that. We need to eliminate this threat as soon as possible; otherwise, your planet as you know it will disappear for good. It is literally a ticking time bomb, and we cannot see how much time we have left."

"Why can't Faith eliminate it with her lightning bolt? You know, the same ability she just displayed? That would kill it almost immediately, right?" Hope asked, over-simplifying the problem.

"She could do that, but funny enough, that is how we got here in the first place." The Man's thoughts were racing, synapses firing as fast as he could force them to. "The problem with the Voidtriss is not that it is impossible to kill, but rather if you do kill it, your problem just gets that much worse. If it dies, it creates a black hole that consumes the planet and everything around it, which is where the Orb of Blood Disdain comes in." The Man pulled the Orb out of his pocket like it was a rare coin and displayed it for everyone to see.

"I don't understand," Hope said, bewildered. "How can the Orb help?"

"If we can get the Voidtriss to swallow the Orb, before we kill it, the Orb should be able to save us and revert any gathering of black matter in the area. This should prevent a black hole from forming."

"And how do you propose we force-feed that thing?" Ron said, internally praying he was no longer needed for the escapades.

"We need to get close and then hope that convenience is on our side," The Man responded.

"I'll do it," Faith said, obviously distracted by something else. Her eyes gave her away. They were blank, widely jittering back and forth, trying to process other information her brain was consumed with. Her mouth barely moved as she muttered to herself. "I'm the reason why this is all happening, so I'll do it."

"We can work together," Hope said, also willing to get close to the Voidtriss. "I mean, if this planet dies, then my people won't have a place to live."

"I just need you guys to create a distraction, and meanwhile I'm going to shove this thing down its throat." Faith grabbed the Orb viciously from The Man and moved towards the back door, dancing around the hole she had formed with her lightning blasts. "I'm going to force-feed it, wait a moment for it to digest this thing, and then it's dead. I'm not going to hesitate too long. This thing has caused enough grief, and I'm pretty sure pictures of this thing are already surfing the Internet. Why can people see it now?"

The Man thought about Faith's question for a moment, then responded with, "My guess is when we reversed time, we removed the parallel plane that was hosting this thing, henceforth allowing people from your world to see it."

"I see, and why aren't there other versions of you and myself already fighting this thing? I thought we were supposed to avoid our past selves; otherwise the planet would implode?"

"There is only one of us, and we are sitting right here; that is my guess, at least. I do not have definitive proof of this, but it seems to me that is the only answer. The timeline has changed. Since I am a Watcher and yourself an anomaly, it must be impossible for us to cross our own timelines. Unfortunately, it creates a paradox, which may also be the reason for the dissonance in this world."

"I see," Faith said calmly, opening the doors and revealing a partial mass of void standing in front of them.

"Miss Faith," The Man said, grabbing her petite shoulder before she could jump out of the vehicle. "Is everything alright? This is the calmest I have seen you in a very long time."

"Yeah, I'm just tired of this day. I want it to end already," Faith somberly said, deflecting The Man's concern about her sudden attitude change.

"I am pretty tired too. It has been a pretty long day today." He smiled and then released his grip to let her jump out of the vehicle. "I think it is about time we save the world."

~~~

Faith kicked off her heels and sprinted towards the looming void ahead of her, holding the Orb of Blood Disdain in her small hand. The Orb filled her palm's crevasses neatly, like she was meant to hold it; designed to fit her hand, and her hand only. The smoothness of the surface was euphoric, something she had never experienced before, encouraging her to keep the Orb within her grasp.

"I wonder how she plans to do it," Hope said as she watched the lady in a torn-up summer dress run full speed toward the mountain of abyss they had been calling the Voidtriss. "How are we supposed to distract it?"

"Miss Faith has a way of overcoming. She will not take no for an answer, and she is not aware that she always wins against calamities such as this, because of her Free Will. I do not think she has a plan other than an inkling, but I can tell you she will win this fight like she has with every other, and tomorrow will bring a new challenge to overcome," The Man said, watching calmly as his friend leaped onto the swinging arm of the Voidtriss and ran up it, like it was solid ground. "Unfortunately, there is nothing we can do. You have all-seeing eyes, I watch over time and universes, and our EMT friends here are normal humans who would rather not be mixed into this. The most we can do is throw stones at it, but they will not hit it, just pass right through."

"What do you mean? Faith is running up its arm right now, so it has to be solid, right?"

"She is able to do that because of her will. She wants to do it and since nobody has told her it is impossible to do, she is doing it graciously. When she learns to control her Will, she will almost be unstoppable."

"I can see the white aura of Free Will around you too; why don't you will that monster out of existence? Certainly, you have more control over it than she does?"

"One would think, but Miss Faith has a stronger Will than I do. Sure, I can control the outcome of certain events to make it seem convenient for myself, but Miss Faith could erase her existence entirely if she wanted to. I do not know any Watcher who has that much Will. Even though the universe despises her existence, it will listen to her in a heartbeat over anybody else."

"Is your friend alright?" Ron asked. His voice sounded confused and worried as he checked Kev's and the man resting on the cot's vitals, to reassure himself they were doing alright after crash landing. "She has all the signs of depression, but she hit the brakes pretty fast on her behavior. Does she suffer from bipolar disorder?"

"As long as I have known her, she has not mentioned it, but I suppose it is possible she has not been diagnosed for it."

"Young man, I would watch your friend, and help her whenever you can. I've seen too many people with bipolarism leave this world before they were ready, because they were having too many down days, you understand?"

"Yes, sir."

~~~

To the surprise of the Voidtriss—if pure blackness could display surprise—the figure of a mite was attacking it. Its bulky arms swung furiously in an attempt to knock the nuisance off, but the mite persisted and continued to climb.

Faith allowed her mind to be empty as she climbed the Voidtriss's arm. Her body moved on its own and the exhausted woman acted without restraint, keeping at least a single foot on the amalgamation of nothingness. She was entirely focused on force-feeding the monster and nothing else, so when one of the waving arms struck her and sent her flying like a rocket, her instincts told her to panic.

Though the panic was apparent, the feeling of déjà vu overwrote it. The familiar sensation of being thrown through the sky at mach speeds was alarming to Faith, as she remembered the last time the Voidtriss threw her; it hurt. *Not again, not this time,* she thought, rotating her body perpendicular with the landmass she was hurtling towards. She was determined not to leave a petite human-shaped dent in the hill this time.

Before her impact with the hill, mere nanoseconds away, a thought occurred to her; it was potentially a game changer if it worked. She was willing to give it a try and figured if it didn't work, she would resort to Plan B, which she knew would.

Faith felt a static discharge from the soles of her feet, similar to that of when she walked up walls, but this discharge was different; it felt stronger, and there was more tickle to it. She intended to build a static barrier between her and the hill, with the opposite magnetic polarity of the Earth, and at the last second she would flip the polarity of the barrier, hopefully launching her away and back toward the Voidtriss.

If her timing was wrong, all the g-forces she was experiencing were going to cause her to die, which was not acceptable if the world-ending monster in front of her remained alive. Her vision was blurred from the speed she was traveling, leaving her to trust her instincts. And at the last possible second, she felt her body crumple down into a squat and propel itself away from the hill just like she had imagined. She was a speeding electromagnetic bullet, shot out of a nonexistent rail gun, flying twice the speed she was just thrown at.

Only the vapor cone Faith left behind her could be seen from the ground below, but everyone watching the event could feel and hear the sonic boom moments later. The pressure from the boom was enough for the vehicles in the front of the traffic jam to have their windows blown out.

Faith's hand was outstretched with the Orb in it. She couldn't see where she was headed, but somehow she knew she was on a direct path to the mouth of the void, exactly where she wanted to be. Before she knew it, it was cold and dark everywhere she looked. Was she blind? Had she ruptured her eyes from flying at least mach 2? It would make sense, but then she heard the growling sound. The sound she recognized as the Voidtriss's growl. She could hear it everywhere, which clued her in as to where she was.

Somewhere inside the monster was Faith, drenched in saliva straight from the void; a disgusting feeling, similar to the look of the sludge people. She was grateful, almost impressed she didn't blast a Faith-shaped hole through the monster's neck, a feat she considered highly probable. *I should have killed this thing immediately going that speed, but instead it catches, and then just swallows me? What's the deal?*

~~~

"Where'd Faith go? I can't see her," Hope said, trying to follow Faith's movements from the ground. "Did she disappear?"

"You saw her get hit by that thing, right, young lady? That's the last time I saw her," Ron said, just as curious as Hope was.

"Miss Faith is using her brain. She was hit so hard by the Voidtriss it sent her flying into that hill over there, but in the nick of time she turned herself, and slingshotted right back to the Void-triss. That is when that sonic boom and vapor cone happened," The Man said, pointing at the sky, where the remnants of the cloud floated, quickly dissipating. "After that, she launched her way into the mouth of that thing. Curiously enough, she did not fly through the back of its head. I have a feeling she is starting to understand what Free Will really means. She knew that if she killed it too soon, we would end up in the same predicament. She slowed herself, somehow, enough to stop safely inside of the monster."

"Impossible," Ron said in disbelief, forgetting he had already seen the impossible more than once. "Especially if she was going as fast as you seem to think she was traveling."

"Sure, for anybody else, but for Miss Faith, nothing is impossible."

"So how long does she have to wait before my people's relic takes effect?"

"That is a very difficult question to answer. It could be seconds, minutes, who knows? Faith will know when the time comes; that is probably why she had it swallow her too."

The Voidtriss began to growl, like it was in pain. Its excessive groaning showed its overwhelming agony as it scratched at its stomach.

"I guess the time is now," The Man stated, watching the Void-triss act as if it had swallowed an active hornet's nest. "We might want to hurry up and get back inside this ambulance. I have a feeling there is a chance of void rain today, and trust me, we do not want to be underneath it."

The Man herded Hope and Ron back into the ambulance as he noticed the belly of the Voidtriss beginning to glow. A white light penetrated the dense blackness, and the absolute darkness, indicating Faith was escaping from her temporary holds.

Bolts of lightning, in all directions, impaling the monster created an extravagant show. One of which would lead to mass hysteria from the traffic holding the road down. A cracking sound, louder than the sonic boom, came from the stomach of the monster as Faith emerged with an explosion of force, eviscerating

223

the Voidtriss in an instant. The force from the explosion upset and lifted many of the vehicles in the jam, nearly clearing the road.

Splatters of darkness rained down on the Earth as the sound of tinnitus rang in everyone's ears for miles. Those who could not see what had happened were left confused and scared, wondering if World War Three had started. The body of the walking abyss had disappeared, leaving only a few remaining smaller chunks, resting throughout the field.

In the moment of silence that followed, sighs of relief were expelled from those who understood what had happened. The calamity had met its end and the day was over; a success for the books.

"I did it," Faith slurred tiredly, holding her fists above her head, like she had just won the fight of the century. Her eyes drooped as she fought to keep them open. The red color she had been misted in had been washed away by the dark saliva she had swum through, leaving her dress soaked and heavy.

In her celebration she missed what was happening in front of her own eyes. The tar that now surfaced the Earth had started to shrink and disappear, like it was burrowing into the ground, but unfortunately, it was not. It was doing something much worse; becoming black hole singularities.

It was obvious that across the land things felt heavier, denser. The Man, with his repaired arm, could feel it as soon as it happened. The stinging feeling that accompanied the feeling of bones grinding together alerted him, but the inability to stand straight up told him there was a gravitational pull that was not there before, pushing down on him. "Oh, no," he said, realizing the day was about to derail.

"Hey, jackass," Faith shouted at the ambulance, displaying a sincere but concerning smile. "I messed up again, didn't I? I didn't wait long enough."

"Miss Faith, do not worry about it. We will fix this, like we always do," The Man said, fighting to overcome the extra gravity.

"And then what? We fix the next thing I screw up? And then the next thing, and the next? I'm a screw-up, we all know that, but it seems to me the world would be a better place without me."

"You are not a screw-up, Miss Faith; bad things happen to you because you are an anomaly. You do not have to give in to what the universe wants. Defy it, every step of the way, show it you have a place on this planet." The Man crawled towards Faith on his forearms, slowly.

"I'm pretty tired of this song and dance. I don't want you or anybody else to suffer anymore in regard to myself. I know you've told me in the past that I have Free Will. I've been thinking a lot lately, pondering my decision. If I never existed, no one would be in this situation. I wouldn't have caused all of this pain and misery."

"Stop," Hope yelled, realizing what was happening, crawling along the ground behind The Man. "You may have hurt some people, but you have also helped tons of people too; just look at me and my Quii family."

"This is my chance to save everyone I care about."

"Do not talk like that, Miss Faith. Think of all the things you have yet to experience. We can do this together. Do not do it by yourself."

Faith began to glow pure glistening white while the sounds of the world quieted down, paying their respects to her. Her Free Will shone brightly through the Goobert's curse, and her presence shrank.

"Miss Faith, do not do this," The Man said, raising his voice in a last-ditch effort to convince her to change her mind. "You do not need to do this."

"I appreciate everything you've done for me, but this needs to happen this way. We've run out of time and you know it. Please don't worry about me. I am sorry to have put you through such misery over the years. Goodbye, jackass, goodbye, Hope it was nice knowing both of you."

With the sway of a breeze, the woman who smelled of daisies and cursed like a sailor was gone, taking the dense heavy feeling with her.

~~~

"Faith!" The Man and Hope cried out in unison as the woman who saved the universe disappeared without a trace.

"Where am I? Why am I here? Who are you people?" Ron asked, looking confused, trying to process what was going on. All he knew was he had a patient lying on a cot, while his ambulance was in ruin, with his partner passed out in the passenger seat. A haze of confusion fogged his mind, leaving him feeling surreal.

"Ron," The Man said, standing in the field, his head pointed toward the sky as he watched the clouds pass by. "Thank you for your help. I am sure Miss Faith would have wanted me to relay that message on to you." He turned and looked at the wrecked ambulance, sincerely, and choked down the lump that had formed in the back of his throat.

"Who is Faith? What happened to my ambulance, and why are there two people in it unconscious? I am sure at least one of them needs medical attention."

"He will be fine; they both will actually. I need you to understand everything is alright now, and everything will be alright from now on. Faith has saved us, and that is all you need to remember."

"Who is Faith? Do you mean religion?"

"Why doesn't he remember Faith? Did he look the Voidtriss in its eyes?" Hope asked, concerned with Ron's amnesia.

"No, Faith is gone. In his eyes she was never here—she never existed, and that is how she wanted it. I understand you are just as exhausted as I am, especially after seeing our friend remove herself from existence, but I do believe we need to talk to someone before anything else happens."

"Who?"

"Faith's mom. She needs to know, regardless."

CHAPTER 20

QUASI-DAISY

The delicate girl who entered the world without realizing she was the most important person on the planet had stepped out of it, just as quietly as she had entered it. She had blossomed into a strong-willed, anxiety-filled, sailor-mouthed woman. A woman who was determined to help those who needed assistance, but most of all, her few friends that she had met in her short journey.

Without Faith, the world exists in a catatonic state. A state so boring, the word adventure is meaningless. She had a charm about her, able to bend the will of the world around her; influence the universe into making her something greater than she could ever imagine. Her existence should not have been, but somehow it was, and in her short journey she called life, the girl who was like a daisy in the end had managed to experience much more than the average human. She had become a light so bright that snuffed out the worry and darkness that surrounded the world; the brightest light, the rays of sunshine that poked through and smiled at the world, encouraging the next day to move forward and to progress into the future.

~~~

"Oh, you're Faith's friend, aren't you? I think I saw you around here a couple times. I have to apologize, she never told me your name, and she never told me she had more friends other than you. I suppose she is lacking in social cues and etiquette. I blame myself on that one," the woman who answered the door said, as she peered at her two exhausted-looking guests politely. "I haven't seen her in a few days; it's like she vanished off the earth, but this is normal for her. You know how she is. Oh, where are my manners, come on in. I am Faith's mother. You can call me Grace."

A man and woman stepped into the house almost in unison. "You have a lovely home and a beautiful name, Grace. My name is Hope," the woman said, pushing her glasses up the bridge of her nose without hesitation. "I haven't known your daughter very long, but she helped me and my friends with something very important to us. You could say she saved us."

"Oh, she is very good about doing that kind of stuff. I'm glad she helped you. Her heart is always in the right place. I'm so proud of her. How can I help you? Like I said, I haven't seen her in a few days, and she doesn't carry a phone with her, so I can't call her to let her know her friends are here. Can I get you anything to drink?"

"No, thank you, Miss Grace," The Man said solemnly as Hope and himself sat on the couch directly facing a recliner that Grace had gingerly sat in. "We are actually here to talk to you."

"What do you mean? Is it about Faith? Is it her cursing problem? I told her she needed to stop being so brash, but she only curses when she gets stressed, so sometimes I just let her do it. For some reason it calmed her down better than any therapy could."

There was a stagnant silence that filled the air while The Man waited for his words to materialize in his throat. He looked around and noticed the pictures that decorated the walls all around him. Every picture had a common theme; Faith. "Miss Grace," he said, as his breathing and heart rate increased. His eyes widened as a thought occurred to him. *She is not gone. There are three people sitting in this room that remember her, and the surrounding pictures are the proof. She is out there somewhere, hiding away. I will keep my promise to her; we will bring her back, and I will protect her from the Goobert's Curse.* "I promise you, we are going to bring her back. We do not know where she is at the moment, but when we find her, we will tell her that her beautiful mother is worried about her. Mark my words, I always keep my promises."

Tears filled Grace's ocean blue eyes. "What are you talking about? Is Faith in some sort of trouble?"

"Miss Grace, have you ever heard the word Panglossian? It is a term that means excessive optimism—all is good in the world. Your daughter makes the world shine and smile. I believe her to be the reason everything is going to be alright. I once made a promise to her that I would protect her from the evils in this universe. I intend to keep that promise, and I intend to keep the promise I just made you. You do not need to worry. I am sorry for frightening you; she is alright, and will always be safe no matter what with us by her side."

Thank you for reading Panglossian: Quasi-Daisy. If you enjoyed it please leave a review on Amazon, and consider telling your friends and family about the story.

There are more stories in the works, so make sure to follow me on my social media.

Twitter: @mobinng
Facebook: facebook.com/mkbingman
Blog: www.brainfoldstoblogger.blogspot.com
Website: www.mkbingman.com

I started writing this story November 14, 2014 with nothing but a simple idea that had been stuck in my mind for years. I had no clue where it was going, but it was stuck in my mind, until finally in 2019 I decided I would stop putting it off and finish the story.

In July of 2020, Panglossian: Quasi-Daisy was finished, nearly six years from when I started it. I am biased but I think it is a darn good story, probably the best I have written in my life, so far.

The story will continue in Panglossian: Quietus